M000284046

THE BILLIONAIRE'S WAKE-UP-CALL GIRL

ANNIKA MARTIN

"A brilliant love affair! Smart, sexy, and passionate, The Billionaire's Wake-up-call Girl is full of hilarity that made me laugh out loud, and yet Annika never fails to pull my heartstrings—her characters so real and vulnerable, I ache for them. I fell for Lizzie and Theo right along with them as they fell for each other."

~Author Trisha Wolfe

Adventure is worthwhile in itself.

AMELIA EARHART

ONE

Lizzie

LOOKING BACK, maybe I should've noticed the red flags.

The unusually large sign-on bonus, for example—payable only after I lasted thirty days on the job.

Who can't last in a job for thirty days? That was my thought when I applied for this position.

And then there were the strange looks my co-workers would give me when I went around introducing myself as Vossameer Inc.'s new social media manager. "I'm here to jazz up our online image," I'd explain.

In the elevator, on the communications floor, down in the sleek and elegant lobby, just these strange looks. Uncertain smiles. One woman's mouth formed into an alarmed "o" before she introduced herself back to me.

At first I chalked it up to company-wide cluelessness about social media. After all, Vossameer didn't even have a Facebook page when I started three weeks ago.

But now as I watch my boss Sasha fret and frown over the

PowerPoint report I created to show how perfectly I nailed my assignment, I'm starting to think a little bit harder about those red flags.

She clicks to a page that shows examples of my successful, industry-appropriate posts and a graph of my stunning engagement numbers.

She sucks in a breath. Winces.

What?

Trust me, Facebook engagement was no easy feat; Vossameer's most exciting product is hemostatic gel for use in traumatic wound-care situations.

Another wince. A frown.

Was I the clueless one all along? Was I misreading the looks I was getting from my new co-workers?

Am I like the traveler in Transylvania who excitedly tells all the villagers about finding an awesome free castle to stay in? *OMG, I have the whole place to myself because the owner only comes out at night. Isn't that wonderful? Score! High five!*

I hold my breath as she clicks from page to page.

Sasha has a severe blonde bob, a love of nautical-looking outfits, and a Cruella De Vil makeup style, though to be fair, it might be a poorly lit home mirror.

"Mmm..." she says finally. And it's not a *yum* type of *mmm*. It's an *uh-oh* type of *mmmm*.

"Is there a problem?" I ask.

She just shakes her head. As though the problem goes beyond words. Like she asked for an interim report and I gave her a handful of peanut shells with the salt licked off.

She clicks to another graph of positive results and again she furrows her dark and dramatically arched brows—I see it in the reflection on the screen.

"The engagement numbers are already better than most of Vossameer's peers," I point out.

Crickets.

Actually, not even crickets. "Crickets" suggests little beings are happily chirping away in a field. What I hear is more like the silent gloom of stones in a forgotten parking lot.

She clicks to the next page. My website mock-up.

"You wanted our site to come up on the first page on Google," I remind her. "Now it does, but we'll do even better once the new site is up. I think people will stay longer."

Trust me, that's a nice way of putting it. The current Vossameer site looks like it was made by depressed robots in 1998.

Of course, when you're Vossameer, a billion-dollar unicorn of a company, you don't need a nice site. Vossameer could have no site at all, and giant health groups would still pay zillions of dollars for their lifesaving medical gel.

But now they're trying to partner with some high-profile charitable foundation—Locke Foundation, part of Locke Construction.

So they have to look shiny online.

Which is why they hired me. That was my assignment.

When you search Vossameer, the top hit is a Forbes article on mysterious CEO Theo Drummond that can be summed up in eight words: *he's an asshole, but his products save lives.*

And it's not the only one. Tons of articles paint Mr. Drummond as a reclusive genius. A gruff misanthrope. A surly asshole.

I've never met the notorious Mr. Drummond, but the asshole thing is not hard to believe. The evidence is all around.

The employees here are fearful, as though they're expecting to be fired at any moment, or maybe beheaded. The environment is sleek gray marble and steel, like an elegant and slightly futuristic prison. No outside decorations are allowed, not even in the deepest recesses of your cubicle.

Even the outside of the building is unforgiving—a mod gray concrete bunker with rectangular windows arranged in straight rows. A study in harsh geometry.

Mr. Drummond doesn't like decorations, Sasha told me once. *Vossameer is about lifesaving solutions, not party streamers.*

I'd brought a giant tub of home-baked frosted cookies to share my second day, and people nearly fell out of their chairs. It turns out we can't bring treats to share. Ever.

This is a workplace, not a potluck, Sasha said.

I've gotten good at sensing the assholey DNA of Mr. Drummond's statements, and I'm pretty sure that was one of them. Same with the party streamers comment. It's something about the sheer jerkiness of it, and also, how Sasha changes her voice to sound breathless and intense.

Everyone here is obsessed with Mr. Drummond. They seem to regard him the way the ancients regarded the gods that controlled the weather and plagues. Angry and vengeful, yet glorious. Never to be spoken ill of.

Also, nobody talks about Mr. Drummond without using the word "amazing" at least once. Maybe that's in the employee manual somewhere.

Sasha's obsession goes way further—more into awestruck love territory.

She speaks his name like she's whispering hallowed secrets to the Greek oracles atop Mount Olympus—*Mr. Drummond this, Mr. Drummond that. Amazing Mr. Drummond.*

"Mr. Drummond is not the most sociable person in the world," Sasha breathlessly informed me the day I started. "He has *extremely* high standards—for himself and for his employees —but his amazing breakthroughs save lives every day. The work we do to support him makes that possible." And then she'd looked me deeply in the eyes and said, *This is the most important job you'll ever have.*

I'd just nodded while making a mental note to stay away from any brightly colored liquid.

I cross my arms. Wait for Sasha to click on through my doomed PowerPoint.

"On the next page are the website hits that come from Facebook," I say nervously.

Sasha doesn't want to see the next page. She levels a long red fingernail at the screen, like a blood-red rocket, and taps on the image of an old man holding hands with a baby. She then taps the faces of happy newlyweds. "Why am I seeing these people?"

"Well, our marketing materials tend to concentrate on the medical effects of our hemostatic gel, but that's not what we're selling, is it?" I say. "We're selling more time with loved ones. We're selling health providers the ability to grant more time to wounded patients. That's our true product."

She actually cranes her head around and looks up at me, like I'm saying something really radical. And not Marketing 101.

"Look at any hospital or pharma website," I continue. "Right now, let's go look. You'll see pictures of happy people living life together."

Sasha pulls out her phone and enters the name of a large local hospital. Does she not believe me? I'm hugely relieved to see an image of a woman leaping in the air, trailing a silky scarf behind her.

Sasha looked surprised.

This place.

That jerk Mr. Drummond runs these people so hard, they have no life. Poor Sasha seems to be up to her neck in press releases and case studies. But seriously, do they not watch TV? Do they not mess around online?

"After all," I say, "it's not as if hospitals are going to fill their sites with pictures of bloody scalpels and ugly surgical scars. Right?" I try a smile.

Sasha doesn't.

She's back at my PowerPoint. A family at a picnic. Old people doing a puzzle. At one point, she sucks in a breath, like the images literally agonize her. "Mr. Drummond won't like seeing all this," she says in the most ominous tone possible. "He won't like it *at all*."

As if I've spent my three weeks filling people's drawers with Ping-Pong balls instead of nailing my assignment.

"Why won't he like it?" I hate how small my voice sounds.

She just shakes her head.

"The thing is, my assignment was to modernize and humanize Vossameer's online presence...and people relate to people," I say.

Cue the crushing gloom of stones.

If I were more mercenary, I'd give them the boring site they want and a sad Facebook feed shunned by all. I'd be long gone by the time they realized I screwed them over. But that's not me. I may only be here for the bonus, but I intend to do a good job for them.

"No, you probably have a point. About the people," she says. "It's social media, after all."

"Yeah, right?" I agree hopefully.

"Mr. Drummond does want this foundation partnership. But..." She gestures at a picture of a happy family. Makes a tiny little sound. A tiny little frightened sound.

Does Mr. Drummond just hate happy families? Will he start throwing chairs if he sees a little boy and his grandfather working on a train set?

And if so, why bother to invent lifesaving solutions?

"Welp!" Sasha straightens up. "Who knows, maybe he'll like

it." Her tone is weird. Far too bright. "Mr. Drummond sees things we don't, does things for reasons we don't always understand. It's amazing he's as patient with us as he is."

"Sure, okay," I say.

"I'll have you present with me," she says. "We'll head up after lunch."

"Wait—what?" I nearly swallow my tongue.

I'm going up to the top? To the tyrant's lair?

"You'll help me explain."

"I thought you liked to present...solo." I've gotten the feeling that Sasha has been passing off my ideas as her own. Not that I care. Again, only here for the bonus.

"You're the expert." She smiles.

Translation: If all goes well, she'll take the credit. If it goes poorly, I'll take the fall.

She looks over my outfit, or more winces over it.

I straighten my blazer. I'm in a gray pantsuit with a white shirt under. It's something a stylish female detective would wear, at least in my imagination. Even my dark blonde hair is contained in an un-fun bun.

Where did I go wrong?

Though to be fair, most maiden sacrifices happen with the helpless victim wearing a nightgown.

"It's fine." She waves me off. "See you at 1:45."

I thank her and make my way down the row of non-visually-distracting cubicles.

I eat my turkey sandwich at my desk, feeling doomed. I open my bag of chips ever so quietly. That's another rule—inmates of Gulag Vossameer must not make excessive non-work-related noise.

What's more, they must never prepare foods that produce an excessive smell. Microwave popcorn is expressly banned.

I have this fantasy of popping popcorn in the microwave—

Orville Redenbacher extra-buttery movie version—while dancing on my desk in a pink mini skirt to Britney Spears's "Gimme More."

But that would have to happen after the bonus is in my bank account. I desperately need that bonus. Beyond desperately.

I just need to last six more business days, not counting today. A person can handle anything for six days, right?

Two hours later, we're waiting for the elevator. Sasha frowns at me for about the tenth time. "Do not speak unless spoken to. You understand?"

"Got it," I say.

"Don't elaborate needlessly," she says. "You tend to elaborate..."

I swallow. "Got it. No elaboration."

I don't have an official marketing degree. I used to own a bakery, Cookie Madness, that got really popular thanks to my work on Facebook and Instagram. I even won some awards. Those awards got me this job—I could tell from the interview.

It still hurts to think about my stolen bakery. My stolen life. My stolen dream. Stolen and destroyed.

We get in. Sasha hits the button for the fifteenth floor. "Not everybody gets the chance to meet him," she says.

Yay? I think. But I don't say that. I just nod and smile.

I worked in restaurants all through culinary school, and I had a lot of jerky bosses. Jerky bosses can be fun because they give the employees a shared enemy to whisper about, to exchange mocking glances over, and that creates a sense of camaraderie, like a workplace version of the French Resistance.

Vossameer doesn't have even that bit of joy. It's sad.

We're stalled at the tenth floor while people try to fit in a cart. Nervously, Sasha checks the time.

I'll admit, I'm interested to meet the elusive and tyrannical

Mr. Drummond on a purely WTF level. Because who runs a company like this?

In my quest to be the perfect leader of the five employees who worked at my cookie bakery, I used a lot of positive reinforcement. If somebody took a risk that backfired, I would still praise them, because I wanted them to feel empowered to try new things. I encouraged individuality and creativity, and it totally paid off—my employees came up with some great ideas.

We hit eleven. The cart leaves.

There aren't many photos of Mr. Drummond out there. Most of them are him standing in large groups, or in a lab wearing protective goggles. I requested a picture for the site, and Sasha told me Mr. Drummond isn't into it. The picture he makes his assistant provide for industry events is a black-and-white line drawing of a chemist's beaker with two bubbles coming out of the top of it.

He doesn't like to draw attention to himself, Bob from HR explained in hushed tones.

Hushed tones.

As though amazing Mr. Drummond might hear his words and feel displeased, and that might destroy his ultra-important lifesaving train of genius thought, and a swarm of locusts would descend from the sky to eat everybody's smell-free lunches.

Here's a hint for the inmates of Gulag Vossameer: you don't have to talk in hushed tones when you discuss Mr. Drummond. He doesn't have godlike omniscience. He doesn't have bat-like hearing. He is not a wizard.

He is but a man!

When you pull aside the curtain, that's what you'll find. A controlling jerk of a man with a machine to make his voice sound loud and boomy. Just like in *The Wizard of Oz.*

Right before we hit floor fifteen, Sasha takes out a compact mirror and touches up her lipstick. She's such a gorgeous and clever tiger of a woman, smart and aggressive. Sure, her aggression is turned on me half the time. Still. I feel bad for her.

I feel bad that this jerky man has made her feel like this. It's not right!

I want to tell her not to waste her time on a control freak like Mr. Drummond. *He's just another man behind a curtain!* I want to say. *There's more power in your awesome shoes!*

But I don't.

For the record, her shoes *are* awesome—shiny and sculptural high heels in severe black. Her dress is a formfitting knit, sexy in an understated way, with a smart wool blazer over it.

She snaps shut the compact and glances at me nervously as the door opens.

I so rarely see her nervous. It's ominous. Like in movies where the most powerful jungle animals start running for the hills.

"Don't mess this up," she says.

"No worries!" I try a reassuring smile. "I got your back."

Sasha's frown is intensified by her severe Cruella brows. Again she surveys my outfit; again she doesn't seem to like what she finds.

We then begin our long trek down the sleek hallway of harshness.

Now, in addition to the presentation, I'm stressing about my outfit. At the bakery I never had to dress businessy. I'm so nervous now that I remove my necklace and slip it in my pocket. Less decoration.

Then a wave of annoyance flashes over me, because *what?* I just spent the last three weeks working my heart out on their online presence. If this company was run at all competently, I'd be feeling pride and excitement, with just a little nervousness. And Sasha would feel it, too. We'd both be eager to hear feedback and use it to create the best site possible.

Instead the mood is *into the belly of the beast.*

We pass a pair of concerned-looking chemists, coming from one of the labs. There are labs on every floor here. That's what you get when a chemist runs a company.

We reach Mr. Drummond's office. Sasha knocks.

A distressed-looking woman lets us into a large reception area lined with file cabinets. "He's expecting you," she whispers, leading us toward a pair of black doors. Even her gray hair seems anxious, the way it wires urgently out of her head.

I smile. "Thanks," I say.

A glance passes between the two of them.

What?

I'm starting to get paranoid. And kind of angry. People here work so hard for him, and how does this guy reward them? By keeping them completely on edge.

The receptionist knocks softly—twice—then pulls one door open.

I follow Sasha into a chaotic office space that's decorated with charts of chemical elements and whiteboards with madly scribbled circles and lines and letters, like the alphabet exploded somewhere nearby.

File cabinets and shelving units full of boxes and binders and bottles line the walls, and taking center stage is a massive worktable supporting piles of manuals and notebooks and a lone coffee cup next to a lone laptop.

In a gloomy far corner there's a broad wooden desk, dark except for one warm circle of light cast by one lonely lamp. Two severe chairs wait in front of it, sentinels at the ready.

But where is amazing Mr. Drummond? Why would his receptionist act like he's here when the office is empty?

A door off to the side is plastered with colorful safety signs, including one that says "Lab Coat and Eye Protection Required." A lab, then. Did he go in there?

I wander past the worktable. "Looks like Mr. Amazing is being amazing elsewhere," I mutter.

"What's that?" Sasha says.

"Looks like he's elsewhere," I say more loudly.

I move closer to the desk. Close enough that I suddenly make out a pair of icy gray eyes staring sternly at me from behind black-framed glasses. Dazzling eyes. Gorgeous eyes.

Mr. Drummond.

Fear whooshes through me. Did he hear what I said? Please, no!

Mr. Drummond stands and pulls off his glasses, still staring at me.

Gulp.

His white lab coat hangs open, revealing a fine gray suit underneath. He stalks toward me with the grace of a large predator.

But that's not what's so remarkable about him.

With or without glasses, he's the most dramatically, effusively, wildly handsome man I've ever seen. His hotness has its own force. It has its own gravity. It has its own zip code, miles past the neighborhood of *stop staring* and deep in the *religious-experience-of-beauty* zone.

Double gulp.

His dark hair is short and thick, with the texture that you know would be curls if he let it grow out, but like everything at Vossameer, it is rigidly controlled.

His brows are sooty. His lips, currently formed into a frown, are dangerously lush, a little banged-up to create a bad-boy pillowy effect that I very much like.

I swallow and straighten up, reminding myself that this is the control freak responsible for the stern and joyless workplace that is Vossameer. The cruel architect of the microwave popcorn ban.

His extreme hotness is just another assholey aspect of him. Another way he controls people. Melts their minds. Makes their pulses race.

"We have the social media and site makeover presentation for you, Mr. Drummond," Sasha stammers. "For your perusal."

He continues to regard me unhappily. Did he hear my Mr. Amazing comment? "Do we have an appointment of some sort?" he asks Sasha, even though he's looking at me.

"Yes," Sasha says.

He shoves ink-stained hands into his pockets. "And you are..."

"This is Elizabeth Cooper. New assistant."

"Pleased to meet you." I half-lift my hand, unsure if shaking hands is a thing he does with mere mortals.

He grunts at me, then turns to Sasha. "Let's have it, then. We'll set up over there." He motions at the worktable.

I quickly retract my hand, curling it around the printout folder. *O-kay!*

When I had a new person join my beloved bakery, it would be like we were greeting a long-lost sibling, not somebody's pet spider that you never wanted to see in the first place.

We go to where Mr. Drummond is clearing a space. He looks up when he's done, and for one hot heartbeat, I have this strange sense he's aware of my secret opinions about him, as if there's some strange conduit between us.

Or who knows, maybe he's telepathic in addition to being the world's most amazing chemist and most horrible CEO.

He takes the laptop from Sasha and centers it where he wants it. His hands are quite large, with long fingers, strong yet elegant. I find that I can't look away from him. He really does have some kind of magnetic gravity thing going on.

Sasha takes her place in front of it and clicks to open the

PowerPoint. The title comes up. Vossameer. Relatable. Human. Engaged.

Then a page with the generic new tag: "Helping to save lives." Sasha thought of it. It's quite the step up from their old tag, "medical antihemorrhagics."

Mr. Drummond frowns, as though he's having trouble making sense of it. Finally he utters one word, dripping with disgust: "No."

Sasha looks at me. Like she's stunned that such an offensive thing made its way to the presentation. "You'll need to get rid of that, Lizzie."

"No problem," I bite out, feeling my face heat.

He clicks deeper in. He's reading everything—all the great results. And he doesn't seem happy.

Sweat trickles down my spine.

It's as if I'm in marketing opposite-world. Good is bad. Down is up. It would make a funny story if it wasn't so important for me to keep this job, to get the bonus.

I cannot lose the bonus.

But things aren't looking good.

I'm suddenly awash in the frantic, helpless feeling I had the night I discovered the life I'd built was imploding. The night I found my bank accounts cleaned out, and then I discovered the bakery eviction notices that my ex, Mason, had hidden from me, followed by the credit card debt from cards I didn't know about.

Mason had worked his way into my trust, little by little, and he'd stolen everything. I know I share some of the blame. I was so in love with him. Blinded by love.

It was too late by the time I called the police. Mason had disappeared, probably to a tropical island, they thought. He'd always dreamed of living in the Caribbean; that's probably one of the only true things he ever told me.

In the days after, I learned the worst of it—he'd taken out

loans everywhere possible in the name of Cookie Madness and my name, too—including a loan from loan sharks.

Actual loan sharks.

Which is why I need this bonus so badly.

"What are these images of picnics?" Mr. Drummond barks. "How is that relevant to anything? I'm running a pharmaceutical gel business, not a Six Flags."

Sasha turns to me. "Lizzie?"

I look at the screen, feeling his eyes on me, willing myself not to die of despair.

The picnic shot is one of my favorites. Manhattan skyline in the background. I love New York, and now, thanks to Mason, I have to move away to cheaper pastures.

As soon as I get the loan sharks off my back.

"People don't care about what's on their bandages," I say. "It's not the quality of Vossameer gel they care about—"

"What do you mean?" Mr. Drummond interrupts, indignant. "Of course they care about quality."

"No," I say, looking him right in the eye. "They care about another chance to be happy, to share meals with their favorite people, to watch them grow. To celebrate together. Lean on each other…" I almost want to cry, imagining all the things I'll miss.

Mr. Drummond's gaze gets even more intense, if that's possible. It's like he wants to bore a hole through my face.

"So actually," I say, "these pictures are relevant. Because we're not selling hemostatic gel. We're selling another day. We're selling possibilities. And giving medical personnel the power to deliver on that."

The air seems to pulse between us.

"It's how all other medical solutions companies position themselves," I add, thinking I've made a compelling case.

Mr. Drummond tilts his head. "Do I look like I care what other medical companies are doing?"

I swallow. "Okay."

"It's a question," he says. "Do I?"

My heart pounds in my ears. Really? He's going to make me answer a rhetorical question? I suck in a breath. "I suppose you don't."

"You suppose right. I don't care what other companies are doing. And all of this...children and their teddy bears and whatnot..." He gestures at the screen, seeming at a loss for words, so heinous is the sight, "it has no place on our website or our feeds or whatever..."

"That's what I've been telling her," Sasha says. "Families don't belong on our site or on our feeds."

I curl my hands more tightly around my file folders. "How about medical personnel? Or could we maybe spotlight the chemists?" There's a whole army of chemists here, ready to do Mr. Drummond's bidding, his personal fleet of nerdy minions. I've spoken to a few of them in the elevator. They talk about the amazing opportunity to work under him. The amazing learning opportunity. "We could have them talk about—"

"How about achieving our goals without a lot of fluff?" Mr. Drummond says, totally cutting me off.

There's this weird silence where I think I could actually come to hate him. I've been working on letting go of my hatred of Mason with the help of a book entitled *Forgive and Be Free,* but I might hate Mr. Drummond. I might even cherish hating him. Miraculously, I manage a smile. "Social media, too? No images of people?"

He raises an inky brow.

"Okay, so the assignment is to modernize and humanize Vossameer's online presence," I begin, gritting my teeth, "and I hear you saying, let's do that *without* using any humans *whatso-*

ever." Is he listening? Does he hear how messed up that is? It's like saying, I'll make some noise without using any sounds whatsoever.

But no. He grunts his approval.

"Very good, Mr. Drummond," Sasha says.

I stare at one of his alphabet explosion boards, willing the meeting to be done.

"So do we have everything under control?" he asks.

I grit my teeth and nod, because I have to keep this job. "Absolutely."

"Of course," Sasha says. "I'll help her figure it out."

We get out of there quickly. Sasha is silent all the way down the hall and into the elevator. Then the doors close. "You were a disaster," she says. "The way you contradicted him on everything. I had to pull it out of the fire for you."

I bite my lip. *Wait out the clock,* I tell myself. *Outplay. Outlast.* "Well," I say, "we have a strong new direction to work with. So that's good."

"Those images. I told you…"

"Consider them pulled," I say.

"And your outfit. It was highly distracting to Mr. Drummond. The employee handbook forbids revealing outfits."

My hand goes to my collar. All my buttons are done up except the neck-choking one, but who does the neck-choking button?

"It's distractingly formfitting as well," she says. "This is a workplace, not a fashion show."

I quickly button the neck-choking button. But it's not the outfit. She didn't like that Mr. Drummond was so focused on me. I want to reassure her that what passed between us was disdain only, but I did find him attractive in an annoying way.

And he *was* looking at me a lot.

This is bad.

Nothing will get me fired faster than if she thinks Mr. Drummond likes me.

"I'll keep it appropriate," I say. Right then and there, I resolve that whatever spark there was, I'll douse it. Stomp it. Kill it.

I'll become utterly invisible and unattractive to him. Mentally I scan through my closet, trying to think of the ugliest, most shapeless outfit possible.

"Even so, I'm going to have to write you up for inappropriate workplace attire," she says.

"What?" My pulse races. Three write-ups and I'm out. With trembling hands I check the rest of the buttons. "I didn't think..."

"Now you will," she snaps.

TWO

Lizzie

MIA, my roommate and best friend in the world, pulls a shape-less gray dress off the rack at the Salvation Army on West Forty-sixth.

"No way," I say. "I'm trying to appease her, not mock her."

"Come on. She'll see you're trying," she says. "This is what she wants. She wants for you to become invisible."

I groan and take the dress.

Mia gives me a really serious look. "This is a code red alarm. We need serious ugly firepower to hide your hotness."

I snort. Did I say she was my best friend in the world? Then she holds out Crocs and a fanny pack.

"I'm going for invisible, not, 'Look at me! I'm having a psychotic break!'"

"Do you want to keep the job or not? Go try it on."

I grab the stuff and head into the dressing room. I catch one last glimpse of her before I close the door. She has her phone out. "I better not see this on Instagram," I say.

"Are you kidding? This is why they invented Instagram."

I take off my short sweater dress and my leggings and boots and pull the sack dress over my head. It's linen with delicate white lace around the collar and sleeve cuffs. I can see how somebody thought it was nice, in an Amish sort of way. I think if you were standing on the prairie with the wind blowing, it might look okay.

I put on the Crocs and fanny pack, even though I think Mia was just joking about those. I walk out with a dorky expression.

"Oh my god!" Mia collapses in a chair, covering her face. "It's perfect. So sad."

"You're such a good friend to me."

She snorts and comes to me, turns me around.

"I'm not walking into a Manhattan office building wearing Crocs. It's not happening."

"Fine. Don't wear them." She arranges my hair in a ponytail at the nape of my neck, then turns me around. "You look like you're in a religious survivalist sect or something."

"Yay?"

She narrows her eyes at me. "There's still your face to contend with," she says. "Your face is still a problem."

"I already don't like where this is going."

"Nah, you just need a little acting instruction," she says. "Think of your favorite snack..."

"Cookies that I frost," I say sadly. "That's my favorite snack."

"No, no, a different snack. Cookies remind you of the bakery and the bakery makes you sad. You like every kind of candy. How about gummy bears? You love those."

I nod. I always get gummy bears when we go out to movies.

"I want you to picture gummy bears. Show on your face how you feel about gummy bears. Right now."

I smile and widen my eyes.

"Okay, pull it back a little. You don't love them that much."

I pull it back.

"There! Now I want you to add something," she says. "Think of gummy bears while looking at my nose. Never my eyes, just my nose. It'll make you seem distant and a little stupid."

"Wow, Mia, if you decide to quit your day gig, you could try for a career as a makeover expert." Mia holds down different jobs during the day, but by night she's an actress. Her career hasn't really gone anywhere, but it's just a matter of time. I think she's amazing.

"It's totally effective. Check it out." She puts on a pleasant face and talks to my nose. "Don't I seem dull now? Who even does this?"

"Oh my god! It's like you're barely there!"

I practice talking to her nose. We talk to each other's noses and laugh in the store. Then Mia gets really serious. "You must avoid looking into his eyes at all times, just in case your pupils grow large and Sasha picks up on it as a sign of sexual attraction. Or worse, if Mr. Drummond does."

"I am not and will not be attracted to that asshole," I say.

"You did say he was gorgeous."

"That doesn't mean I'm sexually attracted to him. I think the Taj Mahal is gorgeous, but I'm not going to stand in front of a picture of it and masturbate."

"Okay, now, that's just disturbing."

"I'm seriously not attracted to him," I say, even as my traitorous mind conjures up his pillowy bad-boy lips. "I'm off guys, and if for some bizarre reason I wanted a new relationship, it would not be with somebody who's more of a controlling asshole than Mason ever was. And what a jerk! Keep your eyes to yourself, jackass!"

We buy three sack-like dresses and head up 46th Street. It's a bright, springy March day, so everybody has emerged from their hovels, walking and lingering. It's the lingering that sets people apart; the natives linger in the zones behind fire hydrants and trees so as not to block the sidewalk, while the tourists plant themselves wherever.

"From now on, if you ever have contact with Mr. Drummond, you must do the opposite of what you did before. For example, you guys had that conflict about photos and you told him why he was wrong, right? You challenged him."

"Yeah, but I was nice about it," I grumble. "Unlike him."

"Still, you challenged him, and a guy like that isn't used to being challenged, so it made you stand out, because clearly everyone there kisses his ass. So if you interact with him again, you have to act impressed. Like he's so amazing."

I groan.

"Hold up." Mia slows in front of a street corner vendor selling knock-off Chanel stuff. "I know it's hard for you," she says, kneeling to examine a bag. She holds up a black quilted purse for me to inspect. "You like?"

"Way too Kate Middleton," I say.

She puts it back and picks up a huge red one.

"Kylie Jenner. No, no, no." I make her put it down and drag her away. "I don't know if I have it in me to kiss Mr. Drummond's ass. It's a lot harder than wearing an ugly dress. I don't know if I can do it."

"I know, but just remind yourself he's not Mason. He's controlling and jerky like Mason, but he is not Mason, okay?"

"Okay."

"You will act impressed and amazed whenever he comes around. You just have to last tomorrow, you get the weekend to rest, and then it's one more week. You can do it."

"I don't know if I can."

"You can." She pulls me to the curb to avoid a guy with a pastry cart. "We're in this together."

I squeeze her arm. "It hugely helps that you would say that."

"I'm always with you. Even when you move back to Fargo. I'll be the devil on your shoulder telling you to have that extra dessert."

I sigh.

"But I think you won't move," she continues. "I think you'll find a gorgeous, dirt-cheap space to rent for your new bakery that you can't pass up."

I look at her sadly. "A gorgeous, dirt-cheap place that they are dying to rent to me with my shitty credit."

"There are still lucky finds out there."

"Not in this city," I say.

She's silent. She knows it's true. Moving out of the city and back with my parents in Fargo is the fastest way to deal with my Mason debt. I could live there rent-free, renegotiate my credit card debt, and run catering out of our family pizzeria for a year and a half. I'd save money like a boss. Come back to the city with the funds to rebuild.

"Don't worry, though. I'll get you such a good subletter," I say. "I'm going to find somebody with a boyfriend or girlfriend who has their own place. And eighteen months later, boo-yah."

"Friends don't let friends say boo-yah," she says.

I give her a fake frown.

"I wonder what Mr. Drummond's like in bed," she muses. "Is he just as much of a control freak in bed?"

"Oh my god! Is this a good question to be asking me? Is this what I want in my mind as I struggle to gaze at his nose while channeling my love of gummy bears?"

"You know you've been wondering it."

"He's probably a deadbeat. His most effusive praise is a grunt," I say. "What does that tell you?"

She gives me a long, hard look. Solemnly, she whispers, "It tells me, *caveman*."

"Fuck the fuck off! Seriously? That's what you put in my head?" I say. "How can I control my pupils now?"

But control my pupils I must.

THREE

Lizzie

THE NEXT MORNING I'm standing in the coolly elegant Vossameer lobby waiting for the elevator alongside a group of well-dressed professionals, and I'm pretty sure they're all trying really hard not to stare at me in my deranged Holly Hobbie outfit. A few lose the battle and do the "room scan" but you know they're really looking at me.

I'd put a belt on it this morning at the last minute to make it look less weird, and I left the Crocs at home. Still.

I text Mia.

Me: Having second thoughts. Did we go too far?

Mia: noooooooo! Just work it.

Me: :/

Mia: Hold your head high, like you think it's hot. Pull it off.

Me: It's a freak dress, not a flubbed line!

Mia: <3

Mia is big on not letting little things throw you. But this dress is not a little thing. It's a tent.

I suck in a breath. I last through today and it's one more week.

I get off on the fifth floor and head down the hall and on to the communications area. Betsy's on the phone. She smiles, and I smile back, heartened.

I head back past Sasha's workspace, braced for the disapproving brows of madness, but she simply glances up, nods, and goes back to work, which I take as approval.

I text Mia as soon as I reach my desk.

She approves of the dress! LOL

Mia texts me back a smiley face, then a cavemen image, and I threaten to put soap on her toothbrush when she least expects it.

But really the dress was the right move. Nothing will stop me from getting my bonus and paying those loan sharks.

I always thought that loan sharks who come to your door and threaten you existed only in movies, but no, they are real, a fact I learned in the month after Mason disappeared, when an actual loan shark got into our building and came to our door to collect the first payment.

I couldn't have been more surprised. Up until the loan shark appearance, the most sketchy characters in my life in the largely gentrified neighborhood of Hell's Kitchen were certain Starbucks baristas and maybe the occasional creepy Uber driver.

The loan shark had a huge moon face and he showed me a paper that Mason had signed, and my name was on there, too, though clearly it was forged. I told him so, told him I didn't sign it, but he didn't care. I told him that I cared, and that's when he showed me the gun.

Mia had come to the door by then, and we both just stared at it. Neither of us had ever seen an actual gun up close that wasn't attached to a police officer's belt. He also had a pinky ring, which made everything slightly surreal.

"Are you literally threatening us with a gun?" Mia asked.

"What the hell does it look like?" He aimed it at my head, and I nearly fainted. "You'll bring Lenny six thousand dollars to Carson's on Third Ave in Murray Hill or this shit gets serious."

"Please," I said, shaking deeply. "First installment, six thousand. Carson's. Got it."

With that, he left. I was still trembling an hour later.

I pulled together two thousand—it was all I had. My parents back home lent me two thousand, and I know that was hard for them—our family pizzeria really struggles post-holidays.

Like a champ, Mia scraped together two thousand dollars, her entire savings.

She's been amazing. She even knew the exact perfect amount of time to wait to point out that the loan shark's name was Lenny. "Lenny? Seriously?" she'd said over wine that night. "Can that be more of a cliché?"

"I know!" I'd whispered.

Another payment is coming due soon—fourteen thousand. An insane sum for twenty-seven-year-old women struggling to pay Manhattan-sized rent.

I'm in other money trouble thanks to Mason, but banks and credit card companies don't go around wearing pinky rings and showing you guns.

That's why Vossameer's sign-on bonus looked so good: a big wad of cash in thirty days—twelve thousand, plus what I earn in my paycheck—deposited into my account. The thirty days hits on Friday, and the rest of the money—fourteen thousand—is due on Sunday.

Perfect.

I pictured myself getting off work Friday and rushing down

to my bank, pulling it all out in cash, and paying Lenny bright and early Sunday morning.

Will this enforcer guy really shoot me if I don't come through with it? I kind of can't believe it, but it's not the sort of theory I want to test.

Once Lenny's paid off, I'll quit Vossameer. Then at the end of the month, I move back to Fargo.

I want to cry when I think about that part of my plan, but there's no way around it, though I do miss my parents. I'm an only child, and the three of us were such a fierce unit.

Once things are at their worst, you get to start repairing, isn't that what they say? I started from nothing before. I can start from nothing again.

I work on new images for Facebook posts for Vossameer. Mostly I'll be using the logo in different sizes and shots of the box that Vossameer's gel products come in.

I eat my scentless roast beef and Swiss cheese sandwich at my desk and think about how it's just seven sleeps until I'm free.

The trouble starts after lunch. That's when I'm summoned to Sasha's cubicle. I smooth my dress, which has not improved with the passing hours, and head across the endless rows of cubicles toward Sasha's cubicle.

I round a corner and my belly flips upside down.

He's there.

Mr. Drummond.

I only see the back of his dark hair over the cubicle tops, and sure, there are other guys here that are Mr. Drummond's height with dark hair, but the air around Mr. Drummond seems charged somehow. As if he operates at a higher frequency than mere mortals.

I get this flash of annoyance, but at the same time, excitement.

A couple of guys from design are there, too, and Bertie the

design intern. Sasha is standing, leaning fetchingly on the cubicle wall. But it's Mr. Drummond I see. He's wearing a regular suit. No lab coat.

I stroll up to stand on the other side of Bertie, farthest from Mr. Drummond. Then I take a breath and imagine gummy bears. I plaster on a vague smile. I stare at his nose.

He looks right at me. His look is direct. Honest. Blunt, even. His gaze sears. It sets my heart pounding. Still I stare at his nose.

You can't see me, I think. *Stop looking, because you can't see me.*

Except my evil, evil brain likes having his attention on me. Because he's beautiful. And glorious. Up close I can see there's a small scar on his bottom lip, and that's what creates the pillowy-and-hot-in-a-dangerous-way effect that his lips have. Like he got in a really horrible fistfight with a guy who landed a vicious punch perfectly placed for male beauty.

Uh.

I turn to Sasha.

Still I can feel his eyes on me. His gaze has weight, pressing on my skin, melting something in me. I catch his scent, the same as before. Melon and pepper.

I want to glare at him, but I'm the opposite of that today. I'm obsequious and dim-witted.

"Okay," Sasha says. "Everyone's finally present and accounted for."

I stare down at Sasha's barren desk instead of Mr. Drummond, even as he begins to speak. "I've been reading up on things," he says. "I wanted to do an Instagram strategy. What do you think about it?"

I intensify my daffy gaze. Because, *Instagram?*

The gothically arrogant chemist has come down from the castle and uttered the word *Instagram.* Does he even have an internet connection?

I kind of want to look back over at him just to ensure those words were actually being formed by his lips and not a practical joker in the office with mad ventriloquist skills.

I don't.

There's a long silence.

Behold, I think, *the sound of five minds boggling.*

"Opinions?" Sasha says. She wants everyone else to go first, so that she can monitor Mr. Drummond's expressions when people say their answers and figure out what answer he'll hate the least. Unfortunately, that's everybody's plan.

Bert the intern takes the plunge. "That's something we should definitely be looking into *vis-à-vis* the Locke Foundation partnership," he says, which loosely translates into, *I want to say something relevant that won't get me fired. Please don't fire me!*

I'm staring at Sasha's desk thinking of the travesty of Instagram for Vossameer, considering we can't mention the word *families* or show people.

What exactly is this guy imagining? Photos of bandages on a dirty sidewalk next to some dirty pebbles?

I think wistfully of the Instagram feed from my bakery. People loved coming in and doing goofy shots of the random-occasion frosted cookies I'd sell. Every day was a different theme.

One of the design guys agrees it's something to look into. He suggests we "go to school" on the competition.

I feel the attention turn to me.

I turn my vacant eyes to Mr. Drummond's nose, channeling gummy bears. I act like I'm pondering his nose. Like it's so amazing, I can't wrap my mind around it. "Excellent idea. We should look into it and make a proposal. Could be amazing."

Something changes in his expression. I'm only looking at his nose but I can totally tell. Is he surprised? I direct my gaze of daffy admiration to the far wall. Like the wall is so impressive.

If he's looking for traces of annoyance, he won't find any. If he's looking for that woman who has ideas of her own and thinks he's the biggest jerk ever, he won't find her.

She's gone. Hidden.

I stare and stare at the wall. *Take that!*

Sasha proposes a timeline.

I look over at Sasha, nodding my head at everything she says. Like I'm hanging on her every word.

Eventually Mr. Drummond's gaze is on Sasha, too. Sasha thinks his Instagram idea is amazing, too. We all think it's amazing, because Mr. Drummond is amazing and every word from his lips is a diamond.

FOUR

Theo

I HAVE a love-hate relationship with uncompleted puzzles. Unanswered questions. Unsolved problems. I find them compelling, yet utterly tormenting.

People say I'm a brilliant chemist, but honestly, I just can't stand when problems that clearly have solutions go unsolved.

I happen to be working on the most important problem of my career: how to create a dehydrated hemostatic agent with vascular repair properties or, in layperson's terms, a dehydrated version of my original Vossameer gel, which helps stave off blood loss. I know it's technically possible. It has to be.

This new formula could save a lot of lives. It would be light and portable, perfect for small first-aid kits. It could be issued to soldiers. Shared with aid workers. Kept in remote villages where medical transport can take days.

It would be my most important breakthrough ever. And with Locke's reach into nongovernmental and refugee organizations around the world, it would instantly go where it's needed the most.

Meanwhile, people die from car crashes, gunshots, farm accidents when they might have been saved by the ready availability of the new formula.

It torments me that I can't work faster, and really, how has nobody else figured this out? The chemistry of it should be so doable. I can feel it right there in the air, waiting for somebody to pluck it out.

But nobody has. So I have to.

I know it's possible.

Needless to say, I'm fixated on the dehydrated Vossameer problem. I eat, breathe, and sleep it. I agonize over it. Sometimes I feel like I'm running a hellish race where, the moment I think I'm nearing the end, the finish line vanishes and reappears in the distance. And then I speed up, trying desperately to reach it, only to have it move again. Forever out of my reach.

Some of my most brilliant solutions come to me in the middle of the night; I wake up in the dark with my mind spinning on the answer, and I'll switch on the light and scribble down a chemical structure. Even that hasn't been happening. But I live in hope, carefully working through the problem as I fall asleep.

But what did I wake up in the middle of last night focusing on?

Her. The new assistant. Ms. Cooper.

The people who apply to join the Vossameer team typically understand and admire the work I do. They're highly driven professionals who crave the opportunity to work in a no-nonsense environment where they help bring lifesaving products to market at a fair price.

Yet Ms. Cooper practically trembled with disrespect toward

me—possibly even irritation. I kept looking at her, thinking I was misreading her.

And I could've sworn she said *Mr. Amazing is being amazing elsewhere,* not *he is elsewhere,* like she claimed she said.

Since when does a Vossameer employee say something like that? About me?

I found it annoying, and then I felt annoyed that I cared.

I did a little digging and saw that Sasha had used part of the social media budget to create a bonus that would attract top talent. Ms. Cooper had won an award of some sort.

So maybe she didn't join up out of a sense of mission.

Still.

Lying there in the middle of the night, I tried everything I could to get my mind off her. Because what do I care what some lowly admin has to say? What do I care about her impudent attitude if she does her work?

But it agitated me enough that I couldn't sleep. When the wake-up service called, I was ruder than usual.

Even then, I couldn't get her off my mind.

Why her? She's pretty, yes, but I'm a man of science. I know beauty is a scam, nature's way of conning us into procreation, no different than birdsongs or peacock plumage.

Though there was something...*activated* about her beauty— it was an angry, burning beauty, jaw set impudently. Hair the color of honey. A dark freckle on her right cheekbone. The freckle ruined the perfect symmetry of her face—normally I wouldn't like that. But the freckle made her more perfect, somehow. And, god, the way her green eyes blazed.

The blaze of her eyes seemed to have gotten under my skin, created this chemical reaction in me that eventually jolted me awake. And there I lay, with the memory of her growing brighter the more I tried to push it aside.

I create lifesaving fucking formulas, and some admin...

what? Thinks my breakthroughs are obnoxious? That I'm some-body to ridicule?

Lying there in the dark of night, I realized, to my astonish-ment, that I found it...hot.

I tried to tell myself it wasn't hot. But it was hot.

I should've fired her, but I wanted to...I don't know what. Get in her face. Reprimand her, kiss her.

I *wanted* her. It defied logic, how badly I wanted her.

I couldn't believe it.

I have better things to do than to obsess over the female of my species, to use my mental energy on an endeavor that barely sets me apart from the cuttlefish.

I tend to have rational, low-maintenance girlfriends who are as career-focused as I am, preferably scientists and technologists who won't give me drama when I cancel a date to stay late in the lab, women who respect that I'll always be more passionate about my work than them.

As I've become more successful and well-known, my girl-friends have tended to get more respectful and compliant. More convenient.

Works for me.

And then she bursts onto the scene. Takes over my entire brain. Some lowly assistant. No woman has ever compromised my focus like this.

No woman has ever compromised my focus in any way.

It's all wrong.

As any scientist knows, you always recreate your experi-ments, see whether you can duplicate your results.

Lucky for me, I did that.

And now, standing at some third-floor cubicle, I see my perception of her yesterday was off.

A mirage due to exhaustion, maybe, because this admin, Ms. Cooper, is as obsequious as anyone at

Vossameer. Good god, the woman's barely able to look me in the eye.

It's not just that. Yesterday there was a fascinating intensity in her gaze. She felt bright, annoyed, slightly thrilling.

Today, she's...vacant. I'm not even sure she understands my question. Caught without warning in her natural habitat, she's utterly dull. Maybe she came off as more confident yesterday because she was repeating something she'd heard. Could that be it? Like an actress in a play, rehearsing for the presentation to me?

Something twists in my belly—a sense of loss. Sadness. I should be happy that my first impression was wrong. I can't be distracted by silly investigations into the personalities of my staff.

Maybe when I awaken in the middle of the night, I'll be running chemical compositions in my head like I should be. Every extra day it takes to perfect my formula costs lives. Actual human lives.

Sasha drones on. A lot of marketing speak I don't care about.

And seriously, what is this Ms. Cooper wearing? She looks like she just fell off a turnip truck. Did Sasha make her wear something business-like yesterday? But now she's back to normal?

This is who I was obsessing over?

I grip the side of the cubicle, angry with myself for wasting precious time. Googling marketing trends for an excuse to come down and see what it was about her.

Nothing, I affirm to myself. The *what* about her is *nothing*.

Though even in her boringness, there's something strangely compelling about her. She's watching Sasha, eager and impressed, but I have this strange sense of her; it's as though I feel her in a way I don't feel other people.

Exhaustion. That's all. I'm exhausted. Overwrought. I saw what I came to see.

"Thank you, then," I say. "Write it up and...make a proposal to me." I turn and walk. Somebody follows. Sasha.

I head out into the hall. Still she follows.

"A few quick questions."

"Walk and talk." I make for the elevator bank.

Sasha comes along.

"The new one's a little quiet, isn't she?" I say. And then I want to eat my words.

"Lizzie? Ms. Cooper?" she asks. "The one I presented with?"

"Yeah," I say.

"She's a little incompetent, I'm afraid," Sasha says, walking beside me now. "She tries, but she's..." She shakes her head sadly. "I've already given her two write-ups. She won't last through probation. I hate to say this, but she's a bit of a moron. Slow-witted. Why do you ask?"

"Just wondering." I stab the up button, mind already on my formula. "You had a question?"

"Yes. Do you have a due date?" she asks. "For the Instagram?"

I don't give a fuck would be the answer there, but this partnership with the Locke Foundation is important to me. And the Locke people don't want to put a logo on their website that doesn't lead somewhere impressive.

Because apparently it's not enough for the Locke Foundation people that we have the most effective hemostatic gel in the world. And it's not enough for them that we want it distributed free to those who otherwise couldn't afford it.

"What's a reasonable due date?" I stab the button again.

"It depends. I'm thinking we could work up a creative brief and strategy, but if you want the proposal to contain a budget, that might add time. We'd need a set of measurable goals and a timeframe to get the budget."

My only measurable goal is me getting into the elevator alone.

But that won't work, so I turn to her. "What would you recommend? How would you prefer to proceed?"

"Let's do goals and strategy by the end of the month. Once that's approved, we'll establish a budget."

Finally the doors open. "Make it so." I step in. Then I slap my hand over the door. "One more assignment."

She raises her brows. "Yes?"

"My receptionist is out today..."

Sasha brightens up. "I heard about that. She'll be a grandmother."

"Yes." Not what I was getting at.

"You need someone...to office up there?"

"No, I'm fine." Better than fine. I enjoy having the entire area to myself. No people. No cheerful greetings or questions or requests to put things on my calendar. "My wake-up-call service is no longer viable. Do you think you could arrange for a new one?" I pull out a card and write my bedside number. "This is not to be used for any other purpose. Have a wake-up call placed to me at 4:30 in the morning, every weekday morning, starting Monday. If I don't answer, it's to repeat. If I answer and hang up, it's to repeat. They need to make sure I'm awake. You understand?"

She nods.

"Thank you."

FIVE

Lizzie

SASHA APPEARS AT MY CUBICLE, eyebrows in full anger mode. "Do you realize you didn't make eye contact with Mr. Drummond once today? Do you think that's polite?"

"Excuse me?"

"He was wondering why you wouldn't even look at him," she says. "What was that? Some kind of elusiveness game?"

Mr. Drummond said something to her? I grit my teeth. It's like the man *wants* me fired. "I was trying to be non-distracting."

"You think that was non-distracting? To so pointedly ignore him when he was speaking to you? This is a workplace, not a forum for testing out strategies best left to singles bars."

I nod obediently, clenching my fists under my desk. She has no idea how hard it was not to look him right in the eye and tell him to lay off the crack pipe, because, seriously? Instagram? Without nice images?

And what was Mr. Drummond even doing coming all the

way down to the third floor to ask about Instagram? He doesn't even like social media.

One of the books I got about forgiveness told me to write letters to people I was angry at. I start composing one to Mr. Drummond in my head. *Dear asshole, please stop looking at me. You and your sizzling eyes and hot lips. Please never come down again. Uhhhh.*

Also, *singles bars?* On the upside, Mia will think that's funny.

When I look up, she's still all angry eyebrows. I brace myself. Is she going to give me a third write-up? God, please no.

"I want you to attempt to write up a credible Instagram strategy. Let's see what you've got. Propose a reasonable set of goals and a strategy to get there."

I sigh, thinking of my bakery, of the fun shots I'd put up of the ironic cookies of the day. "Can we use stories of real-life people who were helped by the products? With the details changed, of course. But instead of people pictures, we could have images like a bicycle if they were a biker..."

The brows go full active. "And run afoul of medical-records privacy laws? Does that sound like the kind of marketing Mr. Drummond would appreciate?"

"Guess not," I say glumly. "Wait, I have an idea," I say. "We do two directions—one that's on the passion of employees here, and maybe even a work-journal blog-type thing on a breakthrough. Even better—you know how Mr. Drummond's working on that new thing? We could send a junior chemist up to take notes on his progress, and get shots of beakers and things, and it would be like an exciting race to find a cure. I bet Mr. Drummond would love that—he's so focused on his formulas, right?"

"Hmm." Sasha folds her arms.

"And then a third direction—a rationale on why Instagram is a waste of money for Vossameer."

"He *asked* for Instagram."

"I think he'd appreciate it if we evaluated it critically instead of just saying yes. '*Why Instagram is wrong for Vossameer.*' I bet he'd love it."

She frowns. Why do I care? But I do. I have this sense that it's exactly what Mr. Drummond would want.

Sasha sighs. "Work it all up, and I'll decide how I feel about it. End of next week. Can you do it?"

I grin. I can put my head down and work like a dog all next week, and that's how I run out the clock. Then I pass go. I collect my sign-on bonus. I do not go to loan-shark-beat-down jail. "I will make this Instagram proposal amazing," I say.

She gives me a skeptical look. "See that you do. Oh, and this." She hands me a business card. The front says, simply, *Theo Drummond. CEO. Vossameer Inc.* The other side is a scribbled phone number. Pencil. Deep, severe lines. "You're to arrange a wake-up-call service for Mr. Drummond for 4:30 in the morning, every weekday morning. Don't screw it up. He's very particular about managing his sleep patterns."

"Is there a recommended company resource for wake-up calls?"

"If there were, I wouldn't be tasking you with it. Find a service on Craigslist or something."

"Okay."

"Arrange the first one for 4:30 Monday morning. Can you handle that?"

"Got it." I give her my most pleasant smile, even channeling a bit of the gummy bear goodness. *Can I handle it?* It's a phone call to order a service. How hard can it be?

Three hours later, after I've called every wake-up service in the state, and then the region, and finally the nation, I discover exactly how hard it can be.

Fun fact: thanks to the invention of alarms and things that slowly turn on your lights, there are not that many wake-up services out there. And the ones that do exist already know of Mr. Drummond, and they won't touch this account with a ten-foot pole, because apparently Mr. Drummond is more of a jerk in the morning than he is normally. And really hard to wake up.

At one point, I actually go down to main reception and beg the woman at the desk to give me Mr. Drummond's receptionist's cell. I put in a frantic call to her and reach her in the hospital waiting room. I tell her the situation and ask her whether she had any contingency plans for when this wake-up-call service quit.

She sounds surprised and unhappy—she thought that service would hold up, and it was the last of the options she knows of. She was thinking of trying services out of Canada or the UK.

I thank her and hang up. It's 5:30. I'm going to end up on the most crowded subways possible because of this. But the Canada idea is good. I go back to my cubicle, and I finally find one that will do it. I make sure they understand the time difference, and that the call is to be placed Monday at 4:30. The woman on the other end assures me they'll place the call, assuming the boss is good with taking international payment.

"What do you mean? We're good for the money," I say. "We'll send cash if it comes to it. We'll send Canadian dollars through the mail if you want."

"I just have to clear it," she says. "I'm sure it's fine."

"When will I know it's cleared?"

"I'm sure it's fine as is," she says. "You're on the docket."

The docket is not inspiring faith in me.

Don't screw it up. Sasha's warning keeps buzzing through

my mind. Just for the heck of it, I arrange for an additional wake-up call to be placed to my phone for twenty minutes before his. Just to make sure.

It'll suck to be woken up at 4:10, but I'm sure I'll be lying awake anyway, freaking out at what happens if I lose my job and my bonus.

SIX

Lizzie

THEY SAY a watched pot doesn't boil. And unfortunately, sometimes a watched phone doesn't ring at 4:10 in the morning. Or 4:15. Or 4:20.

It's Monday morning, and I'm standing in the corner of our kitchen, which is actually the corner of our living room, sucking down coffee, and freaking out.

All because Mr. Drummond apparently can't operate any of the thousands of technological innovations designed to wake people up. Mr. Drummond has to have an old-fashioned phone call. And then he's a jerk about it, or he goes back to sleep.

And now there's no service that will take him. And my repeated emails to the Canadian wake-up-call people haven't been answered.

I thought I was on the docket!

"Damn," I whisper. "damn damn damn."

The only option is to call him myself, but what if Sasha

finds out? She'll fire me for sure. *This number is to be used for wake-up services only.*

Damn.

I look up to see Mia staring blearily at me. "They didn't come through? With the call?"

"I'm sorry," I say. "I didn't mean to wake you."

"I think it was the coffee smell." She pads in and grabs a mug. "It's okay. I have to memorize a scene for tonight." She pours. "You didn't get your test call?"

"No," I say.

She leans on the counter across from me. "You have to call."

"He'd figure out it was me, and Sasha is looking for a reason to fire me. Anyway, I don't even know what a wake-up call says." I check my phone for the hundredth time to make sure the ringer's on and put it aside next to Mr. Drummond's business card. "I can't."

"This is not rocket science," Mia says. "He just needs a call." She grabs my phone and pretends to dial. "Ringing." She puts it to her ear and holds up a finger.

I smile wearily. Mia *would* do role-playing at a time like this. I suck down more coffee. I'm feeling punchy. Tired. I need a plan.

"Yes, hello," Mia says into the phone, modeling how to do it. "This is your wake-up call..."

I narrow my eyes, imagining arrogant Mr. Drummond, so confident of his superiority to the rest of the human race.

I grab it. "Wake up, motherfucker," I say. "It's time to rise and shine, okay?"

Mia raises her hand like she wants the phone back, but it's my turn.

I spin around. "It's another day, full of promise and possibility, another opportunity for you to step over whatever people you step over on your way to wherever the hell you go at this weirdly stupid hour."

Something soars in me.

I continue—with gusto, "Time to start your day of being a complete and utter asshole, a man who thinks he's all that and totally *isn't*. And you need a wake-up call because you're sooooo special. Because for whatever reason, you're too much of an asshole to work an alarm clock like ninety-nine-point-nine-nine-nine percent of people are able to do."

I turn back around to find Mia looking stunned. Maybe she didn't think I had it in me. She's the thespian of the household.

"Oh, wait." I spin back around, continuing in a sweet voice now. "I'm sorry. You're such an important person. I mean, oh my god! The whole world shivers in admiration."

Mia's behind me, grabbing my arm, like she wants a turn.

"The birds fall from the trees when you approach, stunned by your glory. Everybody can't wait for you and your enchanting thoughts." I pause, and then add, "*Not*."

A rumbly voice sounds out. "What?"

I freeze and pull the phone away from my ear. I see that it's a live call. I see that it's been one minute and three seconds of me insulting Mr. Drummond nonstop.

I turn around. Mia's eyes are wide, her hand clapped over her mouth.

"Hello?" Mr. Drummond repeats.

My thumb hits the hang-up button with lightning speed. I throw the thing onto the couch like it's on fire.

"Omigod, I'm so sorry!" Mia says, frantic. "I'm so sorry. Omigod, I thought..."

She thought I knew it was real.

"I know," I say numbly. "It's okay."

"It's not okay," she whispers. "I'm so sorry."

"I should've checked it. You were just trying to help. It was my mistake, my—"

Riiiing. We both jump as the phone rings and vibrates, shifting slightly on the couch like a live thing.

He's calling back.

I hold up a hand. "Don't answer."

"Furthest from my mind," Mia says.

It rings again.

"Please tell me you have generic voicemail on there," she says.

"Yes," I whisper as it vibrates again. "It's a burner. No name. It just says to leave a message." Thanks to Mason, I can't get a real cell phone.

"Good. And when you call me with that one, it comes up NY Cell. It doesn't have your name."

The ringing stops.

Mia looks at me hopefully. "You haven't taken your allergy medicine yet today. Your voice sounds husky. He probably never heard your voice sound like that. He won't know!"

"Of course he'll know," I say. "Once he complains to Sasha."

"Tell her you didn't know they'd be like that."

"What wake-up-call service says things like that? They're going to figure out it was me, and Sasha is going to fire me." I put my head in my hands.

Mia sets a hand on my shoulder. "I'm so so so sorry."

"It was an accident," I say through near tears.

"We'll figure it out. If you lose that bonus—"

"*When* I lose the bonus."

"I'll help you raise what you need."

"I need fourteen thousand dollars," I say.

"I'll prostitute myself down on Thirty-eighth," she says.

"Stop it," I say. "You're not going down to Thirty-eighth."

There's a foot and back rub place there that we always think rubs more than feet and backs.

"I'll wear my green feather boa."

I snort and shrug her off. "I guess if I had to go...saying all those things did feel kind of amazing."

She beams at me. "There's the spirit."

"Though possibly not worth my kneecaps."

She strikes a pose. "Blow jobs for a buck," she says. "See? I got this."

"Don't even." I go to the window and watch a squirrel sneak into the dumpster six stories below. We call it our conundrum window because the dumpster really stinks in the summer. But if you keep it closed, it gets really hot in the place. "Nobody's prostituting themselves."

"Let me at least take you out for breakfast," she says. "We'll get hash browns with hollandaise sauce and eggs on top. And mimosas."

Our favorite naughty breakfast. I wrap my arms around myself, picturing the gun in that guy's hand. "Why? Because I'll be sleeping with the fishes soon?"

"Seriously. Come on."

"No, I'm going in to work," I say. "I'm not fired yet. Maybe if I explained."

She winces. She's heard the Sasha stories.

"What if I explained to Mr. Drummond?"

"Are you joking?"

"I could make it into a funny story maybe."

"It doesn't sound like Mr. Drummond has much of a sense of humor," she says.

"Trust me, he doesn't."

"Tell him it was your roomie," Mia says. "Blame it on me. It's not like he can fire me."

"It wouldn't work. He wouldn't care. No, I'll just tell the

truth. I'll say we were messing around. Surely there have been times in his life when he's messed around."

"We were demonstrating to each other what *not* to say," she adds.

"Dude, he's a millionaire chemist. I doubt he'll go for an explanation like that."

"Well, bottom line, we're in this together." Mia holds out her pinky. I pinky-shake her.

SEVEN

Lizzie

I THINK up different speeches I could give Mr. Drummond as I walk down Ninth Avenue in my shapeless prairie dress. I run through different angles as I wait for the train with the other morning commuters. I rehearse in my head while I ride the crowded car.

By the time I'm emerging on Lexington Ave., I have a funny and perfectly polished anecdote. A comedy of errors, if you will, where I'm being silly with my friend. I play up my utter shock that the call was live. I then go into my determination to make up for it, to work harder than ever on my projects, suggesting my mistake is a win for Vossameer.

If nothing else, Mr. Drummond seems obsessed with efficiency. Silly to fire me now in the midst of important projects.

It's for sure Mr. Drummond that I'll approach. Sasha would fire me in an instant, no matter how compelling I made it.

Walking in the entrance of the bunker-like Vossameer

tower, I'm feeling hopeful about my chance to save my job. Save my bonus. Save my kneecaps.

I just have to get to Mr. Drummond first—before he tells Sasha what happened. It will be our little secret. Me and Mr. Drummond.

A weird little thrill goes through me at the thought.

I say hi to Marley, the security guard, and get into the elevator with a group of overworked, underappreciated Vossameer employees with their gray lanyards around their necks and their grim, driven dispositions. The elevator door closes and we ride silently, reflected as indistinct gray blobs in the elevator door, like a giant mood ring for employee morale.

I get out on the third floor twenty minutes early, heart nearly banging out of my chest. This is the moment of truth; if Sasha wants to talk to me right away, it means Mr. Drummond got to her.

I hold my breath as I pass by Sasha's desk. Her nose is in her computer screen.

"Good morning," I chirp.

She looks up and nods. "Morning." She returns to what she was doing.

She doesn't know! There's still time!

I deposit my coat and briefcase and fire up my computer. I log in to the company intranet and see a green dot by Mr. Drummond's name. He's up there. All systems go.

My plan is to head back out into the hall as if I'm going to use the restroom and hop the elevator right up to the fifteenth floor. I'll burst right into Mr. Drummond's office and beg for two minutes of his time. I'll tell him it's urgent. It's not like I have anything to lose.

I steel myself and set off down the row of cubicles.

Sasha is not at her desk when I pass by. Not a good sign, but she could be anywhere, right?

I turn the corner, and I see her at the front, talking to Betsy, the receptionist. She raises an arched brow as I pass. "Leaving so soon?"

Translation: You should've peed on your own time! Even though I'm early.

I smile. It could be worse. A lot worse! "BRB," I say.

"Wait," she says. "We need to go over the site map with IT." She pulls out her phone. "Does eleven work for you?"

I fire up my phone. "Yeah. I don't have anything set in stone right then."

The door opens behind me. I don't think anything of it until Sasha straightens up, shoulders back, face bright.

I turn.

Mr. Drummond.

"Hi...uh..." My voice is barely a whisper.

He doesn't seem to hear or really notice me at all. "Sasha, do you have a moment?"

Nooooo!

My fingers close around my phone so hard, the thing nearly bends in half. He's here about the wake-up call. He's going to yell at Sasha. And then she'll fire me.

"Mr. Drummond!" she says. "Of course."

I feel a sob well up in my chest. I'm so fired.

If only Sasha hadn't waylaid me! I could've caught Mr. Drummond in the hall. Done the funny-story thing. Appealed to his practicality. Begged. Groveled.

"The wake-up-call service you arranged," he says.

"Yes?" she says.

I wince. He thinks *she* arranged it. This is just getting worse.

Betsy types away, oblivious to the carnage about to take place in her midst. I gather my courage. "So, you guys, a funny story—"

Sasha gives me a shocked look. "Excuse me? Mr. Drummond's in the middle of speaking."

"I just think I should tell you—" I look over to find Mr. Drummond looking equally annoyed. My words die under the heat of his gaze.

He turns back to Sasha. "Was there anything unusual about the way they advertised? The way they described their service?"

I stare at the floor, pulse racing.

Sasha tilts her head. "Why do you ask?" What else can she say? She has no idea what service I arranged.

"It was..." He pauses, seems to search for the word. "... unorthodox. I was curious..."

Unorthodox?!

Sasha looks over at me. I shrug minutely and curl my lips. *No idea!*

She turns back to Mr. Drummond. "Nothing out of the ordinary," she says. "One wake-up service doesn't tend to differ from another."

He scowls into the middle distance as my mind scrambles to make sense of all of this. *Unorthodox?!*

"Is there a problem with it?" Sasha asks. "Should we get rid of it and find another?"

"No!" he says quickly. "Leave it. This service will do for now."

Sasha has a totally pleased look on her face. She seems to be interpreting this as praise. Which...maybe it is?

"Carry on." He turns and leaves.

I watch the door close after him. Stunned.

Sasha turns to me. "Finally you did something right."

I nod. "I'm glad it worked out." More glad than she'll ever know.

"What's the deal? Did you get it off Craigslist or what?"

"That's what you requested," I say.

"Does it have a name?"

"Um...I'd have to check. Something really generic. They seemed...competent enough."

"In an unorthodox way? Do you know what's unorthodox about them?"

I shake my head.

She frowns. "You don't know much, do you?"

"You want me to research it?"

She snorts hotly, like that is such a stupid question. "No, we need to keep the site on track. Get me the deets on the wake-up service after you complete your other duties."

I go back to my desk and sit. I'm not fired. Mr. Drummond was okay with the call. I get the Vossameer website on the screen, then slip my phone into my lap and text Mia.

Me: OMFG he was into it.

Mia: Wut?

Me: You will not have to hock BJs for a buck!

Mia: he liked it? Serious?

Me: he said it was unorthodox.

Mia: Nooooo!!!!! WTF

Me: LOLOL

Mia: OMFG ROFL

We exchange every relevant emoji, which turns out to be most of them, including smiling imps, baby chicks, and gears. When hard heel clicks tell me Sasha and her eyebrows are heading my way, I hide the phone and act like I'm working.

Now that I'm not fired, I'm not sure what I'll do for tomorrow's call, but it seems far too risky to do it myself again. I'm thinking about hiring our unemployed actress friend, Karin.

I spend the day doing user stuff with IT when I'm not working on my Instagram strategy, but I keep thinking about Mr. Drummond's strange reaction.

Unorthodox? It was totally mean. Does he like that sort of thing? Is the man some sort of masochist?

When I really think about it, there's a lot about him that doesn't add up. For example, why is a man who seems to hate people so hell-bent on saving them? Why is he so resistant to fun lifestyle images on the website? Why does he never smile? Why does he run the place like such a prison?

Mia is cross-stitching when I get home. Cross-stitching funny sayings is one of her major new passions. On the coffee table in front of her is a brown paper bag; from the aroma, I can tell that it's pad Thai from the place down the block.

"What's the occasion?" I ask, stripping off my coat.

"I was planning it this morning as a consolation feast. But now it's a what-the-fuck celebration. Because, what the fuck!"

I grin. "Can you even?"

"Not even!"

I rush into my room to change out of my sad sack and into yoga pants and a long T-shirt. I'm excited about pad Thai.

When I get back out there, she hands me the cross-stitch she's working on, stretched across the round holder. "For you." It has a beautifully stitched image of a unicorn, and it says, *Because I'm a sparkly unicorn, motherfuckers!*

"Oh, Mia. I love it!"

She takes it back. "It's almost done. And then I'm going to frame it. And then you can have it. To always look at."

For when you move back to Fargo.

But she doesn't say that part.

We pull out bowls and wine. I open my container and a puff of fragrant steam comes out. I dump it into my bowl and tell her about the scene at the reception desk.

"Did you nearly faint?"

"Rrmm-hmm," I say, mouth stuffed with delicious noodles.

"Unorthodox," she says.

"Four more days," I say. "I can do this."

"Are you ready to do a repeat performance tonight?" she asks.

"What? Of the call? Are you kidding?"

"You have to," she says.

"No way," I say, twirling up another steaming forkful of rice noodles. "I was thinking about saying they quit on me and I'll get Karin to just do it for the next four days, just do a normal wake-up call. Just get me through to the bonus. Though she can stay on if she wants. She might like it as a side gig. She needs the money."

"Wait, what? You can't quit the calls!"

"Why? Karin needs the money. If she won't do it, somebody else will. I should've thought of it in the first place." Mia and I know tons of needy actors and musicians, being that we both worked in Manhattan restaurants. It's how we met.

"You can't just say the mean wake-up service quit after one day," Mia says.

"Why not? I can't help it if they're flakey."

"Don't rock the boat. He liked the mean wake-up call. You have to do it again."

"I can't," I say. "I just couldn't."

"You said it felt amazing."

"But I didn't know I was actually talking to him."

"Set your alarm for four and think about what a jerk he is. How controlling he is."

"He is that." I squirt in a bunch of soy sauce. "His employees work so hard, and he doesn't care. He won't even let us have microwave popcorn."

She gives me an outraged look. Mia's amazing at fiercely outraged looks; it's something that seems to run in her large Italian family along with a passion for Italian cinema and things decorated with sloths. "Microwave popcorn is one of the main sources of office-worker pleasure," she says.

"I know, right? He wants us to be machines like him. He leads by fear. Dude, have you heard of twentieth-century leadership techniques? Seriously."

"See? That's the spirit." Mia digs into her pad Thai. "You just have to replay this whole conversation at four in the morning."

"I don't know," I say. But then I think about his stern face and rumbly voice, and something stirs in me.

"You get to vent to your asshole boss. Do you know how many people would kill for that opportunity?"

"It's risky. What if he figures out I'm somebody from the office?"

"Don't talk about the office. You're a husky-voiced stranger who's tired of the patriarchy."

"It did feel good." I take a swig of wine.

"And he liked it."

"He found it *unorthodox*," I say. "I can't imagine that he likes it."

"Men are weird," she says.

"He does seem to like unpleasant things. I think his favorite color might be gray."

"Gray isn't even a color," Mia says. "It's a shade of black."

"Yeah! It's a shade of black, motherfucker!"

She snorts. "That's the spirit!"

I smile. I'm starting to feel better about the whole thing.

"The secret to improv like this is that you just commit," Mia says. "Whatever comes out of your mouth, go with it."

"So weird. I can't even look at him at work, or Sasha might think I'm flirting with him, but I can call him up in the middle of the night and tell him exactly how I feel about him."

Mia grabs her wine glass. "Best job ever."

EIGHT

Lizzie

I'M LESS enthusiastic about telling Mr. Drummond exactly how I feel about him when my alarm goes off at four in the morning.

I snuggle under the covers, thinking about how handsome and stern he looked when he came out from around his desk in that white lab jacket that first day. The gorgeous chocolatey tone of his hair. His intense and piercing gray gaze, just a little bit angry. And how the air crackled.

And I think about when I first saw him standing at Sasha's cubicle that day. How keenly I felt him, like I could close my eyes and feel his stormy energy.

And then the drowsy pleasure clears from my mind and I remind myself I have to call him and be mean.

I sit up in bed. "Because you can't or won't learn how to work an alarm clock," I whisper into the darkness.

At twenty minutes to go-time, I review scenes of men being jerks to me over the years. There are surprisingly a lot of them. I review how Mason always acted as if my bakery was only successful because of the location. I review how jerky Mr. Drummond was about the tagline. I pull up my PDF copy of the Vossameer handbook and reread the stupidly restrictive rules, and then I put in my earbuds and listen to Queen Latifah's "Wrath of My Madness."

Eventually I'm ready.

Heart pounding, I grab my phone and hit redial. Even though it's scary, it's kind of exciting. I'm weirdly looking forward to it. The phone rings just two times.

"Yeah?" he grumbles, sounding barely awake.

The mellow vibration of his voice warms something deep inside me.

But I have a job to do!

"Wake up, you stupid motherfucker. People are waiting for whatever annoying bullshit you have in store for them today." I'm trying not to smile. I kind of like that he's listening. "Your hapless minions await whatever stupid bullshit flows from your meteoric mind."

A silence. "So that really *is* your technique. It wasn't a fluke."

"You have a problem with it?"

"Not a problem, other than I just wanted to know."

I frown as I register this. Is that why he wanted me to call back? "This is about curiosity?"

"Are you honestly surprised by that? *'Wake up, you stupid motherfucker'*? You're literally the worst wake-up-call girl on the planet. I thought maybe it was a mistake, but no, it seems that this really is how you wake people up. Frankly, I don't understand how you're still employed. Because you shouldn't be. You absolutely shouldn't be."

Fear shoots through me. *Now* he'll get me fired.

"I tried to call back and ask yesterday," he continues. "You wouldn't pick up. You made me wait until now to get my question answered. I don't appreciate it."

What happened to unorthodox? "Well..." I don't know what to say. Now he's going to complain to Sasha, and she'll freak out on me. And fire me. "Um..."

"Yes?" he asks in an imperious tone.

"But if you were calling me back," I try, "it means you were awake, right? Which means my duty was completed successfully. And efficiently," I add.

"No, it means you insulted and annoyed a client. Does your boss know you speak to people like that?"

Asshole, I think as tears cloud my eyes.

"Do you not understand how a wake-up call is supposed to go?" he continues. "Because whatever you think you're doing here, it isn't something I should be asked to pay for. You're supposed to call the person and say good morning. Inform him as to the temperature outside and briefly tell him the forecast."

Fucking Mr. Drummond. He's such a control freak that it's not enough for him to run his own company like Stalin on steroids, now he has to tell me how to do my imaginary job.

Inform him as to the temperature outside.

"Now let's try it again," he says. "Call me again and do it properly."

"Are you kidding me?"

"I'm trying to do you a favor."

"You want me to do some role-play now? And then you're going to get me into trouble with my boss?"

"At least you'll know how to do a proper wake-up call in the future."

"What do you even know about wake-up calls? Nothing."

"I know a lot about wake-up calls," he rumbles. "More than you might imagine."

"No, you know nothing." I turn over, conscious of the feel

of the cool sheet sliding against my skin. "How do you know I'm not the best wake-up caller on the whole East Coast? Because guess what? You are totally awake. I bet you're more awake after two minutes of my awesomeness than repeated calls from any other service. Come on, tell me. Has any other service gotten you to the level of alertness that I've gotten you to?"

He's silent of course.

"I think not," I say.

"That's not the point."

"Oh, it's totally the point. I'm amazing, and you are lucky to have me." I'm committing, like Mia said. What do I have to lose? "However," I continue, "due to your back talk and poor attitude, I'm thinking about firing *you*."

"Excuse me?"

"You're a bad client. The worst."

I can feel the stunned silence through the phone. The slight tenor of his breath. A strange mix of anger and fear and weird swirls through me.

Finally he speaks. "Are you telling me there are people out there who *prefer* this kind of wake-up call? This is just what you do?"

Every molecule in me goes still, because I'm thinking about what he said—he didn't complain yesterday because he had to have his question answered. I lasted one day. Can I last another? "What do *you* think?"

"I don't know. That's why I'm asking you. Are there other people you speak to like this? Are there people out there who prefer a rude wake-up call?"

"That's funny, I thought you were the expert here."

"Answer the question."

There's something wildly sexy about his demanding attitude. In a flash I imagine him in the bed with me, demanding wrong things. And I would be all, buzz off! And then he'd make me do them, and it would be so hot.

And then I blot that mad thought from my mind. Because hello!! It's Mr. Drummond!

"Well?" he grumbles.

He really seems eager to know. Well, he's a scientist, isn't he? Famous for his curiosity. His puzzle-solving abilities.

Can I last yet another day? And then another?

Coyly, I say, "I don't *know* if you *deserve* an answer. What with your attitude."

"Excuse me?" he rumbles.

"You heard me." I steel myself. Am I really going to do this? Yes.

I suck in a breath and glance out the window. It looks cold. I can see little droplets reflected in the orange light from the Royale Hotel looming above our building.

I say, "The current temperature at JFK is thirty-seven degrees with periods of light rain forecasted throughout the day." With that, I stab my finger onto the red hang-up button.

Gone.

I sit cross-legged on my bed, pulse racing, cradling my phone with both hands, cool and heavy, screen perfectly black and a little smudgy. Quiet for the moment.

Suddenly it vibrates. A huge smile takes over my entire face as I hit send to voicemail. And wait.

Beep.

The voicemail icon shows up.

My pulse whooshes in my ears. I click to hear the message. It's short—just two seconds. The sound of a man sucking in a breath, then letting it out. It sounds like frustration. Vulnerability. Heat.

I listen to it a few times more. Even in the one frustrated breath, you can catch the deep timbre of his voice. It feels strange, this little message. Like a little gift. Something of his that's all mine.

I listen to it again, squeezing my legs together, feeling happy and thrilled and turned on.

Wait—*turned on?* I sit up, mortified.

Hell, no!

I toss aside the phone. So over controlling assholes!

I need to survive another day. That's all that matters.

I should try and go back to sleep, but there's no way. The wake-up call definitely woke me up. Mutually assured destruction. I get up and make coffee in our tiny kitchen, careful not to make noise and wake up Mia.

Trying to get his rumbly voice out of my mind.

I bring the coffee to my bedroom and sit in bed with my laptop. I navigate over to my bakery's blog and start working on a post, which always makes me feel serious and sad and not at all sexually aroused.

Sure enough, it does the trick. Because I put my heart into the business, and Mason reduced it to rubble.

Never mind. It won't be easy to rebuild, but I'll do it.

First, though, there are my knees to protect. The safety of my best friend to ensure. My bullet-hole-free skin to keep bullet-hole-free.

Even though I'm sad, I keep things extra positive on my blog and on Instagram. My new post has a picture of flowers with one of my famous random-occasion frosted cookies. Canary Appreciation Day. *We're coming back bigger and stronger!* it says underneath.

Someday soon. NOT, I add in my mind. I duplicate the post onto Instagram.

Last week's post: *New recipe: vanilla-maple glaze, just in time for Paul Bunyan Day!* And a picture of my tester batch. I used a special frosting nozzle to get the red-and-white-checked shirt looking just right.

A few people commented excitedly. One wonders whether I'll be back up and running in time for National Ferret Day. National Ferret Day is April 2nd—just a few weeks away. I answer with a smiley face. *The ferrets will have to go cookie-less this year, alas. #ChocolateferretsFTW*

I didn't tell the customers that Mason is the reason my business crashed and burned, or that he fooled me and squeezed every penny out of my life. It's better that way, image-wise. I don't want people feeling sorry for my bakery. I want them to see it as a place of joy, the way I once did.

I loved going in there in the mornings. I'd laugh with my staff and customers. We'd listen to music and bake and frost.

And then came Mason. Gorgeous, controlling Mason, who was full of ideas for modernizing my accounting systems and things. He'd give me lectures on how much of a slacker I was with money management, how I should tighten this and that.

And god, he was so charming, so out of my league. This sexy suit guy who worked on Wall Street. It was love at first sight the day he came into the bakery. Or so I thought. He seemed to have all this money. Not that I cared—I had my own, after all. The bakery was killing it! It never crossed my mind that the bakery was paying for his nice suits and limo rides.

I wanted to believe he loved me. I was willfully blind.

The police actually knew who he was. They had five names for him. A list of female victims. They said he was one of the best in the business. It was supposed to be a consolation, but it wasn't.

This time I'll stand on my own two feet. No man involved. I'm going to oversee every aspect of my business, or hire professionals I can trust.

I sip my coffee and create and schedule more hopeful posts.

Maybe my bakery is a whimpering little woodland animal, and maybe I'm a whimpering little woodland animal too, but I'll never show it to the outside world.

A few hours later I'm strolling down the sidewalk in the last of my three-prairie-dress rotation, having had not at all enough sleep, yet I feel good. Like the world is fresh and new. I tell myself it's the ionization from the rain, or maybe my fun canary post, but deep down, I know it's a little bit the phone call with Mr. Drummond.

It was so wrong. Yet strangely intimate. I never speak to people like that!

When I emerge from the scaffolding tunnel at the corner, the Vossameer building comes into view, rising up from the ground with all its concrete muscle. Butterflies swirl madly in my belly.

There's the prison I'll soon escape, I remind myself.

But the butterflies aren't thinking prison; they're thinking stern Mr. Drummond's lair. They're thinking sparkling gray eyes glowering out from nerdy glasses. They're thinking lab coat. Bad-boy lips.

Stop!

I force my mind to the Instagram strategy as I ride up the elevator to the third floor. Betsy up at reception is her cheery self, persevering in the face of utter grimness. "You look nice today," she says, a total pity compliment.

"Thank you," I say, looking down at what is basically a stitched-together ream of fabric. "Maybe this dress looked better on the rack."

She holds up a hand. "Been there."

I smile. Betsy is the nicest person in the entire place. I head down cubicle row. Sasha pops up and crooks her finger.

Come here.

Danger bells start clanging.

"The wake-up-call service," she says.

I frown, as though that's the last thing I'd expect her to bring up. "Is it still...working out?"

"Apparently so. Mr. Drummond wants an extra call." She hands me a card. "This is his office line, to be used only for the purposes of an extra call to be placed by the current operator he's working with. The call is to be made at precisely 9:20 a.m."

"Huh," I say with a totally straight face. "Really."

"Yeah, I don't know, maybe he's planning a nap up there or something. And you're to specifically request that the operator working with the Vossameer account be assigned to this job, but it shouldn't be obvious he's the client. Have them PayPal invoice me. Understand?"

"I understand," I say, scrambling to think how I'd ever get away with placing a call from my cubicle. What will I do?

"Unusual, I know. But there's always a method to Mr. Drummond's madness," she assures me breathlessly.

"Of course there is," I say. "But this request is for a call in two hours."

"Are you saying you think you can't handle it?"

"I'll put in the order," I say. "I don't know how they assign things over there, in terms of scheduling the operators. I suspect that they might schedule twenty-four hours in advance."

"Figure it out. Whatever it costs. This is something Mr. Drummond wants, so this is something Mr. Drummond gets."

She turns back to her work, my cue to scram. I take a look at the card, vaguely disappointed to find his office line written in Sasha's loopy and polished hand instead of Mr. Drummond's expressively angular pencil writing. Crisp, dark lines, like he presses really intensely, so deliciously stern is he.

The handwriting of an asshole, I remind myself.

Also, *microwave popcorn ban!*

I head down cubicle row, clutching the card. Trying to think how to handle this.

I know what he's doing, of course. He wants to figure out whether his wake-up-call girl speaks rudely to all her clients. So he's posing as a different client. Scientist that he is, he's set up a wee test.

Hah! He has to wake up a lot earlier than 4:30 in the morning to outfox me.

I smile, just at the craziness of it all. I shouldn't be smiling, but I like that he wants more of the calls. I want to make more of the calls. Because it's so damn fun.

I take the card back to my desk.

The problem is that there's no way to be sure I can get alone in two hours. Sasha might need me. Even if I ran to the bathroom stall, somebody could be there. But what kind of service turns down business? What reason will I give?

It comes to me then that I can just say no. He may be perched up there in his CEO lair atop the Vossameer building, but I run the wake-up-call company.

The answer is no. End of story. No reason. Just no.

It feels good and a little bit revolutionary to tell a handsome and controlling guy no, especially after I spent so long accommodating Mason's requests, always trying to make him feel happy and listened to.

Back at my desk, I press my phone to my cheek and pretend to put in the order for the benefit of my coworkers in the surrounding cubicles.

"You're sure there's no way to arrange it..." I say. "We really would like this call to be made...no, I understand...yes, we are *extremely* disappointed."

I return immediately to Sasha's desk, dutiful employee that I am, and tell her the bad news. "The operator he wants is all booked up. They can't give her any more clients. Do you want me to try for a different one?"

"It can't be a different one. He said her or nobody."

I nod. "I tried everything. They're just like, 'No, Operator Seven is not available for another call.'" I don't know where I pull Operator Seven from. It sounds official, though. "Not at 9:20, not at 10:20, not this morning, not this afternoon..." *Not in a house, not with a mouse.*

"Did you offer them extra money?"

"Of course," I say. "I don't think there's anything that'll sway these people. No dollar figure. Nothing. Looks like I got the last slot open for their very best wake-up-call girl."

She frowns. "I don't understand. Operator Seven won't take one more spot? How hard can it be to place one more call?"

I shrug. "Again, I could ask about a different operator..."

"No, Mr. Drummond was very specific."

I try to appear sheepish, but hopefully not in a way that looks like I think it's funny. Which I do.

Sasha gazes into the distance. "When Mr. Drummond finds something that works, he commits to it fully and completely."

"Yeah. I don't know what to say."

"I don't either," Sasha snaps, turning back to me. "He is going to be very disappointed." This like it's all my fault.

I furrow my brow, mirroring her expression, hoping against hope that she won't want to take a crack at the wake-up-call people herself. Because that would be a total disaster.

How did I get into this ridiculous situation?

"Well, if they won't, they won't." Sasha waves me off.

NINE

Theo

SASHA CALLS WITH THE NEWS—MY wake-up-call girl, Operator Seven, is all booked up.

"I don't see how that can be," I say. "It's a simple phone call."

"My point exactly," she says. "It's one simple phone call. How is that not doable? I even offered to pay extra, but they simply weren't interested. They didn't even want to talk money. There's no more room in her schedule anywhere. It seems that I landed you the last available time slot from their very best and most in-demand wake-up-call girl."

I stab my pencil into my desk, again and again, hard enough to make a tiny divot. "It doesn't make sense. A wake-up-call business sells punctuality, not time."

Or maybe she really does spend ten or twenty minutes talking to every client. It is possible? Something dark twists inside of me.

"Do you want me to try for a different operator?"

"No!" I straighten and pause, get ahold of myself. "Never mind," I say through gritted teeth, circling the lead in the divot now, feeling utterly aggravated. I'm the CEO of a billion-dollar company. I should have the service I want.

I'm amazing, and you're lucky to have me. Is it possible she wasn't bullshitting me?

"Should I seek out a different service?"

"That won't be necessary."

"Somebody here could place the call for you..."

"No," I say. "Leave it."

And why do I even care? She's rude.

But it's more than the rudeness. There was something fiery and genuine about her. Compelling. Sure of herself, yet vulnerable. And she didn't feel like a pro, rattling off lines. She felt... spontaneous. As though she was speaking from the heart. And that husky, sexy voice. "It's fine. I'll survive," I say.

Operator Seven—that won't do. I want her real name. I want to know who she is as a person. I press my fingers to my forehead.

"Mr. Drummond? Is there anything else?"

"Uh..." I feel half crazy. "How's the...uh...Instagram thing working out?"

"Oh, fabulous!" she says. "I think you're really going to like one of the directions I'm having the team create. We're working up a behind-the-scenes view of the formulation process. A tools-of-the-trade thing. Think beakers and whiteboard shots. Race for a cure. But don't worry, we wouldn't bother you with it or divulge trade secrets. We'd have a junior chemist work with marketing on it."

"Hmm," I say. It's actually not a bad idea. The race to develop the new Vossameer formula is far more dramatic and exciting than anything else we're up to. "I'd take a look at that."

"You would?"

"Put something together."

She thanks me, and we get off the phone.

I click over to my most recent molecular model, letting my mind free-fall over the visual data, red and purple on a field of brown. I convert it to a dynamic model that simulates the natural motion of the atoms in a structure, point by point.

I groan. Nothing holds up. Nothing works.

I rub my eyes. I've been up and awake for hours looking at this thing and not seeing it the way I need to see it.

Why should I care about a wake-up-call girl? Just some girl doing a job that could be done by a machine. She's a human being replacing technology. Nothing more.

I go back to the model and start retracing my steps, which is what I do when I don't see a clear answer. I could do this all day. Probably will. There are people out there to whom it literally means life or death.

Sometimes the way forward is hidden in the steps behind me. A faulty choice I made days ago. A discarded data point.

An hour later, I'm pulling up my early notes. Figuring out how to make a more concentrated version of the existing gel without losing its clotting properties shouldn't be so complicated.

The solution exists.

And the maddening thing is, it wasn't thirty-seven degrees at JFK this morning. At no point this morning was it thirty-seven degrees at JFK. The temperature at JFK at 4:30 this morning was forty, and that was the *low*. So what the hell? Did she know the temperature or not? Is it possible she knew the correct temperature and told me the wrong one just to toy with me?

I grab my phone and text her.

Me: Your thermometer is broken.

I wait. No reply.

Me: FYI. The low was forty last night.

I wait. The words NOT DELIVERED appear.

What?!?! She blocked me? *Blocked* me?

Never mind. My sister, Willow, will know how to get around a block.

I click over to favorites and find Willow's number.

I'm just about to call her, but I stop myself. What am I doing? People are dying out there every day for lack of a dehydrated hemostatic agent with vascular repair properties, and I'm putting the full weight of my intellect into tracking down my wake-up-call girl?

I rub my eyes. This stops now.

I force myself to go back to my notebook, but it's no use. I'm looking at it without seeing it. The formulas blur. I push away from my desk, annoyed with myself.

Women never make me lose my focus. Not ever. I enjoy sex as much as the next guy, but in a context of respect and rationality. Not...whatever these calls are.

And how is it that I'm even thinking about her in the women-and-sex arena? Then again, I was thinking about that assistant—Lizzie—the one who dresses like she just fell off a turnip truck in that way, too.

It's exhaustion. Frustration.

I go to the whiteboard, but I can't bear to stare at it any longer, so I slip around it to the window and look down at the people, like so many toy soldiers.

Wake up, motherfucker.

It was so...shocking. But in a strange, and even slightly enjoyable way. I found it...stimulating.

Wake up, motherfucker.

It's been so long since I felt any kind of surprise from a woman. And really, what kind of woman says that to me?

People are waiting for whatever annoying bullshit you have in store for them today. Whatever stupid bullshit flies out of your meteoric mind.

Meteoric. I shake my head at her use of that word.

Meteoric is the entirely wrong word for what she meant. *Meteoric* suggests something spectacular yet fleeting. Transient. I'm pretty sure she was going for something more like *grandiose. Bombastic. High-flown*, maybe.

I'd like to tell her that. If she's going to sass me, she needs to get her terms right.

Of course she wouldn't listen. She'd come back with some insolent remark, and I'd kiss those sassy lips. And then I'd take her over my knee and spank her. Just slide those pj pants down and give her a good firm slap on her bare ass.

I turn away from the window, surprised at the strange turn my thoughts have taken. What's going on with me? Spanking isn't my style.

Except now that I've pictured it, I can't get the thought out of my mind.

I stalk back over to my whiteboard and study a side chemical reaction, but the harder I try to shake free of the idea of spanking her, the more erotic power it seems to gain, and the harder my cock becomes, and suddenly I can't think of anything else.

I'd spank her, and then maybe I'd turn her over and kiss her. I'd grab her hair and trace my fingertip over the impudent smile I can hear right through the phone.

I go back to the window and press my finger to the glass, letting the sound of her sexy, raspy voice echo through my soul.

TEN

Lizzie

MIA'S GONE when I get back home. I check her schedule and I see she has an evening class to go to.

I usually don't mind being alone, but these days I'm a little rattled by the fact that Lenny's collections guy was able to wheedle his way into the building. You need a key to get into the building, and residents are not supposed to be letting strangers in. But this guy got in. He was in our hallway, knocking at our door. He could come back at any time. I have the door locked, but a few good kicks could break it open.

I sleep poorly, even after I hear Mia roll back in.

My alarm goes off at four, but I'm already awake, pulse racing, looking forward to talking with him and tormenting him.

I need to find a way to keep stringing him along, but I have to be careful; eventually he'll figure out that I'm using his curiosity against him.

I pull my phone out of the charger a few minutes early and give myself a pep talk.

My pulse beats excitedly as the time turns over, from 4:29 a.m. to 4:30 a.m. I press the green phone symbol, because Operator Seven is always on time, bitches!

He answers on the first ring. "Yeah."

I feel my face split into a huge smile. "Here he is, folks, answering on the first ring. Who's the best wake-up-call girl in the city?"

He says nothing, but I know he's there. Then he says, "You hung up on me."

"You were awake, *dude*." I put extra emphasis on the word, knowing somehow that it'll bug him. It's like I can feel the edges of his wonderfully prickly emotions. "Did I not tell you the weather? Isn't that how proper wake-up-call girls end their calls? I heard it from a very reputable source."

"Did you? So you know who this is, then?"

"'*Do you know who this is?*' Did you seriously just ask that?"

"Do I need to ask it again?" he rumbles.

I hold the phone with both hands. The volume is just up enough that I can hear. I kind of do want him to ask it again. Partly because his voice is really grumbly and sexy this morning and partly because I have no idea whether wake-up-call people know who they're calling. Do they get little profiles of their clients? Special wake-up dossiers?

"Well?"

"You think I don't know who I'm calling?" I say, making a snap decision. "This is a wake-up-call service. I know exactly who I'm calling—Theo Drummond, CEO of Vossameer. I know everything I need to know about you. Thing one: You're a man who can't seem to operate the modern wake-up technologies specifically created for wake-up functions, so you have to hire somebody to do it for you. And then you act like a total jackalope and tell her how to do her job."

My heart bangs. Did I really just call him a jackalope? I wait for his reply. Nothing.

Was jackalope a bridge too far?

"Is there anything else I need to know?" I ask. "Because that kind of says it all, don't you think?"

He does his hot warning grumble, and my belly melts. "Oh, I don't know about that."

I lie back down and pull the covers to my chest, imagining Mr. Drummond in his own bed, somewhere across town.

He probably has a kingly king-size bed with thick wooden posts on all four sides. Grand arched windows with amazing views. Would he sleep in pajamas? No, I decide. He'd sleep in the nude; he'd see pajamas as a useless convention.

I imagine him nude in a nest of tangled sheets, muscular chest bathed in moonlight. One trunk-like thigh sticking out the side.

My blood races to imagine it. I turn to my side, and my nipples tingle from the brush of fabric, being that they have become keenly sensitive little pellets of need. "Well," I say hoarsely, "now that you're awake, let's see what the temperature is."

"Don't bother," he rumbles.

"But isn't that how I'm supposed to wrap up our call?"

"It's not as if you have any idea of the temperature."

"I can tell you what I think it is, though. Accuracy is so over-rated, don't you think?" I add, just to needle him. I have to stop smiling, or he'll hear it in my voice. I shouldn't be having fun. "Now, let me take a look here..."

"Wait," he says.

"What? You're awake." I set the phone on the bed, just inches from my face. I curl onto my side, looking at it like a live thing. What am I doing? "This marks the official end of my duties," I tease. "You think I don't have other clients waiting for my amazing wake-up service?"

It's a little evil, reminding him of his question.

"So this really is how you wake people up..."

I decide his tone this morning is less of a rumble and more of a velvety crinkle. Soft, yet substantial.

"That's for me to know and you to never find out, Theo." I decide I get to call him Theo. I like calling him Theo.

Judging by his silence, he's not a fan.

"Just tell me," he says finally. "Is this your technique with multiple clients? It's not a difficult question."

"Hmm," I say, imagining his stern expression. No doubt he's reached stern-face DEFCON one, red-alert status.

"What's your name?" he asks.

"Operator Seven."

He grumbles his disappointment. "Fine. One more question."

"Oh, I suppose," I say breezily.

He lowers his voice. "What are you wearing?"

My mouth falls open. Sexy shivers flow over me. "What am I *wearing*?" Everything seems too wild, suddenly. In a good way.

He lowers his voice yet another octave, which I might not have thought was possible, and which I can report is even hotter. In this lower and more delicious new octave, he says, "Tell me."

My skin feels too tight. "Yeah, I don't think so. I don't think I'm going to *tell you what I'm wearing.*" I look down at my sleep set. Silky pants, white with tiny pink flowers.

Silky matching top.

Nipples hard enough to cut glass.

Umm...

"I think you want to tell me, though."

My pulse races. Because I do. "I'm wearing something beautiful." Like a madwoman, I slide a finger over my belly, and just that light feather of a touch unleashes tidal waves of sensation. I could get off so easy right now. "More beautiful than you can even imagine."

I slide my hand over my shoulder. I'm officially going insane.

"Tell me," he says. "Now."

"You think I take orders from an asshole like you?"

"I think you'd enjoy taking orders from an asshole like me."

"Dream on," I say. "In the words of Michael Jackson, U can't touch this."

"That was MC Hammer who said that. You need to take a little more care in terms of precision...Operator Seven."

"Oh, excuse me, Professor Wonderbrain," I say, enjoying the way he said my fake name.

"Tell me what you're wearing."

A glowy warmth spreads through me. "Why do guys always want to know that?"

"I don't know why other guys would want to know that. But personally, I like my woman to have a little bit of clothes on her, so that I have something to rip off of her. That's why I asked. Because I need to know what exactly I'm visualizing myself ripping off you."

I imagine Mr. Drummond hovering over me, savagely ripping off my clothes.

"I'm imagining you in something girly," he continues. "Extra points for pink."

I swallow, mind reeling.

"Have you ever had a man rip off your clothes?"

I think about the guys I've been with. Nobody ripped off my clothes, though Mason once made one of my buttons pop off. "It depends on what qualifies as 'ripping off.'"

"Oh, Seven," he breathes, "if you have to ask what qualifies as a man ripping off your clothes, then a man has never ripped off your clothes. A man has never been so desperate to get at your beautiful tits and your sweet pink pussy that he goes crazy, just taking the fabric in his fists and tearing it off you like a brute, blind with need..." He pauses, as if to catch his breath. "Insane from the need to sate himself with you," he continues as I slide my hand on down my belly. "If you have to ask that, then I promise you, a man has never ripped off your clothes."

I swallow, stunned that Mr. Drummond's talking to me like this. Stunned that he's talking to *anyone* like this!

Also, I can't believe how hot it is.

"You're right about one thing, though," he says. "I am an asshole. And trust me, I could make it so hot."

My breath speeds. I dimly recall having some sort of goal with this phone call, but it's disintegrated into a thousand little bits. Vaporized. Transmogrified into stardust.

I try to keep my voice steady. "If nothing else, you're getting an A for confidence. Or maybe an A minus."

A tiny huff of breath. Did he think that was funny? "You and that sassy mouth of yours. God, if I were there, I'd put you over my knee so fast."

Shivers explode over me. "W-what?"

"I'd put you over my knee and rip those little pj pants right off your ass and give you a good, hard spank."

"Excuse me?"

"You heard me just fine," he says. "You and that smart mouth of yours need to be taught a lesson. Don't you think?"

I swallow. Something wicked inside me says, "Maybe."

"No maybe about it," he rumbles.

In other news, my finger finds its way up to my nipple, pinching and kneading. The sensation radiates all through my body. "Are you so sure I'm wearing pjs?"

"Pretty much," he says. "Matching. A little bit prissy."

"Well, aren't you smart."

"I'm right?"

"Pretty much."

"I'd make you feel so good," he whispers.

"Somebody's feeling presumptuous," I say. Like I'm not completely winging on my nipple, enjoying the thrill of his forbidden dirty talk. "You might be taking the 'call girl' portion of 'wake-up-call girl' a little far."

"Somehow I don't think I am."

I swallow, trying to think of a clever answer, but my mind has gone offline.

"And I promise you," he continues, "I'd know how to handle you. You'd want things good and dirty. So fucking dirty, and you know I'd deliver. You might even like me to hold you down. Can you feel my hands around your thighs?"

"Yes," I whisper softly.

"I am not a man with a lot of mercy in him—that's something you're figuring out right about now."

I close my eyes. He is not a man with a lot of mercy in him. It seemed like such a bad trait before.

"You would give yourself over to me, and I would be every inch the asshole you need me to be. I would push you right up to your edge. Maybe a little bit past it. Just a little, though. Just enough to make it interesting."

"Yeah?" My voice sounds breathy. Operator Seven is getting into this.

"Oh, yeah."

I slide my hand down over my thigh, back up between my legs.

"I can hear your hand right now. Skin sliding across fabric. Something silky, maybe."

"Silky. Pink with flowers."

He huffs out a breath at this extra detail. Like he really,

really loves it. I close my eyes, enjoying the resonance of his pleasure.

"Tell me where you're touching yourself."

I swallow.

"But only if you'll tell the truth," he adds suddenly. "No lies. I hate lies. What I want with you is a little bit rough and real as dirt."

I stare at the phone. *What I want with you.* He wants a thing with me? Also, a little bit rough and real as dirt? The room seems to spin. "Real as dirt?" I manage.

"Do you think I'm the kind of man who gives you flowers?"

I think about Mason. The flowers he'd give me. The lying flowers. "If you gave me flowers, I'd rip them up."

He grumbles. It's that approving grumble again.

"I'd rip them up and throw them away," I add.

"I might enjoy seeing you do that."

I feel my face heat. "Before or after you rip off my clothes?"

"Before," he grumbles. "Trust me, once I rip off your clothes, you won't be thinking about flowers."

"Okay," I breathe.

"I'd have your legs so wide apart. My fingers so deep in you, my thumb plying your clit so perfectly, you'd be seeing stars. Are you touching yourself right now? Tell me you're there."

"I'm not sure if we're actually doing that yet," I say. In truth, I haven't touched myself in a proper way since Mason. A few sessions with the vibrator to blow off steam. Nothing long or luxurious. I'm a little afraid to let a guy in, but I love this energy between us. And luckily, it's anonymous.

"Go ahead," he says. "It's my fingers there, and it's what I'm doing now. I would play you like a harp."

"In a nest of torn clothes."

"You wouldn't care that your perfect pajamas are in shreds around you. You'd just be desperate for what I can give you.

Begging me for more and more. I'd enjoy you begging me for my cock. That sexy, raspy voice of yours would get me so hard."

Mr. Drummond is a complete freak.

And I've never wanted anybody more.

I press my hand between my legs. Total sensation jackpot. "You are so pompous to think I'd beg."

"But I'm right. You know I am."

"Because you're god's gift to women?"

"To the ones I fuck."

I smile. He's such an arrogant asshole, and I so want him. My whole body feels pleasantly warm. "LOL," I breathe softly, picturing him glowering in his white lab coat, all beautiful and evil and imperious.

"I'd get you so wet, your pussy dripping to get me in there. And you'd be begging me so hard, you wouldn't care what you sounded like. You'd do anything to get more of whatever I decide to do to you. And your clit would be warm and slick and a little bit stiff under my touch. God, the way I'd work you..."

"It was your thumb," I say. "You were doing me with your thumb."

"You liked that thumb?"

"I like a certain amount of conscientiousness. Harps require attention to finger placement; that's what I'm saying here."

"Baby, when I'm doing you, you won't be worrying about hand choreography." There's a pause where I think I hear him breathing, like he feels as aroused as I do. "Your entire universe would shrink to whatever I'm doing to you with my fingers."

I slip my hand under the elastic of my sleep pants. My fingers find my clit.

"It'll be all you can do to survive the sheer pleasure overload while I make you ready for me."

"Yeah?" I say.

"Oh, yeah." I hear the smile in his voice. It's like he knows.

"You're wet for me right now, aren't you? You're about to combust. If I were there, I could get you off with one touch. Maybe even a puff of air."

Excitement thrums through me. Am I masturbating on Mr. Drummond's command? This man who runs Vossameer like Alcatraz?

Yes. Yes, I am.

"So presumptuous," I mumble.

"No, I'm realistic. Go ahead. Tell me how wet you are for me."

"I don't think you need any extra encouragement, mister."

"Tell me anyway. Not that you could do yourself as well as I could do you."

"I've had a lot of practice," I say, sawing my finger along my madly tickly clit.

"I could do you so much better. I might even make you say it. Maybe I'd keep you right on the edge until you admit it to me."

"You are such a pig," I say.

"Oh I am. An utter animal. Sex with me is a dirty, savage affair. Utterly uncivilized. It's the opposite of civilized."

Did he really just say that? I let out a shuddery breath. I'm full-on doing myself, and I never want him to stop talking.

"Are you feeling how wet you are? Spread it around. I want you really wet and silky for me."

I make my motion more circular now, letting him direct my fingers. Because apparently it's not enough that he's my tyrannical boss at work.

"If I were there, I'd be burying my rock-hard cock so deep in that pink little pussy, your head would be spinning."

I flash onto Mr. Drummond's big, hands. Massive knuckles. Thick fingers. Is it possible those fingers are wrapped around his cock at this very minute?

A thrill shudders through me.

I hated him so much at that presentation, and I still kind of do, but I like the idea of his big, stern hand holding his cock.

"Faster now," he says.

"You just assume I'm masturbating," I tease.

"God, you and your sassy mouth," he says. "And yes, for the record, I do assume it. I assume you're close, too."

"Such a freak," is all I can manage. It sounds like I'm saying it about him, but I'm really saying it about me.

Lying here at four-freaking-thirty in the morning touching myself. Belly rising and falling. Shimmery sensations shivering over me. Because of Mr. Drummond.

Yes, it's safe to say I've entered freak zone.

A little voice deep inside my brain whispers, *if you come, he'll win.* It's the same little voice that keeps chanting about his evil microwave popcorn ban.

The voice isn't half as exciting as Mr. Drummond's voice is.

ELEVEN

Theo

"SUCH A FREAK," she says.

She has no idea. I barely recognize myself. And I couldn't be more into it.

She's into it, too. Her arousal comes through loud and clear; it's in her breath. In the way she phrases her words. Short clauses. Gusted delivery.

"It's already happening," I say. "You're already there."

Seven snorts. Even now she's annoyed, but she's coming apart all the same. She seems to dislike me, yet she can't stop herself from obeying me.

This blend of dislike and obedience and heat is the most erotic combination I've ever experienced.

I've never ripped off a woman's clothes—it feels irrational—but when I'm talking to Operator Seven, rational and irrational are out the window.

"Such a freak," she rasps again.

"Whatever you need," I say. She has to be close; I can feel her leveling up right through the phone. God, it's hot.

"I love how you think the whole world revolves around you," she says.

I slide my hand over the cool steel of my kitchen island. Dim lights illuminate the subway tile above the sink, all neat lines and crisp corners. "Me, too. I love how it revolves around me, too," I say.

An annoyed gust of breath. Angry and turned on.

She's not the only one. This anonymous girl has me hard as rock, but I won't jack off. I want to concentrate on her. I'd do anything for her right now.

"Are you almost there?" I growl. "I need to hear you come. I know you're close."

Her breath rasps in and out. Soft and sweet.

"You're almost there," I say softly, coaxingly. I'm losing sight of my goals and questions, and for once I don't care. I ball my fists, wishing I could press my lips to her cheek and feel her raspy breath in my ear as she comes apart.

Where in the city is she? An office? A bedroom? A basement hovel? What does she see when she looks around? What's out her window?

"You're almost there, aren't you? And you're all mine."

"Uh," she breathes.

I need to hear her come. It's an utterly senseless need. This woman who's driving me crazy. This woman who fills my dreams, who looms large in my mind when I wake up in the middle of the night, I just need her to come. I need some control back, or maybe just to give her something.

"Do yourself, baby. You're every inch mine right now," I say. "I'll take what I want, and it'll be so good."

I hear her suck in her breath. A short intake of air.

Then nothing. She stops breathing. It's as if everything between us grinds to a halt.

"What?" I ask.

"No," she says. "No, no, no, no."

"What happened?" I ask, feverishly reviewing my words. *You're every inch mine. I'll take what I want.* Was it a terrible thing to say? We say whatever thing comes into our minds—isn't that the agreement with phone sex?

"What happened..." she begins, "what happened...is that you're awake."

"No," I say. "Wait—"

"The weather is cloudy. It's a mild forty-two degrees at JFK."

Click.

I stare down at the screen, blood racing.

Just like that, she's gone.

And I feel bereft.

I clutch my phone. It's the newest iPhone. Fast. Powerful. Precision engineered by the best tech minds in the world.

Utterly useless.

Call ended.

God, is she calling other people now? Talking to them the way she talks to me?

Don't. You can't.

My mind races with visions of hunting her down. Pressing her to the wall, whispering in her ear, making it all right again. I'd taste her lips and make her never want to call anybody but me.

I need her all to myself. Completely to myself.

It's insane, the thoughts I have about her. I'm a chemist, not a caveman. And she's just a wake-up-call girl.

And the only thing I want.

The thought stuns me. I have no idea what this woman

looks like or what she's into or how old she is. She's the only thing I want.

There's a lifesaving clotting gel I'm supposedly in a race to develop, but it's the furthest thing from my mind.

I could call back, but she won't pick up. I may not know anything about her on a surface level, but I have a sense of what she's made of. I know how she'll react to things.

The knowledge that I have of her feels intuitive. Primal.

I walk to my window, stare down at the lights that dot the pathways of Central Park. Like looping dot-to-dots in a sea of darkness, framed by the relentless glow of Manhattan.

According to caller ID, she's in New York City. She's a cab ride away, somewhere out there in the crowds of people marching up and down the city streets, streaming in and out of the subway, lining up for shows, elbowing her way through the produce section at the corner store.

And my need to find her blazes wild as the sun.

TWELVE

Lizzie

I LIE in my bed with weird energy bouncing all through me. I'm hugely turned on, and even more upset and surprised.

What am I doing taking up with somebody like Mr. Drummond? Wasn't it enough to lose myself to one control freak of a man?

You'll let me take what I want.

Screw that!

I pull my robe on and shiver to the bathroom. Feel annoyed at Mia leaving a towel on the floor and all her hair stuff on my side of the counter.

The annoyance is enough to momentarily blot out the memory of Mr. Drummond's rumbly, sexy tenor, still vibrating through me. The way he was just so assholey, but hot and stern.

"Whatever, dude," I say aloud, arranging Mia's leave-in conditioner and hair oil on her side of the sink counter.

Because seriously? He gets to have his empire and entire

company and crazy millions and everybody bowing and scraping in front of him. And his asshole leadership techniques that make life for each and every one of his minions utterly unpleasant. But he doesn't get to have me.

No, I will not let you *take what you want!*

Mr. Drummond is seriously the jackass of the century—that's the thought that is running through my head. But it's not like a normal thought. It's more like a fiery comet, zipping around inside me. And I want to go tell him. I want to claw at his handsome face and perfectly tailored everything with pretty red fingernails between hot, dirty kisses. I don't actually have pretty red fingernails, and I don't want to hurt him, but that's the unruly image that's currently invading my mind.

I get into the tiny shower and scrub my hair really well. I double rinse it. I soap myself up, refusing to imagine him ripping off my pajamas, desperate to get to my pussy.

If I were there, I could get you off with one touch.

"You think you're all that, and you're not," I say as I rinse off with the sprayer, directing the warm, deliciously pulsing jet of water around my body, washing the shampoo and soap away.

Mr. Drummond doesn't get to be in my head, directing my fingers. I can direct my own fingers, thank you very much.

Furthermore, if I want to masturbate, I'll do so without his voice in my ears. Without picturing his chocolatey dark hair. Without imagining the storm-cloud sparkle of his eyes on my bare skin. Without imagining his thick, manly fingers calming the ache between my legs.

The edge of the warm spray is like a soft pulsing laser on my sex. I aim it right on my clit, moving it just so. Uhhhh so good.

Wait, what?

Shit.

But now that I started, I have to do it! How will I concentrate on the Instagram strategy? That's the thing I tell myself as I enter the land of no return in two seconds flat. I come so hard, I nearly fall over and crack my head open.

With shaking hands, I put the sprayer back in its holder. Take that, Mr. Drummond!

THIRTEEN

Lizzie

I ARRIVE at 7:30 sharp in drab dress number one. "Good morning, Betsy," I say.

"Hi, Lizzie," she says, and then she kind of winces and adds, "Sasha wants to see you ASAP."

Gulp.

I tromp down cubicle row. Did I go too far? Did Mr. Drummond finally complain about the wake-up service? But what's he going to say? *I tried to get the wake-up-call girl to masturbate, but she hung up on me before her orgasm!* But then, why does Mr. Drummond do anything he does?

I smile nervously and approach Sasha's immaculate desk. "You wanted to see me?"

She looks up. "IT needs a new site map for our meeting today. Will you put together complete packets with the current map, top-level-page printouts, and our overview goals? All recent edits, PDF and hard copies, five each. Betsy will show you how to tab them up."

"Of course." I nod enthusiastically. I nod and nod. I'm a bobblehead of relief.

She waves me off, and I walk to my desk feeling like I just won a death sentence appeal. Because if Mr. Drummond was going to complain, he wouldn't wait around. He'd get right on it. He's ruthlessly efficient that way.

I put together the files in under an hour, collecting every edit into one place. I zip them up and send them to print. I grab them from the printer and bring them to Betsy. "We're supposed to tab these up?" I say. Because I actually don't know what that means.

"Ah." She grabs a few boxes full of colorful tabs from a nearby shelving unit. We discuss what the different colors should represent, then we create a two-person assembly line, tabbing and collating.

We chat about *The Bachelor* and exchange theories on our most hated contestant, keeping our voices low, lest somebody hears our jubilation and issues a demerit.

People head in and out of the department while we complete our task. It's nothing special that people come in and out. The door opens frequently, and I don't bother to look over my shoulder.

Until the time that I do.

I don't know why I feel compelled to turn and look at the very moment he comes through. The woo-woo answer would be that some strange force field is connecting us because of our weird phone call, like I still feel him inside me.

The more logical explanation is that he's just louder than everyone else. That he practically smashes open the door, enti-tled jackass that he is.

You will give me what I want.

His eyes rivet instantly to mine as he crosses the threshold, and suddenly I'm back in bed, snuggled under the covers, saying things to him I've never said to any man.

I swallow.

He's in his lab coat, of course. He wears it open over a charcoal gray suit with a gray-blue shirt underneath. The color seems to heighten the gray of his eyes, which in turn seems to heighten the color of the shirt. It's like they're in some kind of feedback loop that just gets louder and louder. And the loop is focused on me, and the closer he comes, the more mesmerized I am.

I attempt to stare stupidly at his nose. I attempt to imagine gummy bears.

But instead I'm back in the shower, trying not to imagine the spray is his fingers, sliding between my legs.

One touch and you'd explode.

Did he masturbate this morning, too? I feel like he wasn't jacking off during the call; his attention on the phone felt so strong and fierce. No way was his focus divided. Nothing about him was distracted.

That's part of what made it all so hot. Like he was hyperfocused. The way he hyperfocuses on his chemistry.

He's found me out, I think. *He knows.*

"Mr. Drummond," Betsy says. "How can I help you?"

He comes up to the desk, immobilizing me with his eyes. He should be focusing on Betsy, but he's focusing on me.

Sex with me is a dirty, savage affair. Utterly uncivilized. It's the opposite of civilized.

FOURTEEN

Theo

TURNIP TRUCK STANDS in the front reception area of the marketing and HR department, clutching a sheath of papers, pretty green eyes gone wide, gaping at me. More than gaping; she seems positively frantic with alarm.

You'd think I sprouted fangs, that I might bite her. And for one long and very strange moment, the idea seems enjoyable.

My pulse kicks up. It's the wake-up-call girl, scrambling my mind. Suddenly even Turnip Truck is enchanting.

She wears another one of her plain dresses. Like she stepped out of a black-and-white picture, and all she needs to be complete in this life is a bonnet and a flock of ducks.

Even so, she's beautiful.

I force myself to think about what Sasha told me about her being a moron, so incompetent that Sasha has to do her work for her.

I don't believe everything I hear from Sasha, but I don't see what advantage there would be to her telling me she'd hired a moron if the woman wasn't a moron. It's too bad, because there really is something about her. Something indefinable. Which doesn't make sense, as I have zero interest in moronic women who are easily impressed and frightened.

Turnip Truck is the opposite of my type.

The opposite of the wake-up-call girl.

It's just my lack of sleep. My lack of progress on the formula.

I turn to the receptionist. "I need to see Sasha."

"Let me see where she is," the woman says.

I set my hand on the desk. Turnip Truck's alarmed gaze falls to my fingers.

In the tight moments that follow, I flash on something I haven't thought about for years—a strange cardboard book I had as a child. The pages were cut into thirds—heads, outfits, and shoes, so that you could turn the parts independently of each other and put a clown's head with a ballerina's body and firefighter boots, for example. Or a clown head could have a suit and tie over ballerina shoes.

I always hated that book.

I hated that you could rearrange the clothes to lie about the person. I preferred to arrange it so that the correct heads went with the correct outfits. I remember trying to tape the pages into their rightful configuration, much to the anger of my little sister, Willow, who preferred to mix it up. She thought it was funny to put a ballerina head on a clown body with lumberjack boots.

Turnip Truck glances up. Our eyes meet, and again I have the sensation that her clothes are flipped wrong. That her stare is flipped wrong. But then she turns away and busies herself with whatever she was doing.

"Sasha's on the phone with IT," the woman says. "Should I ping her?"

"By all means. Ping her."

Ping her.

I take a seat in the waiting area, annoyed. I wonder, not for the first time today, what Operator Seven is doing. Is she calling other people? Unease rises in my chest.

I grab a Vossameer newsletter from the little table and pretend to read it, but I can't stop going back over our conversation. The way Seven's voice gets raspier when she's aroused. Her sense of humor. I love how she doesn't take shit from me, but there's that vulnerability to her.

The women shuffle their papers. Turnip Truck seems to be helping the receptionist. Maybe Sasha gave up on her and demoted her. Being that she's so moronic and all.

Finally Sasha finds her way up to the front. "Mr. Drummond! I hope you weren't waiting long."

I stand. "I'm going to need the contact information for the wake-up-call service."

"I hope there isn't a problem," Sasha says.

A flutter of papers behind the reception desk.

"Oh no!" The receptionist disappears behind the desk, kneeling, presumably to gather whatever papers were dropped.

Turnip Truck stands there looking bewildered at this strange demonstration of the principle of gravity, then she, too, disappears behind the desk. Apparently picking up dropped papers is a two-person job at Vossameer Inc. Do I need to fire every last person on this floor?

Everybody except Sasha. Sasha's work has been stellar in the past month. And her ideas for doing behind-the-scenes lab spotlights have really grown on me.

"Mr. Drummond? Are you no longer finding it effective? I could find you a new service. It would be no problem," Sasha says.

"No, I'm happy with this service you found. I just need the contact information. The name of the service. The number."

Now Sasha looks bewildered. Am I speaking in Urdu?

"Will that be a problem?"

"Sure, I could get that for you, no problem." She smiles brightly. "I'll email it."

"I'll take it now, if you don't mind." I nod at the phone in her hand.

She looks down at it. "It's not on here. It's on my desktop."

I sigh. "I'll wait, then."

She looks nervously over her shoulder. "I got kicked offline. I need to go back and reboot it, and it'll be a bit. I don't want to make you wait. I'll email it as soon as I'm back up. The first task."

It comes to me here that Sasha's hiding something. She seems nervous.

"As soon as it's back up," she confirms brightly. "Top of my to-do list."

I frown. "Wouldn't it be more efficient to have started the reboot process before you left your desk? It would be rebooted by now."

"Oh, of course," she says. "But I thought you might be up here with an urgent matter. I'll have that info ASAP."

I sigh. What the hell am I even doing down here? I have work to do. "ASAP."

FIFTEEN

Lizzie

SASHA TURNS to me as soon as the door closes behind him. "Did I not ask you for those call service details yesterday?"

"Yes," I say.

"Yet you didn't see fit to provide them for me. Thanks for making me look completely foolish."

"I'm so sorry," I say, clutching the papers to my chest. Quietly freaking out.

"Don't be sorry, just get me the damn details. Are they on your computer?"

"Yes?"

"Come on, then." She heads toward my desk.

I follow, quietly freaking out even harder. If I was a cartoon, there would be jagged scribbles around my head.

Because obviously there's no contact information for the wake-up service to show her. What am I going to do?

"It might take a bit to put my hands on it," I say, taking my chair and inputting my password. "I'll have to dig around a bit. I'm not sure where I put it..."

"How hard can it be? You got it on Craigslist, right?"

"Uh...that's what you suggested..."

"At some point you were going to have to pass along the details to billing, were you not? Did you not write it down?"

"I guess I was in a hurry at the time. I know I can put my hands on it, it's just—"

"That you're disorganized? And that your disorganization is affecting the people around you?"

One more write-up and I'm fired. And I lose my bonus. I cannot lose my bonus. With shaking hands, I type *Hello Morning Wake-up Service* into the search bar for my local disk.

"That's what it's called? Hello Morning?"

"If I recall."

"You're not sure?"

I hit enter. Hello Morning is a Japanese TV show and an inspirational thing for women. "I might have to dig."

"What about your email history?"

"Oh, good idea," I say. I navigate to my mail, but there's nothing there for that day. "Oh, wait," I say. "I was cleaning my inbox. Maybe I deleted it or..."

"Why on earth would you delete something like that?"

Why indeed.

She waits.

What else can I do? I scroll to my trash. It won't be there, of course. I'm just trying a lot of things. I can feel the tears prick at my eyes. She's going to find out now. Either she'll give me a write-up for not being able to locate the details of the service I hired for Mr. Drummond or she'll give me a write-up for lying and posing as a wake-up service.

And if she knew what really happened, I'd get nine hundred write-ups.

I close my eyes, trying to think what to do. She's criticizing my junk-mail filter. I can barely hear her. I'm feeling mortified and a little bit angry—not at Sasha; she's just doing the best she can, though she could lose some of the Cruella bitch-i-tude.

No, I'm mad at Theo.

What the heck? He couldn't just leave it alone? What does he want with the company information? Is he planning on ratting me out? I feel so betrayed, like we had a little secret together.

I take a deep breath, getting ready to tell her there is no service, but then her phone sounds. A wind chimes tone, which is sort of perfect for her in a weird way.

"I need to take this. Have it to me in five. You understand?"

I nod.

She walks off. I sit there, heart pounding. That's when I get the idea. I'll quickly set up a service. I can do this!

I break land speed records in how fast I sign up for a Yahoo! email account—HelloMorning456@ymail.com. I use the email to set up a Craigslist advertisement. I make the ad very generic—Wake-up calls provided. Prompt. Trustworthy. Effective. I hesitate about the price. I have no idea. I quick Google wake-up-call service prices and settle on one. I hit submit and wait for it to go live.

My heart pounds nearly out of my chest while I wait.

I refresh my email again and again. Finally it's up. But it says when it was posted, dammit.

Nothing to be done.

I do another quick Google search to see whether there's a way to change the date. There doesn't seem to be a way, but I discover that it's a common ploy to delete and repost things on Craigslist to keep them on top of the search.

Perfect.

I grab a link and type a quick note:

Ack! Looks like they took down the old posting and put a new one up—that's why I couldn't find it! Trying to stay on top of the feed I guess :) But this is the service we're using.

I say a little prayer and hit send.

Then I inspect the ad. If Mr. Drummond scrolls all the way down, he'll see the date. But why would he scroll down?

The more I think about it, the more I think he might not. He's too demanding and jerky to sit there and study every inch of the ad. He'll click the email and make a few demands. Mr. Drummond wants what he wants when he wants it.

It still really stings that he's going over my head to my superiors. We had a certain intimacy going.

Then I remember another hole in the plan—they're going to want to set up with Hello Morning in billing.

Shit.

I go to my PayPal account and set up a special section that invoices under the name Hello Morning. Thank you, PayPal! I arrange it so that the money goes directly to my favorite sea turtles charity. They want the button to say *donate*, but I do a workaround to get it to show up as a regular checkout button.

If he finds a way to follow the bread crumbs when I set up with accounting, they'll lead to sea turtles.

Ha! *Go ahead, follow the money, asshole.*

I sit there wishing I'd picked a more outlandish charity. Sad clown fund or something. But sea turtles are worthy. Sea turtles are my favorite cause in the world.

I smile, feeling excited. Energized. Happy.

When was the last time I felt happy? Not since Mason.

I send the stuff to accounting as a new vendor. I give them the address, let them know the rate, and tell them they'll be receiving invoices every thirty days.

My brand-new Hello Morning Yahoo! email address gets a response with a purchase order number. Hello Morning is to put this number on all invoices.

Yeah, whatever!

I write back to thank accounting. I sign it Katherine Mayhold, comptroller. I don't know why I choose comptroller. But why not? I had phone sex with my boss at 4:30 in the morning and now I'm in a prairie dress impersonating a wake-up-call service. Just another day at Vossameer!

I get to work on the Instagram strategy, but I can't help but have the Yahoo! web mail up on my phone. Waiting.

Whatever will Professor Wonderbrain do now?

Report me to my boss? If anything, I should be reporting him. Maybe he wants to apologize. Maybe he's mortified. Maybe he wants to get a different caller.

My heart sinks a little at this thought.

Nearly twenty minutes after I sent the email to Sasha, a new email arrives. An email from Theo Drummond, CEO, Vossameer Inc. Subject line: Query.

I slip my phone into my lap and click on the message, heart pounding.

To whom it may concern:

I'm interested in contracting with you to hire the operator I'm currently working with as a dedicated provider for me and my business. Money is no object. Please call me at your earliest convenience.

Sincerely,

Theo Drummond, CEO, Vossameer.

1-212-555-1561

He wants me all to himself.

My pulse races as I reread it. I don't know how to feel about it.

It's kind of pushy and entitled. At the same time, it's flattering. Is he a little bit jealous? Wondering how I talk to my other clients?

So he's just going to buy up all my time. Make me talk to him.

And I have no idea what to reply. Obviously the answer is no. Operator Seven is booked—we established that yesterday.

But if money is no object, you'd think Hello Morning would find a way to accommodate him.

I wring my hands. I tell myself I don't have to write back right away. Maybe my company is busy calling people around the world. Maybe the CEO is in Bermuda.

An hour later, Mr. Drummond sends another email. *I'm following up on my previous query, copied below. I'm looking to expedite this process. Please respond at your earliest convenience.*

My pulse races. I feel like a fugitive. If I keep ignoring him, he'll just send more emails. Or maybe he'll try to investigate harder. No, I have to answer. I look around for Sasha, and then I pull out my phone and hit reply.

Dear Mr. Drummond:

We appreciate your interest in contracting with Operator Seven, but she is committed to a full roster of clients at this time, and there are no circumstances under which we would break that commitment. We appreciate your understanding and wish you luck with your search for a suitable alternative.

Just to annoy him, I sign it, *The cheerful folks at Hello Morning.*

I send it off.

No email comes back.

An hour later I'm really stressing. Was it too much? Too unbelievable? Who wouldn't at least give him a price for buying out all these contracts?

I cringe every time I hear voices up front in reception,

thinking he'll have seen the time stamp on the ad and figured the thing out.

I eat my smell-free lunch, a peanut butter and jelly sandwich, trying to get into the competitive analysis part of the Instagram strategy, but I feel like this whole thing is spinning out of control.

No, I think, it's not spinning out of control! I'm lasting like a champ. Just the rest of today, then two days to go! I put more work into the Instagram rationale for Sasha. I talk about how people love a little drama, love to pull for the underdog, and this lab journal angle lets them in on that. I suggest a few junior chemists who could log his daily progress. We could do an image of the day—papers and beakers. Explanations in layperson's terms.

Stanley from accounting calls me that afternoon. He wants me to come down and discuss a problem with the vendor I submitted, namely that there *needs to be an address and phone number for payment to process.*

Hmm. I wonder what vendor that could be? *LOL.*

I head down.

Unsurprisingly, the vendor turns out to be none other than Hello Morning. Stanley shows me his computer screen. It's some sort of invoicing program. He points out the fields that need information. Did somebody get a call from his boss?

"This service doesn't *have* an address and phone number," I say. "I think they send emails from a PayPal address."

"We can't pay them from our system without that contact info."

"I see," I say, trying to sound unhappy. "Let me email them and try to get that info."

I go back to my floor. Just for the hell of it, I send an email request for contact info from my company address to my Yahoo! address, and I cc Sasha and Stanley. To show I'm trying.

I compose another email to just Stanley, giving him the link to the Craigslist ad. *Here's the info, Stanley. This is what we're dealing with. The customer service is terrible!*

I hit send.

Good luck getting those jerks to reply!

And nothing comes back. I'm relieved for the first hour, but then the silence becomes ominous.

Is Mr. Drummond trying another angle? Mr. Drummond is tenacious. He was tenacious on that phone call with me. And he's certainly tenacious as a chemist.

In one of the interviews with him that I read back when I was applying for this job, he talked about how he knew the original formula absolutely had to be possible, that he could sense it, like a sculptor sensing form trapped in rock, needing to be uncovered. He kept going at it, striving to figure out its shape, its detail. He couldn't rest until he had it. He slept in thirty-minute intervals while he was going at it. Like a pit bull he went at it.

Apparently people had been dreaming about this advanced type of blood coagulant for years. People knew that it was possible, but the difference is that Theo muscled his way into solving it.

And here, I have the flimsiest of smoke screens. A Craigslist ad. A Yahoo! account. Mr. Drummond could probably place a call to Yahoo! itself and find a crony to give him my info.

But can he do that in two days? No way. And that's all I need: two days.

Sasha comes back a while later. She has her phone in her hand. She sets it on the desk. The ad is on the screen. "Something's fishy," she says. "Look at the date. This ad was put up today." She eyes me. "Today."

"I know, right?" I turn my hopefully innocent face up to her. "It turns out that sometimes the people offering services at Craigslist take down their old ads and put up new ones so that they appear at the top of Craigslist searches. It's a known technique that Craigslist frowns on."

"Hmph," she says. "And they don't even have a website."

"I know, right?" I say.

"Mr. Drummond doesn't like mysteries," she informs me.

I swallow and nod.

"This is frustrating for Mr. Drummond, and therefore it's frustrating for me." She looks at me again, as though I'm somehow at fault, which, admittedly, I am. "Dig a little, okay? Google the shit out of Hello Morning and see whether you can get something. Surely there is something out there. Don't businesses have to register with the state or something?"

I grit my teeth. "I'll check it out."

"Don't just check it out, give me answers. You wrangled this service. You need to handle this. I was counting on you to vet it at least a little, but apparently you didn't do that, and now we're stuck with this disruptive situation. I don't want to disappoint Mr. Drummond again."

"I'm sorry."

"Don't be sorry; be proactive."

I nod. As a matter of fact, I won't be proactive, but I will be remembering that line to amuse Mia later on.

"Have the answer on my desk in the morning." With that, she storms off.

Mia is there when I get home, working at her cross-stitching. "How'd the wake-up call go?" She puts out the peanuts.

"Oh, it went...fine." I concentrate on getting a glass of water.

"Were you just like, 'Wake up, motherfucker'? Did it work again?"

"Yeah, I guess it worked. It's hard to say."

"Well, you still have a job, right? So I'd say it worked." She shells a peanut. "It's a very rare opportunity you have here. I hope you're appreciating it, because you know I am. You're a hero to everyone who's ever had a jerky boss."

I sigh.

When I look back over, she's studying my face.

"What?" she asks.

"What *what*?" I say.

"You have that look like there's something more."

"Why would there be something more?"

"Because of the look on your face. The wake-up call. What aren't you telling me?" She studies me even more intensely, craning her neck forward.

"Screw off!" I laugh.

"Oh my god, there's a *what* the size of the Chrysler Building. What happened on that wake-up call? You're so gonna tell me." She grabs the wine. "You have to tell me."

"Uhhhh." I sink in my seat.

She pours and nudges a glass my way. Our wineglasses aren't the stem kind; they're like petite drinking glasses with a pretty filigree design. We like to think of them as Parisian. "Spill. You made the mean call. Right?"

"Yeah, I made the mean call."

"And?"

"He was into it." *I was into it.* I sip my wine.

"What does that mean?"

I brush off the question. "Here's the thing—he's become curious. He's been trying to get ahold of the firm. He wants to contract with Operator Seven—that's me—for...I don't know. An exclusive contract."

Mia squints at me, like she's trying to make out distant shapes through a thick haze.

"He wants Operator Seven all to himself." I take a swig.

"That's a bit odd. How many naps does that asshole take?"

"It's not the waking-up part that he's interested in." I pause and bite nearly the entirety of my lips into my mouth to keep from smiling. This is not a smiling occasion!

"Does he want more...rude conversation?"

My teeth are keeping my lips from smiling, but the problem is that I need my lips for talking. I release and contort them into their normal shape as best I can before I raise my gaze to her. "I wouldn't say that it stayed *rude* exactly."

Her voice is a harsh whisper. "Tell me what that means."

I look at her straight on. Sometimes, between friends, a look communicates everything.

Her eyes literally double in circumference. "Excuuuuuuse me?"

I return to biting back my smile.

"No. Freaking. Way."

I whisper, "Yes way."

"To clarify—are we talking phone sex here?"

"It didn't go quite that far."

"*Quite* that far? Sexy phone calls with your asshole boss is pretty far." She gestures, seeming at a loss for words. "Did you get to third base?"

"I don't even know what that means. We were on the phone. Are there bases on the phone?"

She downs her wine and pours another glass. "You have to re-enact it. Play both parts. You call. You're lying in bed."

"I'm not doing a one-woman show of my almost-phone-sex wake-up call with my boss for you."

"A true friend would."

I toss a peanut shell at her.

"You have to," she says. "At least help me understand how it segued from 'you're such an asshole' to..." She looks at me hard. She wants at least a line or two.

I cross my arms and stare up at the cracked ceiling.

"Come on!" she says.

I'm not one to kiss and tell, but I can give her something tiny. "First of all," I say, "he has this really rumbly voice. Like it wraps around you. Soft and gritty." I'm suddenly imagining his whiskers sliding along my cheek, my chest.

"Wet sandpaper."

"Yeah. Or else maybe extremely unforgiving velvet ribbon."

"Guh," she says hoarsely. She gestures impatiently for more. "Dude, I had a hard day at work. I need this."

"One of the early highlights: I called him a jackalope."

She straightens up. "This is already delicious."

"Then he wants to know what I'm wearing."

"Ooh. A time-honored classic."

"I was like, seriously?"

"I'm rolling with this completely. Did you tell him what you were wearing?"

"He had guesses. And he was all stern and assholey, but in a good way. And suddenly...we're all sexytimes. So there you go."

"Wait, that's all I get? What are you wearing and then it's all sexytimes and that's that? No, no, no, no, no. I need details."

"Sorry, sister."

"Noooo!" She clutches my sleeve. "One fun highlight."

I sigh.

"Please?"

I fix her with a saucy stare. Mia appreciates a little drama. "'You are such a pig!' I say to him. And then he goes, 'Oh, I am. An utter animal. Sex with me is a dirty, savage affair. Utterly uncivilized. It's the opposite of civilized.'"

She pantomimes falling off her chair, and then promptly begs for more.

"That was your one and only snippet." I fast-forward to the drama of the office and me putting up the Craigslist ad and linking it to a sea turtles charity through PayPal. How he emailed and I rebuffed him.

"You're like a secret agent."

"A secret agent who needs her sign-on bonus."

She rocks back in her chair. "And now he wants you all to himself. His sexy wake-up-call girl. Nobody else gets her! He will search the ends of the earth for her."

"Let's hope not. It was totally entitled and pushy of him to be calling my wake-up agency. Sasha is looking for an excuse to fire me, but does he even consider that? If it was a real wake-up-call service, what would that look like? I mean, it would look utterly fishy. Yes, he's hot, but he's so oblivious to what other people are going through."

She nods. "Mmm."

"I don't need another Mason, involving himself in my life because he wants something."

"Mason was trying to steal your business, doing shit behind your back," Mia points out. "This guy..."

"This guy is a control freak who will do whatever it takes to get what he wants. You can't trust a guy like that."

"They're not all shitty, Lizzie."

"Three words. Microwave popcorn ban."

That shuts her up.

I swirl the wine in my glass. "I'm keeping things short and sweet tomorrow morning. I'll do the minimum to wake him up; then I'm out of there. No more extra activity."

"Extra activity? Is that what the kids are calling it these days?"

"This is serious," I say. "I doubt he'll fire the wake-up service at this point. Two more days, that's all I need. I have to keep this job for two more days."

"You know he's going to try to trace the call."

"Too bad it's a burner. Who knew I'd ever be thankful to Mason for ruining my credit?"

"'Sex with me is a dirty, savage affair. Utterly uncivilized,'"

Mia says. "I want a boyfriend who says that. And he follows through. Would you be mad if I cross-stitched that for our wall?"

I snort.

"Operator Seven." Her grin is huge. "He wants more of her but he shall never have it. He'll have to live on tongue-lashings alone."

"Shut," I say.

Mia snickers. "Hot, hot tongue lashings."

"It," I say.

Mia smiles.

"From now on, he gets me just waking him up and I'm out of there. He'll see he can't always have what he wants."

"I think Operator Seven is looking forward to not giving him what he wants."

She's right. Just the thought of denying the great Theo Drummond sends a surge of energy through me.

You and that smart mouth of yours need to be taught a lesson.

SIXTEEN

Lizzie

I BARELY SLEEP. When I do, my dreams are strange and way too full of Mr. Drummond sternly scowling in his lab coat. Mr. Drummond, discovering my secret.

Or else they're nightmares of angry Sasha and her angry eyebrows firing me. Because Mr. Drummond won't leave it alone already! Nightmares of Lenny's enforcer and his shiny gun. Nightmares of Mia being killed because of me.

By the time my alarm rings at the evil hour of 4:20, I'm in a state—heart pounding, mind racing. It's like I've lost the job already. Like the loan sharks are already beating down the door.

Because of Mr. Drummond!

He picks it up on the first ring.

"Time to wake up, motherfucker," I say. Before he can even say hello.

"Hey," he says. "Good morning." There's a smile in his voice. It softens something in me.

"It's not such a good morning over here. You totally and

completely got me in trouble with my boss." I'm referring to Sasha, but he doesn't have to know that.

"I got you in trouble?"

"You have to stop researching Hello Morning. Stop trying to contact them. Why can't you just leave it alone?"

He lowers his voice. "I was interested in contracting for your time. I'd think it would show you're doing a good job, if a client wants more of the service you provide. That's typically the sign of a good employee..."

"Oh please with your businesssplaining. 'I'd think it would show you're doing a good job'... Well, it's not helpful. You had to rush in there like a bull in a china shop...did you ever give a thought to another person's situation?"

"Tell me about your situation."

"I'm not going to tell you about my situation. I'm going to tell you about yours." I lie back. "You sit there in your lofty office, and you are so oblivious, it blows my mind."

"Oblivious to what?"

"The effects of your actions! Seriously. You don't see what you do or what's in front of you. That's your problem."

It actually is his problem—in the entire way he runs his business. He's clearly one of these idea guys you read about who can't give up control of his company. New York is full of them.

"Tell me what's in front of me." His voice is soft. It's like he actually cares.

Don't fall for it.

"I just don't want attention drawn to me. How do you think it looks when a wake-up-call client is suddenly coming back with extra questions and requests for more time? You need to think a little harder about how your actions affect those around you. And I mean *all* your actions."

"I didn't..."

"Think?" I say.

There's a strange silence.

And then he says the one thing that could surprise me. "I'm sorry."

I can't believe Mr. Drummond would say this. It touches me —especially being that Mason never apologized to me. It's like we're doing some weird role-play, and he's being Mason, finally apologizing to me.

It stops me in my angry-tracks. "You're sorry?"

"Is that so hard to believe? I didn't mean to make things hard for you."

"Well, I appreciate that," I say.

"Tell me your name."

"Oh, I don't think so," I say. I kind of wish I could give it, though. I feel strangely close to him.

Still more silence. He's not used to being bossed around. "Just a name."

"You're paying me to wake you up. Not for my name." I slide more deeply under the covers. I feel warm and good and a little wild. "You don't need my name for what we do."

"What harm could a first name do?"

"I don't know. What if it's really unusual? Like Sassafras or something."

He lets out a grumbly breath. He's hot when he's frustrated. I smile, picturing his lips. And the way he sets his hands on surfaces like he owns them.

Well, he *does* own them.

His voice gets that velvety rumble. "Tell me," he says.

Something shoots through me.

"I can't," I say. I was supposed to be hanging up by now.

"Tell me over dinner tonight."

My heart nearly leaps out of my ribs. "What?" He wants to take me out? I imagine him in a candlelit restaurant. His icy gray eyes. That short, thick hair, just the beginnings of curls that he must contain at all costs. And that lab coat.

"Let me take you out. Tonight."

"Are you serious?"

"I'm always serious."

I smile, because he really is always serious. "You don't even know what I look like."

"I don't have to know what you look like," he says.

"Risky."

"I always know what I want. I enjoy you. What do I care what you look like? I'm a chemist. I care about chemistry."

If I didn't know him to be such a power-mad jerk, I'd think that was halfway cool. Then again, maybe he simply loves a challenge. Going for the unattainable. "Not gonna happen."

"Why? Is it because you aren't single? Because you don't like men?"

"So those are the only two choices? I must be married or not into men if I won't go out to dinner with you? Because otherwise, wild horses wouldn't keep me away? Is that what you're thinking? Because any single hetero woman would totally say yes?"

"Pretty much."

I snort.

"It's just a fact."

Because you're a handsome captain of industry, I'm about to say mockingly. And then I realize he *is* a handsome captain of industry, and most single hetero women probably would say yes.

"Well, you'll have to find one of those other legions of women to ask."

"I want it to be you. Think of a restaurant. Any restaurant in Manhattan. The best restaurant you've never gotten a chance to go to."

I twist in the covers, tempted for one reckless second. "Do

you not have enough romantic challenges in your life? Is that it? So you have to see whether you can land the strangely resistant wake-up-call girl? Is this your version of the Iron Man or something?"

"Anywhere. Anytime," he adds. "Trust me, you'll want to say yes to this."

"Arrogant much?"

"Not arrogant. Just realistic."

I sigh dramatically. "You don't quit, do you?" I shouldn't be smiling. I shouldn't be enjoying this.

"Pick a night."

"Let's see. Let me get out my social calendar." I pause and wait. "Oh my god! I have the perfect spot for you. How about... nowhere and never. Would nowhere and never work for you?"

"That won't work for me, Operator Seven," he says in the low voice that he seems to reserve for stern displeasure. "Try again."

Shivers prickle over me. "Not happening," I say.

A tortured sigh. "Eventually you're going to say yes. We both know it."

I shouldn't love how arrogant he is. "We'll see, Mr. Drummond."

"Did you just call me Mr. Drummond?"

Oops.

I swallow. Probably the only people in his life who call him that are his unlucky underlings. "You've been demoted from Theo. And if you're out of line one more time, you'll be demoted further. To just Drummond."

"Give me one actually valid reason we can't meet. You've been thinking about me. You pictured me while you got yourself off after our last phone call."

My body hums pleasantly with the memory. "Of *course* you would think that."

His voice lowers. "I don't think that, I know it."

"Okay, I'm officially calling you Drummond now."

"If I'd been there in person, you'd've had a much better time."

"Right, I forgot. You could do me better than I could do myself."

"You wouldn't forget that if you went out with me."

I picture his stern face. I picture his hands. I imagine him across a candlelit table in his lab coat. He probably doesn't wear it to fancy restaurants, but in my fantasy, he does. And he leans over and kisses me. And he pulls me into the coatroom and pushes me against the wall and gets me off. Could he actually do me better than I can do myself?

But suddenly I'm picturing Sasha's *I-love-Mr. Drummond* face. Followed up by her glowering *you're-fired* face. Followed by Lenny the Loan Shark's enforcer's *where's-my-money?* face. And his gun's *I'm-all-lethal-n-stuff* face.

"We're not going out to dinner," I say. "It's just impossible. There are crucial business reasons that prevent it."

"How about I buy the company and change those crucial business reasons?"

Which means more research. "How about if you try to do that, you'll never hear from me again?"

"I'll hear from you again. You're my wake-up-call girl."

"You sure I'll stay your wake-up-call girl? Your company ordered wake-up calls. Watch out, I might switch with operator number five."

"No, you won't. You have to call me. You wouldn't trade with anyone even if you could. You like what I do to you."

I lie back. "Do go on."

"You can't get enough. And you know what else I think?"

I suck in a deep breath, full of the crisp, good scent of my freshly washed pillow. I can see half the Hotel Royale sign. "I know you're going to tell me."

"I think you don't talk to anybody else the way you talk to me. I think I'm the only one."

I smile. "You so desperately hope."

He does his disapproving rumble-growl, but I can hear real frustration and desire woven through like delicate threads. There's something so achingly human about him suddenly. Genuine.

I set the phone against the pillow next to me. "Look, I'm going to be honest here, since that seems to be a thing with you," I say. "You are the only one I ever talk to like this. I promise. But you have to stop poking at the company. You really do."

"I'm the only one you talk to like this?"

"That's right. Okay?"

"Why? Why me?" he asks. "Why did you decide to wake me up like that the first day? Was it something you read?"

"I'm not getting into that with you. I'm saying, stop contacting the company."

"How about if I pass along praise for a job well done?"

"I guess there's no harm in saying that you're happy with Hello Morning's amazing service."

"Especially since my wake-up-call girl has agreed to dinner. She knows I need more of her than her sexy, raspy voice."

That's my best disguise, I realize. The pre-allergy-medicine voice. "That had better not be a *quid pro quo*, because it's so not happening."

"It'll happen," he says. "You'll keep calling me. And you'll keep thinking about me after. How dirty and good I can make things for you. You know who I am. You'll say yes."

"I think the only reason you want me to go out with you is because I said no. Everything's too easy for you. And suddenly you come across the one woman who seems immune to your charms. So you've decided to seduce me at all costs. Seduce the wake-up-call girl."

"I already seduced the wake-up-call girl." He lowers his voice the way I like. "Now I need to taste her."

Lust swells through me, infusing my cells with a warm, heavy glow.

"I need to have you under me," he continues. "I need you to talk to me just like this while I fuck you senseless."

"Are we approaching the savage animal portion of the call?"

"We could be so good together."

I should be hanging up. I should be remembering why I'm annoyed with him. Instead, I'm thinking, *could we be good together?*

"Put us on FaceTime."

"I can't."

"Do it," he says in a tone I like too much.

"I'm not that kind of wake-up-call girl. No vid. No texts. No sexting."

He lowers his voice. "I want to see you. Any part of you."

"No go."

"If you had me on FaceTime," he says, "you'd be able to see me up close, and you'd see that I have a scar on the left side of my lower lip."

The sexy scar. I swallow. "And?"

"Are you lying down? Lie back."

"Now you're commanding me?" I slide my hand over my belly. My belly. That's all. Then I turn onto my back.

"You can't see my scar that well, but when you touch it, there's a little edge to it."

"What's it from?"

"Boyhood fight that split open my lip. My point is, can you imagine how it would feel on your nipple? My stiff tongue. My soft lips. And then this little edge. You'd like the way it feels. I would make you enjoy it. With that fucking attitude of yours, you need to be made to feel everything."

"Oh," I say as my hand wanders down to my sex.

"Or maybe," he continues, "...maybe I kiss you and let you feel the scar first, before I put you in a trance of pleasure with my tongue. What do you think? Which one do you think would be best?"

"I don't know which one would be best." I slide my hand up my belly, under the fabric this time. "Maybe we need to get a debate team to take up the question."

He snorts softly. "Trust me, you'll want to decide for yourself." He pauses. Then, "There it is."

"What?"

"Clothes shifting. The slide of skin against skin. Where is your hand right now?"

I hesitate. Then, "My stomach," I tell him, "sliding slowly up to caress the silky skin beneath my breast."

He sucks in a breath.

"And now onto my nipple," I whisper. "Sliding over it."

"What does it feel like?"

"Pebbly. Rough."

He growls, and the compliment in his voice is impossible to miss. "Down now. We're doing this," he says. "Are you with me?"

I slide my hand down under the elastic in my pj pants. "We're doing it."

He lets out this shuddery breath. Things feel heated. Wild.

"How wet are you? Tell the truth."

"Pretty damn wet," I whisper. Because some things I'll give him. "You know I am."

"I know, baby," he says. "Start with a line between your legs —trace a nice heavy line. Nice and slow. Up and down. Don't speed up until I tell you."

"I can't believe you're telling me how to masturbate."

"I'm an arrogant control freak. You're going to hate me even more soon enough. Even as you crave me."

"Yeah?" I breathe.

"I can't wait to get my fingers between your legs. I can't wait to own that pretty little pussy of yours. Really own it in a way you never can. My fingers are a lot bigger than yours. Big and heavy," he says. "I'll have to work to be gentle with you. Because being gentle, once I get my hands on you, it'll be furthest from my mind."

"Right," I breathe.

"Even with me being gentle, you'll be able to feel the ragged energy in my touch. It's dangerous as hell how bad I want you. How savage I want to be with you."

"*Uhng...yes*," I say.

I hear him shudder out a breath. "Don't screw around, now. Get onto the target. Find it and feel it. Are you there?"

"I'm there."

"That's what you can never hide from me. Feel it?"

"Yes."

"Slide over it. Slow and hard. No mercy. Don't lose contact. I wouldn't. I'd keep you going. Just enough. Just perfect."

I slide the tip of my finger up through my folds. Everything feels heightened. My skin is too tight. The sounds of the city are incredibly distinct. The pillow is perfectly cool under my cheek. "And you'd be wearing your lab coat."

A silence. Then, "I'd be wearing my lab coat. Of course I would. I'd strip you naked, but I'd have my lab coat on over my suit."

I slide my finger up and down my clit. I want him to tell me more things to do.

"How does it feel?"

"Intense. Close." I've never been so turned on. I suddenly

want FaceTime on. I want to connect with him. I want him to text me a picture of himself right now. I want to see him. I want to kiss him.

"It was always going to happen," he breathes. "I was always going to have you. But I don't have enough of you. I close my hand over your top, fragile and silky. You're shivering under me, knowing what I'm about to do."

"Oh my god," I say. The clothes ripping.

"You know," he says.

"You can be hard if you want."

"I can't be any other way with you. I yank the fabric, tear it down the middle."

I close my eyes, speeding up. Mr. Drummond, ripping my clothes, so desperate for my pussy. "Yeah."

"It hurts a little when I rip it, because of how hard I have to yank, but you like it. Because this is way too real. I'm ripping your pj pants, destroying your panties. I have your nipple in my lips before you can stop me."

"Ungh," I breathe, getting my other hand into the act, fingers scissoring over my nipple. Am I really doing this?

"How hard?" he asks. "Tell me. I always make you tell me everything."

"Medium hard," I whisper. "A tiny bit of pain. Just enough to surprise me. No more." I pinch my nipple.

"Like that," he whispers.

"Like that," I say, enjoying our dirty mind meld. Like he knows where my hands are. "Yes."

"I'm back at your clothes, pulling them off you. I don't give a shit, I have to get you naked for what I'm going to do to you, how I'm going to use your body. The cool air hits your skin. You're quivering below me. Of course, I haven't even bothered to take off my lab coat."

"Because you're an asshole."

"An asshole who has you totally bared and exposed under him. And I can't believe how beautiful you are like that. I'm doing you how I want."

"And I'm into it, but a little angry, still," I say.

He hisses out a breath. I love that we're co-creating this. And that he's as into it as I am. Is he touching himself? He seems so focused on me, it's hard to tell.

"You can't believe you'd fuck somebody like me, because you hate me a little bit, but it's what you need. My lab coat hangs open over you, and sometimes it grazes your skin. I'm the asshole who is going crazy to fuck you."

"Like some savage," I say.

"I'll make you beg, just because I can. Then I'll make you come until you cry. Because I'm the asshole who makes it good for you. Get on your back. Get your legs wider," he says.

I do it. I do everything he says, there in the dark of my room. "Right here."

"Not yet," he whispers. "I'm not done with you. Not done kissing your pretty cunt. You can feel my scar so acutely. You squirm around, but I clamp my rough hands down on your silky thighs. Press you open to me. So good."

"Yes," I say.

"I can hear you breathing, I know you feel it. Now listen— two fingers now. Go a little harder than you normally would. That's me, taking a good long lick. Again."

I do it again. Shudder.

"You're almost gone. You're trying to hold it together, but you can't. This asshole you disdain has utter and complete control of you."

I'm panting. Going with it.

"You're close, Seven." His voice winds around me, warm and rough. "So fucking close."

I'm shamelessly panting, breath sawing in and out.

Without warning, my orgasm explodes over me. I'm a cluster of stars, spinning into space. Overflowing with feeling.

"Yeah," he rumbles next to my ear. "Come for me. I'm slowing down. Stringing it out for you...that's it." He's panting, too. "Goddamn, you're hot. So hot and dirty."

I close my eyes, floating. I slow my finger over my throbbing sex. Wake-up-call girl: best gig ever!

"I would kiss you right now," he whispers.

"You would?" I ask, sleepy and contented.

"I love kissing you. You're unlike any woman I've ever met, and it drives me wild."

I smile. Floating.

"I get you nice and close to me now. You're soft to me now, and you'll let me do anything. So I pull you close." He pauses. "Maybe I put you a little bit under me. I don't squish you, but I know you like to feel me."

"Yeah."

"Your skin is warm, and there's a sheen of sweat on your forehead. A drugged look in your eyes. You're floppy as a rag doll. That's what I do to you."

I slide my palm over my cheek. There's a sheen of sweat pretty much everywhere on me. Damp skin cooling in the crisp morning.

How did I let him take over like this? What am I doing?

"I feel..." I don't know how to finish the sentence. Maybe *vulnerable. A little bit confused.*

There's a silence; then he says, "Yeah."

"I don't know what this is," I confess.

"Me, either."

And I wish he was with me more than ever. A little bit on me, like he says. It would be nice.

What if I told him? Told all?

A tiny alarm clangs in the back of my head. *You told all to Mason.*

My pulse races. "I should go."

"Wait," he says.

I sit up, shaking off the last of the sexy sparkle. "What?"

"I hope I haven't made you miss your next call."

I smile, alone in the dark. I whisper, "Nothing would make you happier."

"Here's what I don't get. It sounded like you were all booked up," he says. "Yet here you are on an extended chat."

I smile and roll over. He's still wondering how I am with other clients. Did he not believe me when I reassured him? "Maybe I book this long with all of them."

He grumbles, and I smile.

"Kidding. I don't."

"Let me ask you," he says. "Why are you a wake-up-call girl? Surely this can't be what you want with your life."

"You think being a wake-up-call girl is too lowly?"

"I think you're more ambitious than that."

"You don't know me."

"Don't I? I know you said something outrageous during our first call. You were coloring outside the lines. Experimenting. Or maybe it was an accident. I sometimes think that. I don't know why you said it, but you did, and then you went with it. Followed where it led. That's what a creative, ambitious person does. She tries different angles. Turns accidents into advantages. It makes me think you're used to running your own show. Not doing a job a machine could do. You make things happen. You have a strong will. Yet you have integrity, too."

"Integrity. My goodness."

"If you didn't have integrity, I think you would've taken me up on dinner. Or tried to squeeze me for money by now."

"Maybe I'm playing the long game. Maybe I'm just that good."

"You're not working me. No, I'd know if you were working me. What's more, you don't take shit from me. You're capable and you stick up for yourself. So what are you doing making wake-up calls? That's what I keep asking myself."

I twist around to my elbows, stunned. It's as if Mr. Drummond knows me better after a few calls than Mason ever did.

Mason always acted like my bakery's success was due to luck and location, and he sometimes had me buying it. As if building relationships and managing a crew and finding ways to help people create fun experiences through cookies didn't qualify as hard work.

Also, the whole ironically frosted craft cookie thing came out of experimenting. Running with things.

"Aren't you observant."

"I'm a scientist. Observant is part of the job description. Still, what I can't figure out is why you get so nervous when I set my sights on Hello Morning. Why do you care so deeply about a job you're so utterly overqualified for? As if it's a lifeline."

"Do you analyze everyone like this?"

"Just you," he says.

Something warms inside me. Because I love having his focus on me. Though he's wrong about one thing—I don't stick up for myself. Or at least, I didn't stick up for myself when I was with Mason.

Though when I think about it, I do stick up for myself where Mr. Drummond is concerned.

I find that I like who I am on these calls with Mr. Drummond. As if I'm a more ideal version of myself. A more genuine version.

"For a moment, I thought maybe you're homebound, somehow, or maybe caring for somebody," he says. "But homebound or not, with your communication abilities and apparent control over your schedule, you'd be doing something that pays better. Sometimes I wonder whether you're on the run or hiding. That would give you time on your hands, and also explain why you won't go to dinner with me."

I laugh. "And we're back to that, folks! The most baffling question of all."

"It is the most baffling question."

I snort.

"Then I think to myself, are you in trouble?" His voice goes hard. "Is somebody threatening you?"

"Your imagination is definitely running wild now," I say, even as shivers slide over me. What else will he get right? *This is why they pay you the big bucks,* I add.

"Answer me. Do you feel unsafe? Is your boss at Hello Morning the problem? Is it a boyfriend? A husband? An ex? If you're feeling unsafe, you should tell me. You really, really should tell me."

"Drummond—"

"I can be persuasive." His voice has taken on a dark edge.

I'm imagining his stern, powerful self turned out at the world on my behalf. To Lenny and his guy. But it's not for me. I can't have him. Anyway, controlling men "helping" me is how I got into this mess.

"I'm not feeling unsafe," I say. Which is technically true. At the moment.

"You promise?"

"Promise," I say.

If I don't get my bonus, that'll all change, of course.

"All right."

"Just stop trying to contact Hello Morning, okay? And FYI, my boss at Hello Morning is a woman, and she's absolutely awesome. Promise you will only have praise for me and my service. Or even better, leave it alone. Listen to me for real here. The fastest way to ensure you never hear from me ever again is to get involved in my life."

He's silent.

"I'm pretty freaking capable, don't forget," I add. "Things are under control over here. Stop being so serious. This is just a wake-up call."

He's silent for a bit, and I wonder whether he's thinking what I'm thinking—that it's not just a wake-up call.

He says, "I'm not serious, I'm realistic. People frequently confuse the two."

"Realistic, then."

"I see things for what they are. No candy coating."

"What's wrong with candy coating?"

"It's a lie."

"I'm guessing you don't like jelly beans, then."

"I don't mind candy coating on candy. It's everywhere else that it annoys me. Family pictures at Christmas. The smile on the barista taking your order..."

"What, you hate kindness?"

"Kindness is just another survival strategy."

"Oh my god. That is such a sad thing to think."

"Realistic is not sad."

"You know what you need?"

"You at dinner?"

"No, you need some baby goat videos in your life. That's what I'm getting here."

"Baby goat videos? Is that a thing now?"

I snort. "Yes, and you so need them." Of course he wouldn't be on social media. I turn over. I should go. But I want to stay. I could stay on this call forever.

"Tell me something else," he says. "Something small." The way he asks, I think he feels the same as me. Needing to go.

Wanting to stay. "Is there a man in your life? A significant other?"

"That's not small, that's invasive."

"I have a code," he says. "I don't go for other guys' women."

My heart skips a beat. "Nobody's going for anybody here. We're voices on the phone," I say.

"We're more," he says.

"Now who's candy coating?"

"Tell me you feel it," he says.

I swallow. "There's no significant other," I say, because I like that he has a code. It means something to me. "But you can't be *going for me*. This isn't that."

"Tell me another little thing."

"So demanding."

"It's one of your favorite things about me."

He's right. It's weird. Mr. Drummond is a tyrannical scientist, oblivious at work, yet he's so observant on the phone at the crack of dawn.

"You won't let me see you," he continues. "You won't let me meet you. Give me this. What would you do today if you could do anything at all?"

There's something about the way he asks the question that makes me feel sad for him. Like a prison inmate asking what the air smells like on the outside. Does he never get to do what he wants? Or is he just tired?

"No, my turn. What time do you go to sleep?"

"Midnight," he says.

"What? So you get four hours of sleep a night?"

"Four and a half."

"Jesus," I say. "That's not enough."

"It's fine. I drink a lot of bulletproof coffee," he says.

"As if that makes up for sleep," I say. Everything about him has such a hard edge. He's stern to his people, but apparently he's even sterner toward himself. "Hold on, I know what you need," I say. I pull up Facebook and scroll around for something.

"Are you there?"

"Yeah, hold on." I find what I'm looking for. I text him the link.

"Hold on, here. You can text me, but I can't text you? You get to call me and text me whenever you want, and the rest of the time you block me?"

"Correct. You cannot text me, but I can text you. You cannot call me, but I can call you."

I can practically feel him bristling at this. Nobody pushes Mr. Drummond around.

"This is a video," he says.

"Hit play," I say. "I'll only answer your question if you watch it."

"It's baby goats," he says. "Why am I watching baby goats?"

I click play on my end, too. Baby goats hopping back and forth over a sleeping dog. "I think you just need it."

I hear him exhale. "Okay. They pranced."

"Don't you love it? How they kind of pop up into the air? Watch the whole thing."

A soft sniff.

I smile, imagining him watching it. It's a really sweet one where the baby goats play with each other, all prancey little legs and faces.

Silence.

"Come on. How sweetly they play?"

He says nothing.

"With their cute little faces," I say. "You need to see that not everything is about grim survival."

"Their cute little faces are exactly about survival. Baby animals all have large eyes and big foreheads because adult mammals are hardwired to consider it cute and feed them. It's pure, vicious survival. Survival of the fittest. Practically mercenary."

"Oh my god, are you ruining baby goat videos for me?"

"I'm telling you what we're looking at. Over time, adult goats were more likely to nurture babies who fit the look you see here and the goats with those traits were more likely to survive to adulthood to reproduce."

"Wait, how about this." I send him a cat and a duck who make friends. He seems to like that one—I maybe hear him sniff-snort. And then I send him a cat riding a robot vacuum cleaner. I hear him chuckle softly. It makes me feel good in a way I can't describe.

"Okay," he says finally. "I think I did my time. Tell me the one thing you'd do today."

"Bake," I say. The truth. "I'd bake cookies. That's what I'd do today if I could do anything."

"Cookies." This like it's the stupidest thing he ever heard.

"There's nothing like the aroma of baking cookies," I say, remembering his ridiculous work rules. I suddenly can't think of anybody I'd more delight in making cookies for than Mr. Drummond. "I'm sensing you don't like cookies," I say. "What the hell is wrong with cookies, Drummond?"

SEVENTEEN

Theo

I CAN HEAR the smile in her voice. "What the hell is wrong with cookies, Drummond?"

I cross my legs and look out over the park.

I was glad she didn't detect how relieved I was that she didn't have a man. I thought a vein in my head might explode during the endless silence after I asked that question. I've never been the jealous type. And she's just my wake-up-call girl.

"Who doesn't like cookies?"

"They're a useless food," I say.

"It's National Pug Dog Day," she continues slyly. "Did you know that?"

I sip my bulletproof coffee, enjoying the rough sweet tone of her voice. Her smart, snappy cadence. Nobody talks to me like that. Except Willow, of course, but that doesn't count.

"I would bake the cookies and frost them in honor of National Pug Dog Day. And get this—I would spend a lot of time on each cookie. Beautifully and meticulously frosting each for no reason whatsoever."

I can hear the smile in her voice. Her smile makes me smile. It always does.

"A cookie that somebody would eat in a second for the most useless holiday," she continues. "What do you think? What's your opinion on that?"

"I think you're taunting me," I say. And I'm enjoying it. Far too much.

"Come on, tell me what you think."

"What I think is that I can't decide whether I want to shove you against the wall and kiss that smile right off your lips or move right into spanking you."

"I'm sorry," she says in a way that makes me think her smile just got wider. "I'll be too busy baking useless cookies for that. And they will smell so amazing."

I tighten my grip on the phone. I want her up close and personal. *Need* her up close and personal. I tell myself it's just because I can't have her. But it's not that. It's more.

"I would watch my favorite musical while I bake. *Funny Face*. Have you ever seen it? It's a musical with Audrey Hepburn."

"Musicals," I groan. "You just don't quit, do you?"

"I love musicals. The story goes along, and then they break into song and dance." She lowers her voice like she does when she's feeling mischievous. "For no reason whatsoever."

She's killing me. Some wake-up-call girl, probably in some tiny rented room in Queens or something, is finding all my buttons and pushing them like a pro.

"And she wears this red dress and sings on the steps of the Louvre. It's the best," she says. "And cookies are a valuable food."

I balk. "Hardly."

"Did somebody slip you a bad cookie?" she asks. "Did somebody have a traumatizing cookie experience?" She pauses, and then, "Never mind. I'm sorry."

Something in my chest deflates, because I know exactly what just happened here, exactly why she retreated. When you Google me, the top few results are magazine features that make much ado of my past. The boy whose parents died in a car crash when he was just fifteen. Sister adopted without him. In and out of foster care, all alone in the world, nobody can reach him. He invents the solution that would've saved his mother's life, but he can never bring her back. Such bullshit. "Just don't," I say.

"Don't what?"

"Don't do what you just did. Assume that my dislike of cookies is because of a tragedy that happened half a lifetime ago. Apparently there can't be an article written about me without some armchair psychologist weaving that narrative about my never quite recovering from that. As if it drives everything I do. It's ignorant..."

"Well, you *did* invent the one thing that might've saved her."

"Yes, maybe it would've saved her, who knows, but this bullshit story that I heroically dedicate my life to Vossameer to spare others the pain and so forth...it's simply not accurate. I promise you. It's not how it was, and it's not how it is now."

"Okay."

"It's fucking annoying," I bite out.

"Sorry."

I suck in a breath. I've come on too strong, and I can feel her withdrawing. I'd kill to be able to reach out to her, grab her, pull her to me, make her stay. The world is full of people to do my bidding, but not the wake-up-call girl. Never the wake-up-call girl.

In desperation, I give her something—the only thing I can. The truth.

"When people say that about me, when they go on like that, it makes me feel...alone." My blood races with the strangeness of saying it aloud after all these years. It's not something I ever told anybody. Not even my sister.

It feels...liberating.

"Makes you feel alone," she echoes solemnly. As though she's really taking it in. Not pushing back. Not telling me I'm great.

She doesn't flinch, this woman, and I have this sudden and exhilarating sense that I could peel back all my layers and she still wouldn't flinch. For the first time in my life, I want that. Instead of hiding my layers, I want to show them.

"I don't know why," I continue in a rush. "It's as if those fake stories that paint me to be a heroic phoenix, rising from tragedy or some such shit—it's as if they're about somebody else. They're painting a picture of somebody else. And they leave me feeling alone. I want for somebody to not do that. One person."

"Isolated," she says. "The stories isolate you."

"Yes, exactly."

My heart pounds in the silence that follows. "I'll do it," she says. "It's official, then. You're no hero. Just Theo Drummond."

I swallow. "Thank you."

"Theo Drummond. Just some jackalope on my roster of calls."

"Well, no need to go that far."

"You and your innovations. Whatevs, dude."

I smile. It feels so easy—so right—to confess things to this nameless, faceless woman.

I tip my forehead to the window. "You want to know what else is messed up about it?"

"What?" she asks. There's rustling in the background.

Where is she? What does she see when she looks around? What does she smell like? What does she dream about?

"A little-known secret about being a so-called hero," I say. "When you go around saying you're not a hero, people are even more eager to call you one."

"Heroes *are* notorious for saying they're not heroes," she says.

"It's like one of those finger traps that tighten the harder you try to pull out of them."

"Maybe you need to walk around like, 'yeah, I'm a hero, biotches. Screw you all. I'm the greatest hero in the world!'"

The window feels cool on my forehead. Central Park is a sea of brown, washing up against the stone building faces on the West Side. She's somewhere out there. To the west, I've decided. Maybe just because my window faces that way, and I want to think she's in my view. "I suppose that would do it."

"Too extreme?"

I press my hand to the window. "Where are you right now? Kitchen, bedroom, office..."

She pauses like she does when she's not sure whether to answer. Then, "Bedroom."

"What does it look like?"

"I think I need to take a broom to the ceiling."

"What color is your ceiling?"

"White. It's got gorgeous crown molding, though."

"You like a nice ceiling." It's a statement. It's something I know about her. She would appreciate old buildings, this one. All the unnecessary flourishes around the windows and doorways. She's so impractical.

"My favorite is the pressed tin ceilings. The real ones."

Of course. I smile. "Come on, you'll go out to dinner with me eventually. Why not just say yes?"

"Yeah, well, I hate to say this, but..." She lowers her voice. "I hear you're not the hero everyone makes you out to be."

"I'm something better. I'm an asshole."

"An asshole, and you'll make it SO good." It's almost a whisper.

I love that she remembers that. I'm pacing. When did I start pacing? She needs to tell me her name, give me some way to contact her, or at least stop blocking me, but if I demand it, she'll retreat. Every time I push, she retreats. "I'm the asshole who'll never candy coat things for you. But I can give you what you really want." Then, "Tell me your name."

I realize, in the silence that follows, that I've gone too far. I squeeze my eyes shut.

"The weather," she begins.

"No." But it's too late. She follows through. I like that about her.

"The weather at JFK is forty-five and partly cloudy." With that, she's gone.

I stand there for a while, holding the phone. As if she might pop back in by some telecom magic. She's probably blocking me now. Though on some phones, when you block people, you can still call and text them. Maybe she has that kind of phone.

As wake-up callers go, she's effective. There's no doubt about that.

I've barely slept for three days.

I walk across the parquet floor to the veranda. I step outside into the bracing morning air. The stone pleasantly cool on my bare feet.

I take in a deep breath. I feel energized. Alive. Good.

When was the last time I felt like this? I think back over the months and years, back to the moments when I made my biggest breakthroughs. The day my patent was finally approved. I was pleased in those moments, I suppose, but I can't quite remember feeling like this. Happy. Excited.

This woman. I need more of her. I need to know her. I have to find her.

And the answer is out there. I'll crack this puzzle like I crack every other puzzle. I'll find her name. I'll find her address. I'll find her.

EIGHTEEN

Theo

I HEAD INTO WORK EARLY, reviewing my notes and some of the lab's data on the subway.

Nothing's working.

I get off at my usual stop and take my usual route in. Even at six in the morning, the city is at full swing. I nod at the security guys and head up.

Chemistry problems are like jigsaw puzzles in a lot of ways. I've been working on making a specific piece fit, sure there's a way to get it to work.

But the surreal mystery of this woman, the unexpected delight of talking to her, of directing her in the way I have, it's as if it's loosened something in me. Shaken up my world. Relaxed my white-knuckled grip—enough so that when I walk into the office, my vision is clear enough, or maybe my perspective is wide enough, that I see the problem.

One glance at the whiteboard and I see it.

I've been focusing on the wrong part of the molecule.

I put down my bag, stunned.

I was focusing so hard on the wrong part of the molecule that the shapes of the other pieces had become obscured. But now I'm seeing it all. And there, on the sidelines, is the right piece.

I shrug off my coat, never once taking my eyes from the board.

What. The. Hell.

I have to start over, but I don't let myself despair. I have new information—I know what won't work. I have a promising new direction.

I flip the board over to the side where I have the entire structural formula sketched out, and I step back. Cross my arms. Think loosely about synthesis. Back on the hunt.

Three hours pass like wildfire.

Willow arrives at nine thirty, and that forces me to take a break.

We go to my desk and I show her the email.

To whom it may concern;

I just wanted to let you know the wake-up-call operator with whom we contract here at Vossameer, Operator Seven, is doing a truly outstanding job. I'm extremely satisfied with her performance. Would still be interested in a long-term contract. Is that possible?

Yours truly,

Theo Drummond

"What do you think?" I ask.

"Good. Except you have two *whoms*. Who says *whom* anymore?"

"I do." I hit send.

She rolls her eyes at me with the passion only a little sister can muster. "Whatever. I'm not making any guarantees here."

"I know. Anything you can get," I say. "Anything. Every shred of info. I want it all."

"Of course you do." She clicks over to the Craigslist ad. "I'm curious, too. This whole thing is weird. The discrepancy with the date, the fact the old versions of the ad aren't present on any of the Wayback sites. Not that the caches are infallible, but come on. And I think it's weird that they don't have a site. If they're a real company, they should have a site."

"You'd think."

She's staring at me again. "Come on, tell me. What's your interest in this?"

"Having my answer without a lot of explanation, ideally."

She makes a face at me and clicks again. "I might not get anything at all."

She has to get something. I feel her staring again. Willow's a whiz with computers, but she's nosy. She always has been.

"Spill," she says.

"Maybe I don't like unanswered questions. Sorry to disappoint."

"Oh you're hardly disappointing. I haven't seen you in this good a mood in forever."

"You think this is a good mood?"

"For you it is." She refreshes her screen. "You seem almost happy."

"Must be all the baby goat videos I've been watching."

She sniffs, like that's a joke, and sits up on my desk.

Seven could've asked anything of me at the moment, and she asked me to watch baby goat videos. It's insane. And she bakes and meticulously frosts special-occasion cookies. Gives them to her friends or family, probably. Though she doesn't sound East Coast. She didn't grow up here; she feels too easygoing, somehow. A transplant. She'd send them to her family. She'd be close with her family. Sentimental.

I stare at my screen while Willow scrolls through her phone.

Frosted cookies. What's the point of pouring time into making something that's going to be consumed in five seconds? She should have more respect for her artistry if that's what she loves to do.

I think about telling her that, challenging her on that, on the next call. She'll probably think it's arrogant. She likes to keep control. And then I'd make her touch herself, because she likes to give it up, too.

"What's up with the daffy look?" Willow asks.

"Refresh it again."

"Not until you tell me what's up."

"I have this wake-up-call girl that I...have questions about."

"*Questions*," she says. Like that's not the right word.

"Yes, questions. And it's using up bandwidth I need for solving dehydrated Vossameer."

When I look up, her expression is tender, a little bit somber. "You get to have things for yourself," she says.

"I know."

"Yeah, I don't think you do. You deserve to be happy even if you don't nail this new formula."

I give her a hard look.

Willow holds up her hands. "Fine. I'm shutting up. Here's me shutting up, okay?" She stabs the button, refreshing again. "I mean, they may not email back forever."

"Judging from the correspondence so far, there's a better than fifty percent probability they reply in the first ten minutes," I tell her. "Otherwise, some point today."

"Is this something you've worked out scientifically?"

"Not that hard," I snap.

She smiles.

I refresh. "Nothing."

The email will come back to both of our machines. She's set

something up where replying to the email I sent will give us information about the location of the sender. A little extra something hidden in the email that will get it to bounce off a specifically honed server. Or something. She's the computer whiz, not me.

She thinks we can get the IP address for starters, but depending on what kind of email setup the boss of Hello Morning is using, we could get much more. An intersection. An address. Maybe even a name.

"I'm just saying, you're more than your innovations," she says.

I give her a dark look.

"What if it's an address?" she asks. "Do you march down there?"

"I'll know what to do when I see what you get. It would be stupid to decide how to act on information when I don't know what that information is."

"Sorry, Sherlock," she says.

"I think of that approach as more Michael Faraday." I refresh again.

"Four minutes," she says.

I probably will march down there. I picture myself storming into the office. Or maybe it's some asshole operating out of a shared workspace. Or a storefront in Brooklyn. I'll see what I'm dealing with. Probably put my PI on it. I said I wouldn't get involved, but I never said I wouldn't put a private investigator on it.

She grins at her phone. "Gotcha!"

I check my inbox. The email is there. I click it. Terse, as usual.

Dear Mr. Drummond,

There is only one type of arrangement: the one you are on currently.

We appreciate your business.

Sincerely,

The cheerful folks at Hello Morning

I look up. "Did you capture anything?"

She grabs her own laptop, hits a few keys. "Theo." She sounds surprised.

"Don't jerk me around. What?"

She lowers her voice to a dramatic whisper. "The email is coming from inside the building."

"Are you sure?"

"Now you really do have to tell me what's going on."

"I don't have to tell you dick." I get up and look over her shoulder. I don't know as much about IT as she does, but it's not rocket science to see the return IP is Vossameer Inc.

"It's one of your employees acting as a wake-up service. It seemed fishy to you because it is. Let me guess, you've burned through every wake-up service out there trying to hold to that mad schedule of yours, and some desperate employee took it on herself to do it for you. I hope you didn't abuse the person too much."

"Not too much," I say, head spinning. I'm thinking about how cagey Sasha acted when I asked for the information. An hour later the Craigslist ad was up. Is it possible it's Sasha? But then, who else could it be? She's the one who arranged the service.

"Mystery solved," she says, eyeing me. "That's what's going on, right? You could tell it was a fake thing because it is."

I sink into my chair.

"So who's the unlucky caller?"

"Probably Sasha Bale. In marketing. You've never met her. Except the caller didn't sound like her," I say hopefully. "This caller has a more raspy voice."

"Yeah, there's an app for that. There's a dozen apps for that."

"It was so realistic—"

"App," she says.

"But the way her voice would—"

"App."

"Damn." My heart sinks. I loved that voice. The smart, raspy snap of it.

Time to start your day of being a complete and utter asshole.

I loved her sassy comebacks. I loved the rich rush of her breath when she was getting herself off. God, it's embarrassing that it's partly due to an app. Crushing. An app wielded by a woman I feel no chemistry with.

Willow's watching me, waiting for me to say something.

"I suppose she gets points for resourcefulness," I say. "It's just that she doesn't seem like the type to..."

"To invent a wake-up-call service out of desperation for her demanding boss?"

I was more thinking about her heat, her annoyance, the long, interesting conversations. The goat videos. All of it. "She did seem flustered when I asked her about it. Like she had something to hide. I wondered about it at the time."

Willow smiles. "And then she writes that ad. After you ask."

I was having phone sex with Sasha Bale in marketing.

I should feel happy I figured it out. Maybe I'll wake up at night working on dehydrated Vossameer instead of wondering why Seven's a wake-up-call girl or analyzing the sounds in the background for clues to her life.

I run through other things she said. Getting her in trouble with her boss by snooping—that, too, makes sense. She didn't want me to know. I'm her boss.

Except, in my few interactions with Sasha, the impression I always got was one of very eager admiration. On what planet does this woman make a rude and abusive wake-up call? Does she have a different personality when she's on the phone? The way certain people get road rage behind the wheel or become trolls on the internet?

Willow grabs her coffee. "I gotta go."

I heave myself up and walk her to the elevators. She gets in and turns. Wags her finger at me. "Don't be too hard on her. She was probably desperate."

I head back to my office feeling agitated. Sasha Bale? My feelings say no, it can't be her, but the facts say yes. What kind of chemist would I be if I went with feelings over facts?

It's just that I'd felt sure that if I met Seven in real life, I'd recognize her deep down, that I'd feel something powerful— some sort of pull, or an emotional charge.

A silly notion. I'm a scientist, not a starry-eyed romantic. What's next? Writing love poetry and learning to play the lute? This needs to stop. I need to confirm my findings and be done with it.

I sit down and send Sasha an email.

Are you free for a quick lunch at Siefer's at noon? I'd like to run something by you.

I don't say what. Will she know she's busted? She'll suspect it. She's bright. But what's she going to say? No? I'm her boss.

Which is, I suppose, what legions of sexually harassing bosses have thought to themselves. Though I think it's safe to say that we've left sexual harassment territory far, far behind. We've traveled galaxies beyond anything HR would ever approve of.

I settle back into my chair and study some data.

I guess Sasha wasn't lying when she said I'm the only one she talks to like that. And the lab coat. There are old images of me in a lab coat online, but it's what she sees me in every day, so it makes sense.

I try to put Sasha's face with Operator Seven's voice. Operator Seven's words. The honesty and vulnerability that seems to flow so easily between us.

I pull up her employee file from the HR database. The file doesn't contain many personal details. She's worked in the marketing department of several nonprofits. Attended school at the University of Colorado. Member of the debate team. The knot in my gut loosens as I think about that comment of hers about debate teams. I need to give her a chance.

Her work *has* been good lately. Her Instagram ideas. She's a beautiful woman in her way. Not that it matters. Except I imagined Seven so differently.

You don't see what's right in front of your face.

Apparently not.

An email notification pops up.

I'll be there. What is it regarding? Should I bring anything specific?

~Sasha

I send a short reply.

No need. Just a little brainstorming.

~Theo

I arrive at Siefer's at 11:30, well before it's flooded by the office crowd that it caters to. I grab a coffee and choose a booth in the corner where we'll have a bit of privacy. That also enables me to handle some phone business while I'm sitting there.

But a few minutes later I find myself Googling Sasha. There's almost nothing I couldn't have gotten in her employee file. I go to Facebook. I have an account there that I never use, set up by Willow, of course. I'm using it now, though—to look up Sasha Bale.

I get her picture. Lots of shots of her with a young girl—her niece. Herbs in small pots along a kitchen window. Not much else. *To see what she shares with friends, send her a friend request.*

What does she share with friends? Is the real Sasha there on Facebook? Does she swear and laugh and complain about her boss? Does she call people motherfuckers?

The place starts to fill up with the nine-to-five crowd, some of them vaguely familiar. Employees of mine, I suppose. It's not as if I make a habit of memorizing their faces.

I loosen my tie, hot. I've worn my lab coat as a little inside joke between us.

"Mr. Drummond?"

I look up, and she's there, smiling.

I stand. Put out my hand. "Thank you for coming, Sasha."

She takes my hand. "My pleasure." Her eyes sparkle. She pulls off her decorative scarf and drapes it over the back of the chair. "Are you eating? Should we order first?"

"I'll handle it. Do you know what you want?"

She looks up at the chalkboard menu. "Are *you* eating?"

This feels all wrong already. I want us to talk the way we do on the phone, the feeling of being in perfect sync. Maybe it's too much to expect. Willow always talks about social niceties, how I don't pay enough attention to social niceties. They comfort people, she always says.

Social niceties, then. I check the menu. "I'm having the soup of the day."

"Tomato basil. I was thinking about that. Make it two."

"Any dessert?"

"I'll see how I feel."

I nod and head to the counter, feeling as if I'm in the dating version of Jekyll and Hyde. It's her voice. Her hesitancy. Even her order. Seven's such a contrarian, she'd never match my order. But maybe she loves tomato basil soup. What do I know?

The line moves slowly. I look over to where she's sitting. She smiles. She really is pretty. I should be glad. She wears a blue suit. Brass buttons, with a little trio of ribbons on the front pocket. Like a sexy admiral.

I put in my order and pay. The kid gives me a number on a small stand. I grab the silverware and head back to the table.

"Thank you," she says. "I didn't know you came here."

"I don't, typically."

"The soup here is always delicious. And they have this rosemary bread that's incredible," she says.

I search her eyes for that spark of connection. "Excellent."

After an uncomfortable silence where I think I need to say something, she updates me on the Instagram behind-the-scenes lab journal. It's tedious, and I'm barely listening.

Is Sasha playacting? Is she just that confident her cover isn't blown?

A woman comes by and sets down our soups.

"People love a story," Sasha continues, settling her napkin into her lap. "They love a little drama. They love to pull for the underdog, and this lets them in on that. We've identified a few junior chemists who already run things for you who could log your daily progress—nothing proprietary, of course. We'd get an image of the day—papers and beakers or whatever. Communications could tweak the write-ups to get them into layman's terms."

I break off a bit of bread. Steam rises up. I note the flecks of rosemary. I try it. When I look back up, she's watching me intently.

"Yeah?" she says.

It takes me a moment to understand that she's talking about the bread. I give her a nod. A quick smile. It's just food.

"Right?" She starts in on the soup. "So this Instagram story, maybe we create a header or a name."

This is me, I want to say. *You can be real.* I clear my throat, preparing to change the subject, but she keeps on.

I give up and try the soup. "I like that it's about the process and the product," I say. "That's what people should focus on."

"Exactly." She smiles. "But I guess that's not why you called me here, is it?"

"I think you know why I called you here," I say.

She cocks her head, spoon poised over the fragrant soup. Outside the window, the world rushes on. "To brainstorm..." she says, conspiratorially.

"The calls," I say. "I *know,* Sasha."

"Are they...still working out?"

"You know they're working out."

She studies my face. All innocence. "Do I?"

"Drop the act. They're amazing, and you know it, because you're the one making them. They're my favorite part of the day. Let's talk about the calls."

She studies my eyes, as though searching for something. Then she smiles, and in that moment, she looks beautiful. "You're right. I think they're amazing, too."

"So come out to dinner. You know you want to."

Her eyes widen a fraction.

"I get it, I'm your boss," I say. "If you don't want things with me to move that way, then I'm fine to drop it here and now. But if your constant refusal to have dinner or to let me help you is because you think there might be some trouble at the company... look, I'll rewrite the corporate rules right now."

She studies my face.

"One dinner. See how it goes."

She stares at me strangely. *Say something,* I think.

"It is tempting."

"So..." I say.

After an awkward silence, she says, "I knew you would...

figure it out." She tilts her head. "But just out of curiosity, how did you?"

"You corresponded with me as Hello Morning from inside the Vossameer building."

Her eyes sparkle. "Oops."

"The way you sounded when you were making yourself come this morning...Sasha..."

She sucks in her lips. What is she thinking? She's so hard to read. She looks around. "This place...I feel like we're in a fishbowl..."

"So come to dinner."

"Hold on, I just felt my phone go." She pulls her phone from her purse. "Work meltdown. I absolutely have to handle this."

"What is it?"

"It's nothing that needs to be your problem." She stands. "A fire to put out."

"Dinner," I say. "Tonight. Does seven work?"

She grins. "Am I crazy to say yes?"

"Probably."

"Fine. Let's do this! Name the time and place."

I stand. "I'll text you. You'll have to unblock me, of course."

She narrows her eyes. "You know what? Email would be better. Way better."

"You're not going to unblock me?"

"It's a long story." She looks at the door, back at me, seeming torn. "I really do wish I could stay."

"I'll email you." I watch her leave.

NINETEEN

Lizzie

I'M WORKING on the Instagram strategy when Sasha messages me to meet her in the marketing meeting room.

The marketing meeting room is an enclosed space with a nice view that would be a perfect spot for putting out bagels and coffee in the morning for the team, maybe with a big stuffed chair or two for nice breaks and creative collaboration. It would be a great place to set out cake and balloons for people's birthdays. Maybe even a Ping-Pong table and some Nerf basketball action.

This being Vossameer, of course, this perfectly nice room is where meetings with business vendors happen. It's where the team is gathered to be yelled at. And most of all, it's where people go to be fired.

With shaking hands I grab my phone. I text Mia one word.
Fuck.
Mia: **Wut?**

Me: **Surprise private meeting with Sasha. In the firing chamber.**

Mia sends me back several empathetic emojis. I send her a black sideways heart, then I silence my phone and put it in the pocket of my ugly dress. If there's one thing you can count on with ugly dresses, it's really good pockets.

Sasha is in the room when I get there. She's sitting at the head of the table that will never hold a birthday cake. Her phone is on the table next to a yellow legal pad, over which her pen is poised.

"Take a seat," she says.

I take a seat on the long side, leaving one chair between us.

"Do you know why I've called you in? Can you guess?"

I shake my head.

"How about taking a guess," she says.

I shrug. If she's going to fire me, I'm not helping her.

"The wake-up-call service. There isn't one, is there?"

I frown, like I don't get it.

She puts on a sympathetic face. "It's you. It's been you all along."

How did she find out? Did Mr. Drummond spill? No way. He wouldn't have.

I sigh. "I can explain—I really can," I say, the three words that never lead anywhere good, but I try. I tell her how I had the Canadian service all set up. How I ordered a call for myself just to ensure it came through, and it didn't. So I had to do it.

"Well, I wanted to tell you that I appreciate your ingenuity."

Sasha appreciates my ingenuity? Hope begins to flutter in my heart. "You're not going to fire me?"

"Of course not. Why would I? Mr. Drummond appreciates the service. Most men would be paying ten bucks a minute for calls like that."

I'm flooded with shame and embarrassment. How much did he tell her? "Uh..."

"You think I wouldn't find out? You impersonated a wake-up-call service that escalated to you masturbating and climaxing on the phone, with your boss..." She's watching my eyes. "With him telling you what to do."

My mouth goes dry. Heat steals up my neck. He gave her details?

Mortified, I think back to the last call. Coming on the phone. I'd felt so connected with him. Like we were in on something magical together.

I feel sick.

"I don't get it. I'm not fired?" My voice sounds small.

She gives me a sympathetic look. "Lizzie, I'm sure you didn't mean things to go that way. Right?"

"Not at all!" I say. "It was the furthest thing from my mind. When that Canadian place flaked out on me, I just wanted to replicate an effective service. I only wanted to keep my job."

"Of course." She gets this little smile. "Though it did start out rather *unorthodox*, you have to admit."

I'm barely listening. I felt like Mr. Drummond and I had a relationship. I loved how we were together, and he totally betrayed me. Was anything he told me even true?

"Right?" she prompts.

"It wasn't supposed to be like that—I swear. I meant it to be boring and normal, but my roommate and I were goofing off, and when I said all those mean things, I didn't know he was there."

Her lips quirk. "So what exactly did you say?"

Okay, so he didn't tell her all of it. Just the most intimate stuff. "I really didn't mean it."

"You're not fired," she says. "But I should know how it started. Just in case."

In case of what? I wonder miserably. But does it even matter? "Well...I said, *'wake up, motherfucker.'* Something like that. *'People are waiting for whatever bullshit you have in store for them today.'*"

She looks stunned. "You said that to Mr. Drummond?"

"I honestly didn't know he was there. And...actually I think it might have been *'stupid asshole'* that I called him. Jackalope. I don't know; it all blends in."

She looks amazed.

I'd like to call him a few new names now. I can't believe he spilled the details to Sasha!

"So I guess that'll wake a guy up."

"I should think so!"

I toy with the hem of my shapeless dress. "When I realized he was on the line, I thought for sure I'd be fired. When he came down here and called it unorthodox, you could've knocked me over with a feather." When I look up, she's beaming at me. "You're really not mad?"

She snorts. "It's a little bit funny, you have to admit." I'm stunned. I never thought she had much of a sense of humor. "So he enjoyed that?" she asks.

I look down, uncomfortable with her weird interest. "I don't know that he enjoyed it. I don't know, maybe he was more... surprised. Maybe he's sick of everyone kissing his ass. I think his interest was more about curiosity. What kind of a wake-up caller says that? That's why he didn't fire the service. He's a puzzle guy."

She's watching me intently. "Very true. Theo does not like a puzzle he can't crack. So then what?"

I shrug. "It was just phone sex." I'm done giving her details. I'm not an asshole like Mr. Drummond. Sure, maybe I gave Mia one juicy line, but Mr. Drummond gave Sasha the entire, uncut, XXX-rated version! "One phone sex call is pretty much the same as the next."

I feel this little whimper inside me, though. Because it really felt like more. To me, anyway.

I tell myself it's an important lesson. I promised myself I wouldn't trust a man after Mason, and what did I do? I trusted one. Such a fool.

She raises a perfectly shaped eyebrow. "So that's all?"

That's all? It was a huge amount of sharing. "Yeah, that's all."

"Okay, then." She pulls out her phone and taps the screen a few times, then puts it to her ear. "I need somebody up in marketing. No...no...there's no problem, just an escort out of the building."

Everything in the world seems to fall away. An escort? *She called security?*

Sasha clicks off. Gives me a hard stare. Every trace of warmth and humor is gone from her face. "I'm going to have to ask you to get your things and exit the building."

"You said I wasn't getting fired!"

"You can't be fired; you're not a real employee yet. You're on probation, and that probationary period is now over."

I stand. "Sasha, please. Tomorrow's the last day for me to get my bonus. One day."

"I'm sorry." Sasha points a weapons-grade red fingernail in the direction where my cubicle is. "You were given an opportunity to do the most meaningful work of your life—"

"I did do meaningful work! Think of all the great work I did. The engagement numbers. The Instagram strategies. Please, I'll do anything. I'll work an extra week with no pay. I just need that bonus tomorrow."

"The bonus is for employees who don't commit fraud and

pull the CEO into compromising situations. He could bring you up on charges of fraud and pandering."

"What? No. It wasn't like that." I feel sick.

"No? Maybe it was all fun and games for you, but Mr. Drummond is angry and disgusted, and really, how could you blame him? He doesn't want you calling him anymore. Not ever again. You contact him one more time and he really *will* look into pursuing further action against you."

My stomach feels queasy. Pursuing action against me? So he really was just toying with me, then? Teaching me a lesson? I can't believe it. But why else divulge so much to Sasha?

She points at the door.

By some miracle I'm able to stand. I head across to my cubicle. I don't pass go. I don't get my twelve-thousand-dollar sign-on bonus. I don't dance on my desk to Britney Spears while making microwave popcorn.

I grab my coat and bag and the fun notepads I defiantly bought. I mumble goodbye to a few of my other neighbors, who've popped up from their cubicles, looking alarmed and interested. I just shake my head and trudge up front. They'll find out soon enough. Maybe Mr. Drummond will write it up for the Vossameer newsletter.

In a brave display of affection in this thankless place, Betsy gives me a big hug. I clutch onto her, more grateful than she'll ever know.

Sasha and the security guy look on, like she might be passing me a shiv or something.

I spin around. Face Sasha. "I want to see Mr. Drummond." I've decided I want to tell him he's an asshole right to his face.

"Mr. Drummond doesn't want to see you. Trust me. You don't want to push your luck."

I grit my teeth. I have enough problems without adding in legal charges. "Well, at least I'm free," I say. "This place sucks, and you know it. And if you don't, you need to pull your head out of your ass."

"Let's go." The security guy gestures at the door.

"Don't worry, I know the way." I storm out. Somehow I'm in the elevator with the security guy. Somehow the door is closing. Going down.

All this work for nothing. Lenny's guys will come for the money, and I won't have it. Do I leave town? Do they chase me? But then, what about Mia?

And the worst thing of all? The tears threatening have nothing to do with any of that, and everything to do with the way Mr. Drummond utterly and completely betrayed me.

I thought we had a connection. I loved our connection, so full of risky, thrilling, heartfelt honesty.

Our connection felt real. It felt beautiful.

To me, anyway.

He warned me, though, didn't he? The world revolves around him. He'll take what he wants.

TWENTY

Theo

I PUSH ASIDE the notebook full of half-baked ideas and focus on my phone, sitting front and center on my desk. "It can't merely be a good place," I tell Willow. "I want a great place. Something stylish, but not too fussy. She's the kind who'd be into comfort food, but with flair."

"Okay," Willow says. "Comfort food with flair."

"Stylish and fun," I say. "It can be slightly quirky, but not all-out weird. Not quirky for quirky's sake. And the food has to be excellent. Taste-wise, but also in terms of how it looks. The plate has to look beautiful. And above all, elaborate desserts."

"What have you done with my brother?" she asks.

"Will you help me or not?"

"You really enjoyed those calls."

"Do I have to ask somebody else?"

"No, I'm sending you a link. The Blue Stag Club. But it'll be impossible to get a table..."

"Thanks," I say as the link comes up. "Got it." The place is important. I want Sasha to feel comfortable enough to be her sassy, snarky self.

THE BLUE STAG Club is in the East Village. I walk in just before four. The place is everything Willow said it would be—colorful and cozy, but not overdone. A sense of humor, but nothing wacky. Exactly what Seven would like.

There are a few tables with diners—lunch stragglers, maybe. I venture in and stop at a corner table. Private. Near the window. But that's not what attracts me. It's the baby goat picture above the table.

The maître d' comes up behind me. "Can I help you?"

"I'm hoping for dinner reservations," I say. "Seven tonight. What do I have to do to get this table for seven tonight?"

"It's not possible."

He's wrong. Everything is possible. I haven't felt like this in a long time.

I pull out my wallet and start peeling off bills.

"Really," he says. "We have a policy."

I keep going. And eventually it's possible.

I get out of there and email Sasha with the plans. I tell her I'll pick her up at 6:30. I'm about to tell her where we're going, but I decide to leave it as a surprise. She'll probably call me an asshole when she finds out how I secured our table.

I smile at the thought. I've never felt so connected to a woman. Though it's Operator Seven I'm feeling connected to, not Sasha. I need to work on changing that.

I head home and grab a little time in my study, updating computer models, but I'm incredibly distracted. I answer emails until it's time to get dressed, dithering over what tie to put with my black-and-gray-checked bespoke suit. I'd typically go with a black tie, but this is Seven. I grab a yellow tie with pineapples on it, fix my cuffs, and head down to the street where the limo is waiting. I give Sasha's address.

I've never been one to get overly excited about the possibility of fucking, maybe because the opportunities are always so plentiful.

But you'd think I'd be excited by the chance to finally be with Seven, considering how many times I've imagined it. I close my eyes and picture getting an earful of her snark before pressing her to the wall and tasting her lips, her neck, enjoying the sound of her moans as I get her off.

It's still the faceless woman on the phone I'm imagining. Still her husky voice, even if it is an app.

Damn.

I grab the bottle of scotch from the backseat bar and pour myself two fingers.

Eventually we arrive at Sasha's building, an ultra-contemporary high-rise near Astor Place. I double-check the address. I'd imagined Seven in a prewar place. Something with heft and history. An ornate elevator that only works half the time. I suppose it's possible the ceilings in there have crown moldings, but they wouldn't be historic.

Sasha's grinning as she crosses the sidewalk. I get out and open the door for her.

"The jackalope has arrived!" she declares.

I manage a smile. I should hardly be put off—she's called me worse, but it's always been…different, somehow. "You look lovely," I say.

She raises an eyebrow. "So do you, Mr. Drummond."

"I'm back to Mr. Drummond?"

She stares blankly at me, then shrugs. "Oh, that whole thing…" She waves, as if to dismiss an unruly subject. "I say we start from square one."

I smile politely, though I really don't know what she means. "Ready?"

"Sure am."

I take her hand and help her into the back of the car, and get in after her. I offer her a drink and tell her we're going to the Blue Stag Club. "Have you heard of it?"

"Heard of it? Of course!" she says. "I thought they were booked out for months."

"They were. I did an in-person visit to get a table. I was...persuasive."

She beams at me. "It's perfect."

I gaze out the window, disheartened. I hoped she'd be less... something out of the office environment. More how she is on the phone.

"Gorgeous," she says as we walk into the Blue Stag. I take her coat and hand it off, and we're led to our table.

She doesn't seem to notice the baby goat picture. Maybe it's for the best. It'll be a good thing to draw her attention to later during a lull in the conversation.

The waiter brings our drinks—a scotch for me and a dry martini for her.

"You're so full of surprises," I say.

"What do you mean?" She pulls out the stick and slips an olive between her lips.

"I wouldn't have guessed a dry martini."

She tilts her head and smiles. Her smile is pretty. She's pretty. I have to give her a chance. "Why not?"

"I would've guessed something sweeter."

She rolls her eyes. "Such an asshole."

"Excuse me?" I say.

She narrows her eyes. "You heard me."

I drain my drink as my mood deflates. I, of all people, should know that reality never matches the pretty surface of things.

The phone calls were magical. Utterly magical—a word I never apply to anything but they were.

And I had to break the spell. I had to take more.

Worse, I feel like she knows it. I can feel her nervousness.

"Can I ask you, what made you call me like that in the first place?"

She grins sheepishly. "There actually was another service set up. A Canadian service. But I was so nervous they wouldn't come through that I set up a call for myself for ten minutes before that. And they never came through." She goes on to tell me a funny story about her roommate, about the comedy of errors that led to her calling me a motherfucker.

It's amusing. I'm laughing.

"I was so paranoid when I saw you next. I thought for sure you'd fire me. You could've knocked me over with a feather when you said the service was unorthodox!"

The appetizers and more drinks come. We're actually having fun. I never imagined her with a roommate, either. I push the last bruschetta her way. "I'm saving room."

Her eyes sparkle. She reaches across the table with a napkin and dabs at my lapel.

"Uh-oh," I say. "User error?"

"Just a little one. It would be a shame to ruin this beautiful jacket."

"I had half a mind to wear my lab coat. Maybe I should've."

She snorts. "To the Blue Stag? Why on earth would you do that?"

"I thought you might appreciate it."

"Well, you know I do." She smiles. She seems about to say something more, but then our entrees come.

This is all wrong. Is she feeling as unenthusiastic about our date as I am?

"Talk to me," I say as soon as the waiter leaves.

"What do you mean?"

"This is me. We're here. Cards on the table. Are you feeling weird about this? I want you to tell me if you are."

"Why would you think that?" She tilts her head. "I'm happy we're out, finally. It's just all...so unusual."

"It is," I say, adjusting my napkin in my lap. "The phone calls—that's not something I do every day. Or ever. And I want you to know, I'm not expecting anything. We're just out for dinner."

Hurt flashes across her face; she quickly covers it with a bright smile. "It had to happen," she says. "I mean..."

"Well, you were pretty against it."

"Can you blame me?" She picks up her fork and spins a bunch of pasta.

"I suppose not."

I dig into my steak, unable to shake the feeling that something isn't right. That she isn't right. She used a voice-disguising app, yes, but it's more than her tone. She's so much more formal and tentative in person.

I ask her about her family, and she brightens up, talking about her niece. I like her most when she talks about her niece.

We chat all through dinner. It's nice enough. Even so, I can't imagine kissing her.

Our waiter is showing the dessert tray to the next table over. There's cake and pie, some sort of custard, and a small group of unfrosted cookies. I tip my head at it. "What do you think about that situation over there?"

"The dessert tray?"

"Those cookies?"

"Probably shortbread." She shrugs. "Meh. I'm not a dessert person."

I sit back. What? Not a dessert person?

She looks back at me and smiles.

"So tell me," I say, "what's your favorite movie?"

"*Gone with the Wind.* What's yours?"

My pulse races. "How about your favorite musical?"

"Why?"

"Just...need to know."

"I don't know. I suppose I like *Grease.*"

My blood races. "*Grease* is your favorite musical?"

She searches my face. "You have something against *Grease?*"

"You're not her."

She looks like a deer in the headlights. "I like all kinds of movies. What I like at any one time is dependent on my mood."

I put my napkin on my food. "Why are you pretending to be her?"

"What on earth are you talking about? You think I'm pretending?"

I give her a look. "You're not her."

She's white as a sheet.

"Why would you pretend? Who is she? I need to know."

She puts her napkin on her food. "Okay, fine. Cards on the table. I'm worried about you. You invited a wake-up-call girl you never met to dinner."

"And you impersonated her. Look, just give me her contact information—the real contact information—and we'll go back to how things were. No harm, no foul."

She gazes across the restaurant—hurt. Maybe even angry. She did go to an extreme length to get a date with me, and now I'm rejecting her.

"You're a beautiful, charming woman."

"Save it," she snaps.

"Why create the fake front in the first place? Please tell me, is Operator Seven somebody you know?"

Still she doesn't look at me, but her expression is harder. Her eyes are shinier.

"The information," I say. "I want it."

I can see the gears turning in her head.

And now they're definitely turning in mine.

There's this long moment when we're both thinking through scenarios of how this plays out. What happens if she refuses. What happens if I then push it. I've asked her out to dinner. Dirty-talked the wake-up-call girl. If I threaten her job over this, the potential legal and PR disasters boggle the mind.

"Just a name."

She stands and grabs her purse. "Forget it." She leaves. Without giving me a name.

I drain my scotch.

TWENTY-ONE

Lizzie

I SPEND the night baking cookies, plain vanilla round ones. Most of them I frost as frown emojis, but a few are sob ones.

I watch *Funny Face* twice and sing along with my favorite songs. Cookies don't typically go with beers, but they go with them tonight.

Mia gets home around ten. Wordlessly I hand her the plate.

"Nooo," she says. "Fired?"

"It's not technically a firing when you're still on your probationary period. I learned that today."

"Honey." She grabs a sob cookie, takes a bite out of the cheek. "What happened?"

I tell her about the duplicity of Sasha and the betrayal of Mr. Drummond as she eats three entire emoji faces.

"I liked him. I trusted him. It felt so...real. But it wasn't. How did I not learn my lesson about trusting guys like that?"

She curls her legs under herself, smooshing into my arm.

"Screw it. Trust is an act of bravery. So he can just fuck himself."

"I felt brave around Mr. Drummond. I went places with him I never even went with Mason. But it wasn't really about that—it was like I had this feeling of discovery with him. Like Amelia Earhart, traveling through new territory. Except not alone. We were a team in a way I can't explain. That's how it felt, anyway."

"Amelia Earhart perished over the Pacific."

I groan and grab a frown cookie. "And I perished over Lexington Avenue. Because he takes what he wants. He warned me, even. He took and took and took, and then he didn't even bother to fire me personally. What kind of an idiot am I?"

"It's beautiful to trust. It's beautiful to open your heart. Don't let that asshole take that away. He's small and mean, and you're huge with your beautiful, amazing heart."

"And in the end it's the least of my problems."

"Blow jobs for a buck?" she says with a wistful, hopeful smile.

"It's not even funny. I'm so sorry," I say.

"What do you have to apologize to me about?"

"Um, being the cause of angry loan sharks about to invade our home when I don't have their money? I have two days until thugs with pinky rings and guns come to collect money I don't have. I don't want you in the crossfire."

"Crossfire? What crossfire? Don't tell me you'll be packing heat, too."

"Not funny." I stare at the ceiling.

"If they think they're gonna clip you for that fourteen G's, they've got another think coming," she says.

"What are you even saying?"

"I'm boning up on my mobster talk," Mia says.

I roll my eyes.

"There's a smile," she says.

"That wasn't a smile. I want you to start thinking about where you'll sleep while I deal with them."

"What do you mean, deal with them? What does that mean?" she asks with a horrified expression. "Lizzie..."

"Not *that*," I say. "I only whore to strange men on the phone."

"Mr. Drummond should pay. He's the one who got you fired. Make him help you."

Sasha's words run through my mind. *He's disgusted....* "I'm the last person he'd help. He's not who I thought he was. And I'm serious. You need to crash somewhere Saturday night." The money is due on Sunday morning.

"I'm not leaving you. If you stay, I stay. Also, I totally have to see the kind of cookies you frost for it. They'll be epic."

"You're not staying. If something happened to you, I'd die."

"Goes both ways, sister. We're in this together." She gets up and heads to the refrigerator. It means everything that she wants to stay. It really does.

She holds up two beers: Sixpoint Crisp, our house fave. "Want?"

"You are the best friend ever."

She tosses one over the small island that's supposed to imply that the kitchen isn't the same room as the living room. "So does this mean I have to take it down?"

"What?"

She points her bottle at the wall next to the conundrum window. A new cross-stitch in a wooden frame hangs here.

I go over. There, between two beautiful and elaborately embroidered flowers, is a meticulously stitched saying: *Sex with me is a dirty, savage affair. Utterly uncivilized.*

"Oh my god! You have finally gone insane."

She takes it off the nail. "It's stupid."

"No!" I grab it out of her hand and hang it back up. "It's funny. At least he gave us a laugh."

She pops the top off her beer.

Back on the couch, I Google *do loan sharks really kill you?* I get the same answers I got when I Googled it ten times before. Sometimes they do kill you, but sometimes they just hurt you. Sometimes they make you act as a drug mule. One guy on one of the threads said they carved up his arm.

I'm trying to decide between having my arm carved up and being a drug mule when Mia starts telling me about her most recent date. "He smelled like a body spray factory and made an assholey actress joke," she says. "Next."

"Like what?"

She sighs. "How many actresses does it take to screw in a light bulb? One to screw it in and ninety-nine to stand there and say, 'it should be me up there!'" She swigs her beer. "Soooo funny. Fuck off."

"Fuck off," I agree. Mia has been going to lots of auditions and not landing parts. "What an asshole."

We drink beer in silence, noodling on our phones. Then I just drink beer and watch Mia noodle on her phone, feeling intensely lucky for having a friend like her.

I've lived with her for seven years, since the age of twenty. Not living with her for eighteen months is going to be hard.

I miss her already.

I've already interviewed and ruled out a few subletter prospects. One woman seemed like a party animal. Another had a Kid Rock tattoo.

My ideal person is a serious, quiet type who has a demanding job or a significant other who has their own apartment. I want to do the best for Mia.

I find myself wondering whether Mr. Drummond has close

friends like Mia. He feels alone when people put him in the hero box. Or was that just bullshit?

I go to bed a few hours later, but I don't get much sleep. I keep thinking about that enforcer. If he was a regular person, I'd explain and try to work out a compromise. But he has a gun, which tends to be the accessory of choice for the man who isn't up for working out a compromise.

The later it gets—or earlier, technically—the more worried and scared I feel. Loan sharks hurt people. It's a thing. A thing doesn't become a thing without there being some basis to it.

I'm wide awake when 4:20 rolls around. I watch the time feeling sad and angry; 4:20 comes and goes, then 4:30.

The phone rings at 4:43.

I nearly jump out of my skin. It's him. Did I accidentally unblock his number? Did that motherfucker get around my block?

I'm outraged, but some stupid little part of me is happy. Excited.

And I have to crush that part. I answer. "Go fuck yourself," I say.

I want to hang up, but it's not dramatic enough. So I throw the phone across the room. It bounces off the wall, clatters across the floor, and comes to a stop. I can still hear his voice, rumbling urgently. I don't know what he's saying, and I don't care. That's what I'm telling that happy-he-called part of myself.

The phone is a hunk of metal and glass making noise on the hardwood floor, and I want nothing to do with it.

Nothing!

I get out of bed and shove my feet into my cowboy boots as he rumbles on. I go over and bring a wicked cowboy heel down onto the thing. The crunch is incredibly satisfying.

I catch something that sounds like *Hello? Are you okay?*

Seriously? Do phones only break when you don't want them to?

I bring my boot down on it again and again, really hard, smashing it into little bits, severing our connection for good. Eventually the voice is gone.

So done with him!

He can never call me again.

I can never call anybody again, either, but never mind.

It felt amazing.

TWENTY-TWO

Theo

WILLOW FLINGS OPEN HER DOOR. She's wearing her bathrobe and an angry look. "It's six in the morning."

"It's 6:10," I say, handing her a mocha cappuccino. I walk into her place.

"What's going on? Did you confront the woman in marketing?"

"It wasn't her. We need a plan B."

"You were so sure."

"What can I say? It wasn't her."

She narrows her eyes. "You seem happy about it."

"I don't know. I don't know anything right now."

It's a strange thing for me to say, but she doesn't make a big deal out of it. She's my sister. She's on board. "Aaaaaand you need your brilliant sister to find your wake-up-call girl some other way."

She puts out a plate of scones.

I take a seat at her table and tell her how I called this morning, and Seven said "go fuck yourself," and then it sounded a lot like she smashed the phone. Did Sasha instruct her to do that? At any rate, the number is out of order. The email bounces now, as if the account was closed, but it was probably Sasha anyway.

Either there's an actual service, or it's somebody Sasha knows.

"Theo," she says. "The woman said 'fuck yourself' and destroyed her phone when you called. Magic 8-Ball says...she doesn't want to talk to you."

"Something else is going on. She wouldn't just cut things off like that."

Willow winces.

"Yes, I know how that sounds, but you don't know her, and I do. If nothing else, I want to make sure things are okay. Did Sasha come down on her somehow?"

"And there's the thing where you still want to go out to dinner with her."

I shrug.

Willow sips her coffee. "Let me ask you this. How were you paying for this service?"

"I already hit up accounting. They don't have the contact information."

"Right, but how were you paying?"

"PayPal."

She smiles. "I say we pay them, then."

"Why?"

"So we can follow the money. Assuming the PayPal account is still there." She grabs her laptop and we access the accounting department records. It's there. Willow has me make a thirty-dollar test payment to the specified PayPal account.

"We probably just paid Sasha thirty bucks."

"I know, but you have to look at everything. Sometimes

when you do that and you look at your statement, you get a business name."

We sit back.

Sure enough, she gets a receipt. From O. Waves. And a string of numbers.

"Is Sasha's last name Waves?"

"No, it's Bale."

"Interesting," Willow says. "Sea turtle avatar. Huh."

"Let's Google O.Waves."

She gives me a look. "We have something better, Mr. Bond." She opens up a search engine I don't know. "Deep Web." A few clicks later, it turns out the payee is Ocean Waves, a 301C that supports sea turtles.

"Wow," she says. "She covered her tracks."

"Damn," I say. Total dead end.

"Sasha won't take a bribe to tell who the caller is?"

"She tried to impersonate her, then refused to tell me. I've been in business long enough to know when somebody can be bought. All Sasha's getting is a pink slip as soon as I figure out how to do it without HR up my ass." I push my palms to my forehead, despondent.

"She could sue you so hard."

"Forget Sasha, I need the caller. We know the caller might work at Vossameer, but not necessarily."

"You have hundreds of employees."

"We know she's a she."

"You don't know that."

"It's an assumption. Will you accept that?"

It's when I'm walking home that inspiration strikes.

There was a charitable giving event at the beginning of the month where employees were asked to nominate charities for Vossameer to give to. Everybody got a nomination form. I head back to the office. It doesn't take long to get the list. I want to see whether Sasha suggested the Ocean Waves sea turtle charity.

I look it up. No go. Sasha suggested the United Way.

Just for the hell of it, I go down the rest of the list, one hundred and eighty employees. One person did suggest Ocean Waves.

Lizzie Cooper.

I know I've heard the name. It takes me all of three minutes to put it together.

Turnip Truck.

My head spins. Could it be?

I think back to the burn of her gaze that first day. *Maybe Mr. Amazing is being amazing elsewhere.*

It's her.

Something in me recognized her that first day. And then the next day, she'd seemed different. Clothes all wrong. Doltish attitude all wrong.

She was hiding. Hiding in plain sight.

You're so oblivious.

God, I even stood there imagining that flip book I'd had as a child. The wrong outfits and shoes on the wrong people. Because she was all wrong.

Operator Seven.

She hid herself. Why?

I put in a call to her extension. A woman answers. "This is Amy."

"I'm looking for Lizzie Cooper."

"She's not here," she tells me. "Is there something I can help you with?"

"When will she be back?"

"She's gone."

"Gone? What happened?"

"I'm sorry, who is this?"

"It's Mr. Drummond," I say. "And I'm asking you to tell me what happened down there."

"W-well, all I know is that she walked out of here saying this place sucks and..."

"And what?"

"That we all need to pull our heads out of our asses?"

Sounds about right. "Thank you," I say.

I grab Lizzie's address from accounting and call Derek.

An hour later, he's parking a half a block down from her home. It's a prewar building in a gloomy section of Hell's Kitchen. No doorman. Not a good neighborhood.

I figure out her windows are on the fifth floor, probably the last two windows on the side, overlooking the courtyard.

This is more like where scrappy Operator Seven would live. Lizzie Cooper. Lizzie. She feels right. Absolutely right in every way.

Derek doesn't ask why I make him sit out there. He doesn't question me. Hardly anyone does.

Except her.

I wait, desperate for a glimpse of her. I want to see what she looks like when she's not trying to be invisible, to feel her breath against my skin and hear her whispered words, know what she loves, how she lives, everything.

Googling turns up dozens of Elizabeth Coopers. I forward her HR file, which conveniently contains her Social Security number, to my PI for an expedited background check.

My impulse is to go right up there, but I stop myself.

She hates to be pushed, controlled.

I have to do this right.

TWENTY-THREE

Lizzie

I SPEND Friday morning making cheerful posts on my bakery blog, and then I make Facebook posts that link to them.

One of the posts is a discussion of why cookies sometimes spread into an ugly mess (usually too much sugar, because sugar retains water, or a too-hot oven). And then a lighthearted update on my ongoing experiments in baking with tea. Maybe if I make enough of those cheerful posts, the fabric of reality itself will be altered.

As soon as rush hour's over, I take the rings my grandmother left me when she died to the pawn shops, something I'd hoped I wouldn't have to do. It's an utterly distressing task, but better than being maimed or killed or made a drug mule.

I walk out with two thousand dollars and a heavy heart.

After that, I go around to caterers to see whether there's anyone who'll pay me up front for three weeks of work—that's how long I have in the apartment. My ads for a subletter all say it starts the first of April.

The caterers all turn me down. I think my desperation scares them.

I'm back just after noon, making a new list of caterers to hit after lunch. I'm cheap and good—it'll be a perfect deal for the right caterer. It won't be enough money, but it'll be something to show Lenny I'm trying.

Meanwhile, Mia can't be around for whatever fallout there is.

My plan to keep her out involves installing a sliding bolt on the inside of the door. Literally locking her out. I've arranged to have her stay on a mutual friend's couch. She'll be pissed as hell.

But safe.

So that's my plan. I look at the pristine skin on my arm. What does it mean to carve up a person's arm? Do they carve a message, like, *pay up*? Or just stab it a bunch of times?

I nearly jump out of my skin when the buzzer sounds. I go to the panel, heart racing, unsure whether I should answer. They can't be here already. It's Friday. The money isn't due until Sunday morning. "Hello?"

"Delivery for Ms. Cooper."

I'm freaking out now. I haven't ordered anything in a very long time. Is this how the loan sharks think they can get in? Or maybe it's a dead rat or black roses. Or a horse's head. So far, the loan shark guys have shown zero originality.

"From who?"

"Vossameer."

I frown. Did they courier over some severance stuff? Maybe my pro-rated salary? It won't be the twelve thousand dollars I still need, but it'll be something.

I whip down the stairs.

Down in the lobby, a delivery boy hands me a large white box with a white ribbon. What? I give the kid a few bucks. Not like that's going to make a difference at this point.

I happen to look out, across the street just then, and I nearly throw up when I see Lenny's enforcer leaning against a car out there. He smiles.

I hurry back upstairs and lock the door, then I set the box on the kitchen island and grab the scissors. There are three white boxes inside the main box—one large, one the size of a shoebox and one quite small. I open the large one first. It's something soft wrapped in gray tissue paper. Something velvet. My heart begins to pound as I pull out a red velvet dress.

Not just any red velvet dress; it's a beautifully made strapless dress with satin detailing around the bodice. And a matching wrap. So gorgeous, I can't breathe.

But that's not what shocks me.

It's a lot like the dress that Audrey Hepburn wore at the end of *Funny Face*. A slightly updated version.

Mr. Drummond. It has to be.

Why would he send me this? He told Sasha our most intimate secrets. Had her fire me. He betrayed and embarrassed me.

Is this some psycho way of saying he's sorry? Or is he being weirdly mocking?

I clutch it to me. I should be angry, but mostly I feel tired. And sad for all my lost dreams. For how hard I try all the time.

I hold it to myself. My size.

I shouldn't open the card, but something perverse inside me forces my fingers to open the little envelope.

Tonight. Six. The Blue Stag Club.

I stare, dumbfounded.

Does he really think I'd go out to dinner with him after all of this?

"Screw you," I say to the card.

The shoebox-sized box is, of course, a shoebox. It has two pairs of Audrey's shoes in it—seven and a half, the other in eight. I'm an eight. What did he do? Study the security tapes to get my size?

He did, I think.

I assume the smallest box will be a necklace of some sort. Some mocking costume jewelry.

It's not. It's a cookie with mostly chocolate frosting but just enough pink and green to create a cellphone. There's a card, too.

Happy wake-up-call girl discovery day.

I sink into the chair. All my life I've baked special little cookies for people, commemorating things that are important or unimportant, but nobody ever made one for me.

And now this. I get a mocking one.

He wants me to go out to dinner at the Blue Stag? I should go, just to rip up the dress in front of him. And maybe I could set fire to the shoes and leave them burning on the table.

Or maybe I wear the dress and shoes. I walk in and give him the sassy mean smile he probably wants from the likes of me. He would sit there in his dinner jacket thinking I've capitulated. And I make him buy the most expensive champagne, and then I throw it in his face. *In your dreams, asshole!*

I adjust my vision of the scene to him sitting in his lab coat. He's all hot and scowly in his lab coat. And then I toss the champagne in his face.

Or maybe I drink the champagne and toss the water.

Hell yes!!

It's just about the chase with him. He thinks he can fire me? He thinks I'm such a beggar for him that I'll wear this dress and eat with him and fuck him now?

I break off a corner of the cookie and taste it. Just the perfect amount of vanilla in the dough. Only the best for Mr. Drummond.

I grab the dress. It really is like the one in the movie...except better. I hold it up to myself. I could just try it on...

Ten minutes later, Mia gets back. Her eyes grow wide as saucers. "Lizzie...Oh my god."

I smooth my hands down the bodice. I'm thinking about saying something funny about looking good for when the loan sharks carve my arm, but I don't have it in me.

Mia just looks upset. "Lizzie. No. Whatever you're thinking. You don't have to resort to that."

"What?"

She just widens her eyes.

I snort when I get what she's thinking. "Dude. No."

"What? I come home and you're all dressed up..."

"You think I'd wear this to prostitute myself? I don't know if I should be insulted that you think I'd actually do it, or that you think I'm insane enough to pick *this* out for the occasion. It's not like I'm whoring myself to the ladies of the Audrey Hepburn Appreciation Society."

"I don't even understand anything of what's happening here. Why would you buy a beautiful gown?"

"This dress is more dimensions of assholery from Theo freaking Drummond." I hand her the note.

She reads it. "He has some nerve."

"Like I'll go to dinner."

"Go. And demand the sign-on bonus," she says.

"On what grounds? The contract says I have to last thirty days. I didn't last the thirty days."

"He sent you this dress. Maybe you should go."

"That's what he wants, don't you see? This is not a dress. It's a power play. He thinks I'll go. And even if I go with elaborate fantasies of telling him off, he thinks he can get me to sit down to dinner. He thinks he can get me to kiss him. To sleep with him. Get me to the next step. He probably had me fired so he can make it all happen without fear of a lawsuit. This guy plays to win."

"That is cold."

"And arrogant. And ruthlessly efficient, which we knew about him. This is the man who doesn't even want his employees to be comforted by treats or decorations lest it detract from their efficiency. I mean, really? Now I'm going to sleep with you? You think you're so hot and amazing with your lab coat and your bad-boy lips that I'll just sleep with you after you fire me?"

"The hell with that!" She crosses her arms and frowns in solidarity with me. "He has bad-boy lips?"

"Shut it," I snort.

Mia stares at the dress.

"I should do something drastic to the dress," I say, "like cut it up and send it back to him, but he's not worth the energy."

"Wait. Come here."

I glide over. "At least I look good. If you're going to be beaten by loan sharks, you should at least look awesome. That's my new motto. What do you think?"

"Turn around."

I turn. She unhooks the back. "Oh, hell, yes," she says. "This is an Iggy Miyaki!"

"Iggy..."

"Miyaki. A dress designer. Socialites love her stuff for the big parties. I heard about her when I nannied. You even see her stuff at the Oscars." She turns me around and looks me in the eye. "This dress could be worth several thousand dollars."

"Really?"

"*Several* thousand."

"You think they'll let me return it for cash? I highly doubt it."

"No, but they'll let us return it for store credit."

"And that helps me how?"

"You'll see. Mia has a plan," Mia says, unzipping the dress.

"Should I be scared that you're undressing me and talking about yourself in third person right now?"

"Scared of how brilliant I am, maybe."

We pack the dress back up and put on our best clothes.

Not an hour later, we're in one of those West Side boutiques where they serve you champagne the minute you walk in the door. "I wish they would do this at Target," I say, taking a glass.

"God, that would be dangerous."

She straightens her spine and marches up to the counter. She talks to the woman in a low voice. Before you can say *sweetheart neckline*, we're in possession of a store credit. Five thousand dollars' worth.

I finger the card. "This would be the perfect thing...if Lenny was a high-fashion cross-dresser."

"Part two." We go outside and sit on a bus bench. She makes a few calls and eventually locates a woman who is willing to pay four thousand dollars cash for the gift card. "Little-known secret," she says, pocketing her phone. "Rich women are the ultimate penny pinchers."

An hour later, we have four thousand dollars cash from the dress and two thousand from the rings. We head to the bar in Murray Hill where Lenny's crew is. It's long and windowless and lit entirely with colorful neon beer signs, which makes everything slightly pinkish.

Lenny's hunched over a beer at a booth in the back.

I slap the money down. He flips through the corner of the stack instead of counting it like a normal person. "Six large," he says. "Where's the rest?"

"Since this is two days early," I try, "I thought maybe I could get a few extra days for the rest."

He gives me a look that means no.

"I'm doing my best."

He looks down at the stack. "I don't want anything to happen to you, but..."

"A few more days."

"I've given you a few more days." He looks me up and down. "You want to work it off?"

"Do you have need of a baker?" I ask hopefully.

"Does the baker know how to lie back and spread her legs real nice?"

"Uh!" Mia grabs my arm. "She most certainly does not!"

"Thousand a night, two guys per. Eight nights. It's a good deal," he says.

"She's not even thinking about it." Mia drags me out of there. "You're not even thinking about it," she instructs me.

We catch a train back home. Mia's cutting it close to get to her workshop.

"You're not thinking about it, are you?"

"You're a good friend," I say softly.

She grips the overhead strap and puts her free arm around me. "Oh my god, it's after six. He's at the restaurant right now," she says.

"Oh, right," I say. Like it hadn't crossed my mind.

"Sitting there alone. I hope he feels like an idiot."

"I hope so," I say.

"You can't always get what you want, asshole," she says.

"He wants what he can't have. He wants to win," I say. "Just like Mason. Mason was always jealous of the bakery. And now Mr. Drummond is ruining my life because why? Just because he can? So done with jerky guys!"

"You'll get through this, and you'll find a non-jerky guy. Not that you even need one."

I sigh. I liked when Mr. Drummond was jerky during phone sex, but I didn't want him to be an actual jerk. Is it so impossible to have one without the other?

"Here's what's amazing to me," she says. "They always show loan sharks on TV having an unnatural ability to count money just from flipping through the corner of the stack. And it turns out that that's a real thing? Did you notice that?"

"I know, right?" I say, glad she noticed it, too.

"Do they make them practice? Is it part of an initiation? Do they have to demonstrate that they have skills in accurately counting a stack of bills just by flipping through the corner and shooting somebody in the face?"

"And what if a guy has really good skills in shooting somebody in the face, but he can't count the money like that? Is he disqualified?"

"So weird," she says.

"I'm glad I at least got to wear it."

"It looked beautiful on you."

TWENTY-FOUR

Theo

I GIVE HER FORTY-FIVE MINUTES. In that time, I drink two scotches and go through the bread basket. I'm about to close out the tab when I see the email come through. A return processed. Iggy Miyaki on West 31st.

Returned the damn dress.

It was the most personal, most non-oblivious gift I could come up with. It took two personal shoppers working round the clock to find it. I thought she'd love it.

Hoped she'd love it.

Apparently not.

If she's trying to drive me insane, she's succeeding.

I throw down my napkin, pay the bill, and get out of there.

We had a connection. I wasn't imagining it. Something happened.

I direct Derek back to her place, back to the spot we parked at last time. "We're going to sit on it for a while," I say.

He nods.

What I really want to do is storm up there, but I can't be reckless. There's something I'm not understanding.

I sit back and watch her window. Lights on. What does it mean?

Insufficient data.

According to my PI, Elizabeth Cooper, aka Lizzie, moved from Fargo to New York City right after high school. She attended an elite baking school on a scholarship and went on to land an apprenticeship with one of the top people at a Michelin-rated restaurant. She started a little pop-up bakery after that, then got a permanent storefront just before she turned twenty-five. Cookie Madness.

The place became quite successful. She got a few write-ups praising her offbeat cookies. An article from the *Times* food section has an image of her grinning, holding a huge tray of brightly frosted cookies up to the camera. Young hipsters in baker's hats—her employees, presumably—are gathered around her. But the strange thing is that none of them are looking at the camera, they're looking at her—beaming at her—with undisguised affection.

Another article has a photo of her next to a blond man with movie-star looks and a smile for the camera that I don't like. Or maybe it's the way he drapes his arm around her shoulders. Or maybe I just don't like him. The article identifies him as Mason West, who, according to Lizzie's interview, "pitches in with business expertise."

Some business expertise—the bakery imploded around two months ago, and Mr. West bought a one-way ticket to St. Thomas the same time.

Did Mason West have something to do with the collapse? Or was he a fair-weather boyfriend who left as soon as the gravy train ended?

And why did things go bad? My PI is still digging. He said it looked fast and furious. Gambling debt, bad investment, relative in trouble, or embezzlement—those were his guesses.

It can't be too dire, though—her blog is full of glowing plans and ideas. Vossameer was clearly just temporary for her. She quit with no notice. She would've gotten a great bonus if she'd stayed. What happened?

A face at the window.

Her.

Does she see me down here? No chance; even if I weren't in the back of a town car with shaded windows, I'm a full block down. She seems to be looking at something directly across the street.

Discreetly I get out and take a look. Right away I see it—two guys leaning on a car directly across from her. Staring up at her window. Just standing there, eyes on her windows, no phones.

She grabs the curtains and yanks them shut. Angry? More like scared.

"Wait here for me," I say to Derek.

"Sir," he says.

I button up my coat against the cool March air and head for the guys.

They're still standing out there, still looking up at her window.

I'm taken back to a time I'd prefer to forget. My dad had gotten into another jam, but this one was bad. Guys just like this outside our house. Watching. Dad acting nonchalant. *They just wanna know they'll get their money,* he said.

But he wasn't the one who had to deal with them—he was blacked out by the time they came to the door, so it was Mom and me. She'd wanted me to go to my room, but I was in my early teens, too big for her to boss. With trembling hands, she gave them the secret money from the soup can, with promises to bring more later on.

Is Lizzie in money trouble? It would make sense, considering her credit report. And if so, why blow off the bonus?

They become aware of me half a block down. Or at least that's when they show me they see me.

I smile as I approach them. "Evening," I say.

They're both looking at me hard.

I show them my hands. I come in peace. "You have business with Ms. Cooper?" I ask.

"You a cop?"

"Just a friend of hers," I say.

"And we care why?" the one guy asks.

"I might be in the mood to clear it up, maybe save everyone a little trouble, if I can get a sense of what it is."

"Maybe you're just nosy," the one says.

"Maybe. Or maybe I handle this and you guys get to go out for wings and beer instead of sitting here."

The guys exchange glances.

"It's a money thing, right?"

No answer.

Yes, I'm thinking. "Is there somebody I can see about it?"

The somebody turns out to be a middle-aged loan shark named Lenny. The cost is eight thousand dollars, due on Sunday morning. I tell him he'll have it tomorrow afternoon if he pulls his guys. He agrees, and I arrange for my PI to deliver it.

"She a relative of yours?" Lenny asks.

"Employee," I tell him.

He gives me a rumble of understanding. Insinuating I want to fuck her. I suppose he's right, but it's not how he thinks.

I want to fuck her, sure. But really, I want to do anything with her. I want to know her. I want to talk to her, laugh with her, watch idiotic goat videos with her. I want to know her on every level possible.

He tells me he'll pull his guys back for the time being. There, but not visible, as a courtesy. They'll be back if my PI doesn't show.

I knock on the table and leave.

TWENTY-FIVE

Lizzie

WHAT DOES it mean that they're gone? I almost liked it better when I could see them. Are they watching secretly? Are there mob guys everywhere now? I have at least thirty-six hours, but I don't trust them not to come early.

Just to be safe, I've installed the bolt lock. I've texted Mia to let her know her key won't work. We had a texting argument that ended with me saying I'd be sleeping with earplugs in and wouldn't hear her pounding on the door.

At least she'll be out of danger.

I don't know what to do when they come. I could run out the fire escape, but they'll just come back. And what if it's when Mia is here? No, I have to face them.

So I've been cleaning.

It's probably silly to clean for gangsters, but I have this idea that if my place is messy, they might feel more at liberty to hurt me. The way people are more likely to throw litter on a trash-filled street.

I have on a red Henley shirt and a sporty little plaid skirt that's good for summertime walking and that, for whatever reason, struck me as the garment least likely to inspire gangsters to carve up my arm. Which is, admittedly, not a high bar for a skirt.

Just as I begin straightening our books and pulling out the ones I want to take to Fargo, there's a knock at the door.

It's not exactly loud, but it feels like a crash of thunder inside.

They're here.

I thought I was ready, but my heart's bongo-ing, and I'm not feeling brave anymore. I tell myself it's probably just a final warning or something, but I'm not sure that I have it in me to open that door.

I creep over, careful to avoid the creaking floorboards, and peer through the peephole.

A man's profile. Strong nose, perfectly straight. Whisker stubble leading up to an imperious cheekbone. Pillowy, slightly thuggish lips.

Mr. Drummond!

My mind whirls.

Mr. Drummond? *Here?*

My heart bongos a new tune. It's an angrier and more excited tune than the *Mobsters are coming!* tune.

"Yeah, you can just fuck off," I call through the door.

Slap. Palm meets door. Eye meets peephole. "Open up. Come on." Still so arrogant. "We need to talk."

"You need to stop sniffing chemical fumes if you think I'm ever going to talk to you."

He slaps the door again, more softly this time. "Open up. Please."

"Why?"

"Because we can't have this conversation like this."

"We already had it. That was our entire conversation."

"Just open it," he says.

"You think you're still the boss of me? I cannot even..."

"Seven..."

"Oh my god! You don't get to call me that. Seven is dead." Angrily, I jerk back the bolt. "You killed her!" I fling open the door.

And come face-to-face with Mr. Drummond, larger than life in a dove-gray suit and bright yellow tie.

My heart stutters.

It's weirdly wonderful to see him.

I grip the knob, reminding myself how mad I am at him, how he told Sasha about us, how scared I am of the loan shark guys.

"News flash," I bite out, "you don't get to order me around ever again. And if you think we're going to fuck right now—or ever—after you told Sasha every intimate detail of our phone calls. After you told her to fire me? Being that you didn't even have the courage to do it yourself? Soooooo not gonna happen."

He narrows his eyes. "You think I told Sasha about what we said...and then told her to fire you..."

"Unless Sasha's psychic. Because she seemed to know a whole lot of *details*."

He swears softly under his breath and waves his hand, indicating he wants to come in, and suddenly I'm backing up, and he's crossing the threshold, closing the door, leaning back against it, gazing down at me with those stormy gray eyes.

Everything in me comes alive. It's wrong, wrong, wrong. I cross my arms over my chest. "You think you're staying now?"

He takes a deep breath. "I thought it was her."

"What?"

"I thought Sasha was *you*—the caller."

I frown. *Sasha?*

"The Hello Morning emails were coming from inside Vossameer," he says. "I confronted her, and she more or less confessed that she was Operator Seven. And...she inferred a lot from our conversation."

"Wait." I widen my eyes. "Sasha pretended to be me? To your face?"

He gives me a grim look that makes me glad I'm not Sasha. "I wouldn't have told anybody about our calls. And please believe that I did *not* tell her to fire you. It's the last thing I'd want."

"Oh." My pulse races.

"That's not the kind of man I am," he adds. "I didn't even know it was you until this morning."

Sasha impersonated me?

I think back on our firing conversation, going over the whole strange exchange. "When Sasha fired me, she pumped me for all sorts of information."

"I figured. She seemed to know a lot. *Jackalope*, for instance."

I bite back a smile. "You thought Sasha was Operator Seven."

"Not for long." He looks down at me, leaning back on the front door, large and glorious in our humble apartment. He lowers his voice. "She could never be you."

Heat licks over my skin. "Oh," I whisper.

"Nobody could be you."

Nobody could be you. Did he kiss her? Of all my problems, like a crazy woman, I focus on that.

"I invited her to dinner," he says. "I was already suspicious, but when she told me she didn't care for dessert, I knew for sure. And then I discovered her favorite musical is *Grease*."

"I would've expected *101 Dalmatians*."

He looks confused. Even confused, he's gorgeous, maybe more gorgeous, because his guard is down.

I say, "You should've known the minute she said yes to dinner."

"I should've known before that—way before that," he says. "They told me you quit. That you stormed out, saying how much Vossameer sucks."

"Well, I *did* say that. But I sure didn't quit."

"Because you needed the bonus. For Lenny."

Something in me turns upside down. "How do you know about that?"

"I had a conversation with those guys out there. They're gone, by the way. The debt is settled."

"Wait—what? They're not coming back?"

"No. The debt is handled."

"Did you...handle it?"

His voice gentles. "Seems I owed you money. You'll get the rest, too."

"Thank you," I say. "Really. Thank you. And, um, the dress—"

"Forget the dress," he rumbles. "I don't care about the dress."

Butterflies flutter madly in my belly. "Oh...okay."

His gaze is fixed on me, not in an aggressive way, but more like he's assessing. "That's not what I care about, Seven. That's not why I'm here."

Lust and nervousness swirl inside me. Of course I'm thinking about the whole savage-clothes-ripping thing. Is that why he's here? That's who I am on the phone—it's who we are on the phone. It's blisteringly hot on the phone, but I never did anything like that in real life.

But that's what's between us now. It's huge between us now. A wild river.

"What do you care about?" I manage to ask, even as I remind myself that I shouldn't go down this path. That I'm still reeling from Mason. That I'm leaving town and can't get emotionally invested.

He searches my eyes, like he's really concentrating on me. He says, "I care about the way I felt when I was talking to you. I liked the way we felt together."

"I liked it, too," I confess. Because apparently I'm all about confessing things to Mr. Drummond.

He comes nearer. His Adam's apple bobs in his throat, inches from my lips now. The air between us feels charged with electricity; a frisson of aliveness plays across my skin. "It's not how I usually am."

"You're not usually like that? Savagely ripping women's clothes off?" It's a joke, but not.

He reaches out and touches my shoulder, slides two fingers down the waffle-weave fabric covering my arm. Just that tiny touch and I'm breathless. Dizzy. The floor seems to dip.

"Not usually. But everything's different with you," he says. His breath comes hard—I can tell by the rise and fall of his chest. By the way his yellow tie moves in the light. "Everything with you was real and true in a way I never had. New."

"Me, too," I say. "With you." The truth. And just like that, things feel intimate again, like our calls.

His finger is still on my arm, nearing my elbow, but something's happening. The few atoms of oxygen left between us have changed. I feel him on my belly. I feel him on my thighs. I feel him in the stretch of my Henley shirt over my wildly sensitized nipples.

"I would've moved heaven and Earth to find you."

"I can't believe that Sasha tried to..." My words fade out and he lifts his fingers from my elbow and touches the nook of my throat. He slides those fingers slowly, slowly, down until they hook over the top of the unbuttoned V of my shirt.

He lets them hang there. The backs of them graze my breastbone as I breathe. The brush of his skin on mine burns—just that tiny point of contact.

His cuff link catches the light, seeming to pulse slightly, maybe in time with my breathing. Maybe in time with his. Maybe we're breathing together.

He says, "Everything with you feels like a new discovery. Not of lands or continents, but something more. What it's like to connect. What it's like to want somebody so bad..."

"So bad that you rip off her clothes," I say. "Because you need her pussy so bad..."

"So bad," he rasps.

We both seem to still. To wait. Horns honk and helicopter blades chop in the world outside, but the small apartment feels pin-drop silent.

And I'm squeezing my pelvic muscles so hard, I might make myself Kegel-come.

"You rip off her clothes," I say.

"Yeah?" he says, voice rough as sand.

"So desperate. And you haul her over your shoulder and carry her to her bedroom. And you throw her down there. You don't even care, you just throw her down." I lower my voice, "like a brute."

His gaze roams heavy and hot over my lips, my neck.

I glance over at my bedroom door; then I look back at him.

It's here I realize I'm trembling. Good trembling. Alive trembling. Like really crazy-alive trembling. That's what we have together—scary honesty and aliveness.

"You totally ravish her," I add.

His fingers curl more tightly over the V of my shirt. Just that little movement sizzles. What would it be like to really touch?

He's wondering it, too. I feel him in a way I don't feel other people.

"God, Drummond," I pant, "you need to rip off my clothes and fuck me already."

Something changes in his eyes. He doesn't do it right away, though, power-mad jerk that he is. He uses his grip on my shirt to pull me to him, slow and strong, eyes on mine until we're too close to see each other anymore, and then it's just his lips consuming mine in a slow, hungry kiss—lips to lips, tongue to tongue.

I clutch his arms through his suit coat, shocked by the ferocity of his kiss and my breathless response.

He spins us around and presses me to the door, cupping my face, kissing me senseless. One steely thigh presses brazenly between my legs.

"Oh my god, I love this already," I gasp into his mouth.

My hands find their way under his jacket, fumbling to get his shirt free of his belt, desperately seeking skin.

He lets off long enough to shrug off his suit jacket. It disappears and he's on me again. I press my fingers into his warm, muscular back.

He nips my lip, then kisses me some more, like he can never get enough. He kisses my cheek, my nose, my other cheek, my forehead, and then he's back on me, pressing into me deliciously.

I whimper a little, moving with him—much as I can, considering most of me is flattened by his big, hard body and wonderfully cucumbery cock.

He slides his hands under my skirt, palms my ass, and hauls me up.

I swing my legs around him, wrap my arms around his neck. I'm a lust-crazed barnacle, totally glomming onto this guy. "Yes," I whisper.

He whomps me against the door and we make out, all dirty and sweet. He holds me tightly, giant hands on my ass, fitting us like two pieces of the most urgent puzzle in the world.

His fingertips curl into my butt crack through my panties as he squeezes my ass cheeks, pressing and squeezing, which does something insane to my clit. "Fuck, you're wet," he grates.

"I'm gonna come right now," I gasp.

"Not yet." The room spins, and suddenly we're moving.

He carries me around our little couch and on into the dim hush of my bedroom. He bangs the door shut behind us and continues on, throwing me down on the bed.

I pant like a trapped animal, excited, aroused beyond capacity.

His chest heaves under his white shirt, tie half loosened. The darkness in his eyes hits me like a drug. Without warning he's on me. Rough fists grab the top of my shirt. He rips it down the middle.

I gasp. Cool air hits my belly.

He just keeps going, brutally ripping my shirt. His tie trails over my skin, a wicked feather to contrast with his violent movements. It's the hottest thing ever.

He yanks down my bra cups and presses his warm, whiskery face to my bared chest.

I groan as he devours my breasts, all rough whiskers and urgent sucking. I grab on to his arms, hard like rock. I'm burning up.

Mindlessly he sucks. My swollen sex aches with need.

He pauses only long enough to yank off my skirt and obliterate what's left of my poor panties. With clumsy movements, I take off my bra and toss it out of ripping range. Because, bra shopping.

"I like you like this, perfectly naked to me," he growls. He kisses my bare belly, hands roaming everywhere. "Every inch of you is hot."

Without warning, he slides his finger through my wetness.

I gasp and arch under his touch.

"Look at you, so naked and wet. Waiting for me." He does me with his finger, eyes fixed on mine. "Waiting for me to take you."

"More," I rasp.

Instead he takes his finger from me and slides it lewdly into his mouth and sucks.

He sucks off every last bit of juice like it's the last sustenance left on the planet, because that's men for you.

Slowly he draws his finger back out, gazing down at me. "Mine."

Warmth spreads through me like honey. Amazing Mr. Drummond.

His eyes drop to my lips, and suddenly the pad of his finger is there, a whisper of a touch on my bottom lip, the weight of a butterfly.

I close my lips over the tip of his finger and suck. Like it was always meant to be, like me sucking on his fingertip was predestined. Unavoidable as air.

Lewdly, he pushes his finger deeper into my mouth. Just invades it. "Suck it," he commands in his stern Mr. Drummond tone. "Show me how you're going to suck my cock."

I give him a look that says, you are SUCH an asshole! Being that his finger's in my mouth, the look's mostly in my eyes and a little bit in my cheeks.

"I know," he says softly. "But I'll make it so good."

His other hand is on my knee. He's pressing it wide. He takes back his finger so he can grip my other knee, spreading me open.

The cool air hits my clit. Time seems suspended as he kisses down my chest, down my belly. Lips hot and dangerous. A shuddery breath comes out from somewhere deep inside me as he reaches my pussy.

I'm so exposed to him. More exposed to him than I've ever been to any man.

He pauses there between my legs, and then I feel it—his tongue like a wet, hot finger on my seam. He licks me lazily but firmly. He sends tremors of heat all through me.

My eyelids flutter shut as the room lurches sideways.

He licks me again. My sex heats and swells. I grab onto his hair. His fingertips dig into the flesh of my thighs, pulsing slightly as he licks. His fingers will leave marks. I want them to.

His tongue invades my folds. Every lick sends heat shivering over my damp skin. "Holy shit," I breathe.

Suddenly he sucks something down there, a sharp surprise. I gasp. Then he licks me some more, and then I think I feel his bad-boy lip scar and my mind explodes.

"Do anything," I say. "Or everything." I barely make sense anymore. And why try?

He continues to consume me, holding me the way he wants me. I pulse my hips against his greedy mouth, undulating into him.

He groans, a hot rumble against me.

"I can't...not..."

"Do it, then; do it," he grates into my folds, licking me, driving me higher. He's a predator, hunting down my orgasm and pulling it out of me. "Come, Seven."

I have no choice—he shoves his fingers into me, licks me again, and I cry out. I'm spinning, breaking into blobs of white heat.

He licks me into oblivion.

I clench his hair. "Softer," I rasp.

He lightens up. Then he just rumbles into my pussy, words or maybe moans.

He kisses my trembling thighs—slow and scalding. Then he kisses my still-sensitive post-orgasm pussy, like a sweet electric shock.

I hiss and nearly pull his hair out.

"God," he whispers into my still-quivering sex. "God." Like he's going crazy. Maybe he is. "You are the most beautiful woman in the world."

I want to make some joke about how he is literally staring at my pussy while he says that, but it comes out as "Uhhh."

He sits up after a while, heavy hand on my calf, sliding it around, watching me. "Is this where you call me? From this bed?"

"Yeah."

He looks around, taking it all in, then turns back to me. "Lying right there?"

I nod, still breathless.

"Touch yourself," he says hoarsely. "Like you do on the calls."

"Drummond..."

"Go ahead," he grates.

"It's kind of soon."

"Do it anyway."

Tyrannical Mr. Drummond.

I slide my hand down my belly, shaking a little. I'm following his command, but I feel strangely powerful. "Is that part of the fantasy?"

"Are you kidding?" he says. "I only wake up in the middle of the night imagining it. Or in the middle of reviewing data. Working on the new formula." He says it all like he's annoyed. Like I've been driving him insane.

It seems evil to love that, but I do love it. I slide my hand between my legs, letting him watch me. It's like a dream.

"Do you imagine it?" he asks. "Me here?"

"Yeah."

"What do I do?"

"You burst in and discover me, and you're so stern and angry."

He gets off the bed and walks around to stand at the side, still fully clothed. He looms over me, darkness in his eyes. He pulls off his tie and drops it. "Wider." His voice is ragged.

"So presumptuous," I say, letting my knees fall loose.

He fumbles open his cuff links. He strips off his shirt revealing a broad, muscled chest. He undoes his belt and yanks it free. There's a dull clink as it hits the floor. "What else?"

I slide my finger lightly around my folds, enjoying the way he watches me, so dark and hot. "You're so feverish to get to my pussy that you're savage—worshipful, but feral. And sometimes you bite me a little bit. And you sometimes wear your lab coat."

"My lab coat." His pants come off. His giant cock springs up, thick and blunt. "That's what I wear?"

"W-what?"

"Focus. You like to imagine me wearing my lab coat?"

"Sometimes," I say, mesmerized by the taut beauty of his cock. He wraps his hand partly around it, cradling it. It's hot, watching him touch himself so casually.

"And?"

A bolt of heat shoots through me when he starts rolling a condom onto himself. "And I drive you so crazy, you can't *even.*"

"You think it's funny to drive me crazy?" he rumbles in the stern voice I love.

I slide my hand up my belly, unable to look away from his cock. "No, I don't think it's funny at all," I say. "I think it's fucking hilarious."

He grumbles angrily. The bed dips as he crawls over me.

I press my hand to his chest—not to stop him, but just to feel him, to feel his heart, to get all of him I can.

He takes the hand I'm touching him with and presses it over my head along with my other hand. He holds them together and watches my eyes. "You think it's hilarious? To torment me?"

Everything in me sparkles. We've built a sexy secret that nobody knows about. Like a secret sandcastle. "Very," I breathe.

He growls like he really is being driven insane by me, still holding my hands above my head. He fits my fingers to the middle plank of my headboard. I grip it obediently.

I'm stretched out for him, naked for him, more excited than I ever have been in all my life. Was this how sex was supposed to feel all this time? And we're not even having actual sex yet!

"I should take you over my knee," he says, palming my breasts, brushing his thumbs over my nipples, sending dark spikes of pleasure into the needy ache between my legs.

"Well," I breathe. "Uhh..." I like that idea, too, but I don't want him to stop doing what he's doing.

He grunts something else, panting, settling between my legs. I grip the headboard harder. I can feel him there, nudging my opening with the thick crown of his cock.

"God, yes," I say, aching for him to be in me.

And then he is, gazing into my eyes as he pushes into me, slow and deep as the ocean.

TWENTY-SIX

Theo

I SPENT endless hours picturing what she'd be like. Waking up with erotic images cascading through my brain.

My fantasy Operator Seven doesn't even come close to the reality of Lizzie. She's delicious and maddening and stunning in every way.

And so hot I want to die. Her skin is damp, burning under my touch.

I'm large for her, so I'm moving slowly, rocking into her, letting her get used to my size. It's all I can do not to devour her.

I change the angle of entry, watching and listening, until I have her panting harder. I like that she's feeling as unhinged as I am.

I slide all the way in and come to a stop. For one moment there's nothing else in the world, just her pussy clenching me, hot and tight. "Seven," I whisper. "Seven, Seven, Seven."

She pulls me to her by the hair and takes my mouth. "Yes," she says between kisses.

I move into her, caging her with my arms, listening to her breath, enjoying the way her fists tighten and loosen in my hair. Remembering something she said, I press my teeth to the little mound of flesh between her breast and her shoulder, taking a small chunk of skin between my teeth. A little point of pain.

"Aagh," she gasps. "You remembered."

I remember everything she ever said. Her words are on constant repeat in my brain. The only soundtrack I care about these days.

She groans. "Yes. More. Yesssss."

Her breath becomes erratic. It's delicious. I pull her around on top of me and lose myself in her all over again.

Women are all composed of the same basic material— oxygen, carbon, hydrogen, nitrogen, calcium, and phosphorus. Yet this woman is another breed. Another universe.

It's just by the sheer backward recitations of the periodic table that I'm not losing it like a schoolboy. But I'm not making it longer just for myself. I love concentrating on her pleasure. I could do it forever.

I change my tack again—the way I'm fucking her now is all about me rubbing her clit with my cock. I'm kissing her, pushing her over the edge. She wants the teeth back.

She gets the teeth. She gets what she wants. Whatever she wants.

"Yes," she sighs every so often, so softly you can barely understand it.

It makes my cock feel like granite, that soft sigh of hers. Usually stoking a woman's pleasure is transactional, the price of admission.

Not this woman.

I could happily stay where we are, enjoying her pleasure, knowing I'm making her sigh like that.

She holds onto me, even as she rides me. "So good," she says.

"I know, baby."

I'm fucking her, turning her into tinder, flammable to my touch.

I fuck her and ravish her until her breathing tells me that she's at the edge. Until the way she says "yesss" sounds new. I hear everything in her voice—that voice that's echoed through my dreams. I've learned her to the minutest fraction of pleasure.

A gust of pleasure—she's coming. Crying out.

I'm panting, thrusting into her, feeling her, loving the way her sass falls away and she's just mine. There's no turning back —not for me, either.

My orgasm rips through me. Harder than any I've ever experienced. I come with a cry, nose pressed to her damp skin, insane with the pleasure of her.

I don't know how long we stay joined, coming down together. Time seems useless. I never want to let her go.

In chemistry, just the smallest adjustment—the addition of one atom—can be the difference between inertness and an explosion. We have that something. We really are combustible. Sexually, and in every other way, too. I'm so used to everyone hanging on my every word. Scurrying at my every command. Lizzie stands up. Talks back. Meets me in a way nobody ever has.

She was right there under my nose all that time.

I brush back the damp hair from her forehead, thinking back to that day in my office when I first felt the sizzle of her. Heard her say *Mr. Amazing is being amazing elsewhere,* like the utterly impudent woman she is.

And later on, like a fool, I let myself believe I misheard. I let her hide and be hidden.

I let myself not know what I knew about her.

I lower myself down next to her. "How did I not see you?" I whisper.

She smiles over at me. "Umm...it starts with an 'O'..."

"I mean it," I say. "I didn't see you."

"I didn't want you to."

"Why not?"

She twists the covers around her. "Okay, more like, I didn't want Sasha to see you see me. I was trying to keep my head down. Do the work, earn the bonus. Pass GO and all that."

"I'm going to take care of Sasha."

She slides a finger over my lip. "I can't believe I'm about to say this, but Sasha works her ass off for you. She's like a million percent Team Vossameer. I don't know if you should let her go. Why don't you try praising her once in a while? That would make her feel more secure and less psycho."

"I pay her a lot of money."

"That's not praise."

"I praise her."

"You grunt approvingly."

I grab her finger and kiss the tip of it. "She impersonated you."

"Well, yeah," she says.

My gut twists when I think how mistreated Lizzie was, in my name. "When she was first claiming to be you, but not being like you, I wanted to shake her. I wanted to say, 'It's me!' Because everything felt off. But a scientist doesn't ignore evidence just because he doesn't like the result."

"I can't believe she doesn't like dessert."

I twist a lock of her hair around a finger. In the low light, her hair look more brown. I slide my fingers through it, enjoying the softness. Usually at this point in a hookup, I'm working on my exit strategy. But lying here, I'm working on a stick-around strategy. "Those dresses you were wearing."

"Fake." She grins. "You are too easy."

Just then her phone rings.

"I thought you destroyed your phone. The last time I called," I say.

"Yeah, and it was awesome. Except I had to get a new one." She rolls over and takes a look at it. "I have to grab this."

She sits up, back against the headboard. "Hey," she says. Her mussed-up hair grazes the tops of her pretty breasts. There's a twinkle in her green eyes when she catches me staring.

"It's all good," she says to the unknown caller. "Lenny is handled, and his dogs are off. Yeah, I swear it!"

She smiles and sets a foot on my chest in the silence that follows. I grab it and kiss her toe.

She snorts at something the caller says. "No, Mr. Drummond gave me my bonus after all...I know, right? Oh yeah, and it was..." She gets this mischievous look, and I know she's going to be sassy again. My cock rises to attention. "The bonus was...adequate."

I go to the base of the bed, grab her ankles, and pull her down.

She giggles. "Yes, I have company. You've never met him. But you can come back," she says to whoever's on the other end. A roommate, maybe. Women like Lizzie have roommates.

I take this opportunity to glance around her room. White walls with cracking paint. Tall ceilings with the historic crown molding she once described. Bright scarves are draped over fixtures. Colorful prints adorn the walls—turtles and elves and a girl whose face is half wolf. An old tin sign that says Cooper's Pizzeria. A framed album cover—some boy band, from the looks of it. A National Parks calendar.

"Well, the bolt is off, anyway," she says.

It's late. Is this somebody coming home?

I crawl over her and lean down, whisper in her other ear, "Lose the caller."

She grins up at me. "Nothing," she says. "That was nothing."

I smile. Meet her defiant eyes.

She kills me.

I kiss her. I slide my palm up her stomach. She's not a washboard-abs girl; she's real. She eats cookies. Like a madman, I press my face into the sexy swell of her belly. I drag my lips up over it, squeezing her hips. She's delicious.

Even her imperfections are delicious. Actually, her imperfections make her more delicious.

Still gripping her hips, I slide my face up her chest, aware that I'm giving her a little bit of sandpaper with the whiskers. From the way she wriggles, I can tell she likes it.

I make whisker contact with the underside of her breast. Her skin is literally like silk. I slide my cheek along the curves, enjoying her, taking my lazy time to get to her nipple. I've never done this, just enjoyed a woman without any goal, except maybe her pleasure.

When I come up for air, she's watching me with unfocused eyes. "What?" she says to the caller. "Ahhhh, okay."

I'm up over her on my knees, enjoying her eyes on my cock. I give myself a few yanks, just because I can, cock swelling above her sprawled, naked body. I locate another condom in my pants pockets. I rip open the silver packet with my teeth.

"Gotta go," she gusts. "Okay, okay," she adds.

I pull out the condom and toss the wrapper onto her naked chest. Her eyes flare.

I bite back a smile and slide the sheath over myself, nice and slow, letting her watch me handle myself, because she seems to like that. I give myself a few yanks. Her chest rises and falls.

But enough about me. I lean down and palm her thighs, rough and casual, like I own them. Her eyes twinkle. "Okay, later..." she mumbles into the phone, doing something that hopefully gets rid of the caller.

I shove her legs apart with a growl.

The phone slips from her fingers and hits the floor just before I enter her. "OmigodfuckYES."

TWENTY-SEVEN

Theo

THE NEXT THING I KNOW, she's whispering into my ear. "Wake up, motherfucker."

I come to with a jolt, surprised to see that it's morning. It's light out.

Lizzie stands over me in jeans and a bright pink T-shirt that has a turtle outlined in sparkles. She's holding out a cup of coffee.

"What the hell?" I pick up my phone. It's after seven.

"It's a little thing called morning."

I sit up and take the coffee, stunned I slept through the night. I usually spend the first few minutes of my mornings adding clarification notes to my middle-of-the-night brainstorming scribbles, but there was no middle-of-the-night brainstorming. I look down at the steaming mug, feeling unmoored.

"Black. Right?" she says. "When you're not drinking bulletproof?"

"How'd you know I drank bulletproof?"

She rolls her eyes and shoves in beside me. Like it's too ridiculous to explain how she could've known.

She has shoes on. "Are you going somewhere?" I ask.

"Out," she says teasingly.

I pull her to me. "Come back to bed."

"What? I can't," she says. "This was great, but...it can't be. This can't be a thing."

My heart races. I'd imagined everything would change now. The idea that she might not want to see me again never crossed my mind.

"Come out to breakfast. You have to eat, right?"

She looks away. "I don't know about that."

"It's breakfast, not a date," I say.

"It just really can't happen."

I set my coffee on the nightstand; then I take her coffee and set it aside, and roll her back into bed, getting her beneath me.

"If you rip this shirt, I swear to god..."

I kiss her breast through the pink cotton.

"I'm serious. Dates are off the table with me. I can't do a relationship of any kind."

I kiss her shoulder. Her neck.

"I'm off guys," she says.

"You don't seem like you're off guys. In fact, you were quite recently on a guy, if memory serves." I kiss her again. "And around a guy."

"And I'm moving in three weeks."

I still. "Three weeks?"

"I'm moving back to Fargo."

You can't, I'm about to say. *I just found you. I won't let you.*

I bite my tongue. If there's one thing I know about Seven, it's that she doesn't like to be pushed.

But I can't let her leave. We have something special. "Why move?"

"To get back on my feet. Financially."

Finances.

Finances are nothing. Finances can be solved. I go back to kissing her. "It's just breakfast. And you know you can't resist me."

Her chest rises and falls as I strip off her shirt. "And I don't do relationships."

"Forget relationships. This is nothing but proximity to food supply," I say. "Satisfying my animal needs. Using you for your smoking-hot body. Do you have a problem with that?"

She still looks unsure. I have my hands all over her. I can't get enough of her. I can't think of anything but to find a way to keep this going.

"No commitment. No expectations," I add.

She hesitates.

I prefer to go into business deals not needing a yes. The fastest way to a yes is not needing it.

But for the first time in my life, I need a yes from a woman. Need it like air.

I tell myself it's because she's so elusive. Nothing like scarcity to make a person desperate. But that's a lie.

I need her. End of story.

"You're just my wake-up-call girl."

She puts a hand on my chest, holding me off. She looks serious.

"Everybody needs to eat." I slide a knuckle down her arm. I may not be able to talk her into what I want, but one touch and her skin comes alive; I can see it in her eyes. "Everybody needs to fuck. And you know I'm the best you've had."

"Jay-zuss," she says, but I know she thinks it, and she knows I think it, too. Something real happened last night.

"And you haven't gotten your spanking you so richly deserve."

Her eyes widen, just a fraction. Other people might not see it, but I do. The tides are turning my way. I kiss her neck in the spot she most likes. "Fuck buddies only. Three-week fuck buddies. Nothing to lose with a hard stop like that."

"I don't know, Drummond," she whispers. Which tells me she's thinking about it.

I slide my hand between her legs and watch her eyes go fuzzy. "Theo," I say. "Say it." I press on the spot she loves, stoking her pleasure.

"You're playing dirty."

"I know."

She grabs my wrist. "Three-week fuck buddies," she says. "And you won't try to control me or get involved in my business in any way. You don't meddle in my life. And no more home visits like this."

I kiss my favorite freckle—the dark one at the very edge of her cheekbone. Who tried to control her? Who meddled in her business affairs? Was it that Mason West guy? Is he the one who ruined her? Has anybody made him sorry?

"I'll stay away from your business." I kiss her other cheekbone, for purposes of symmetry. Then I kiss her rosy lips.

I put my hands back on her. Maybe it's not fair that I'm seducing her while we make this deal, but I'll use every advantage I have.

"Just sex," she says.

"Pure animal need," I say, ignoring the little voice in the back of my head that points out what an utter lie that is.

The little voice whispering that this doesn't qualify as animal need.

An animal in need of food will eat anything. An animal lost

in the desert will drink almost any liquid. An animal in heat will fuck anything.

My animal need is for her and her alone.

I have to find a way to make her stay. That's what I decide as I bury myself in the most perfect pussy on the planet.

TWENTY-EIGHT

Lizzie

MR. DRUMMOND—THEO—MAKES a phone call, and a few minutes later, a town car is waiting outside my building. He directs his driver, Derek, to a place called Reena's, which turns out to be one of those secret East Side restaurant gems that only beautiful, wealthy people seem to know about. It's airy and bright and everything is local and organic. We sit in a corner booth and order coffees and eggy things.

"This place opens at five in the morning," I say. "Is this where you go? After you get your obnoxiously early wake-up call?"

"No, I work out."

"At 4:30? Like it can't wait until a human hour?"

"Nope," he says, eyes sparkling.

I'm starting to get that he's even more of a hard-ass toward himself than he is toward his employees. More extreme, more demanding.

A waiter brings the coffees and a little sugar dish of something brown. "What is this?" I ask. The waiter gives me a long explanation that basically means *not sugar*. "Do you have sugar?"

"I'm sorry, no," he says.

I thank him and eye the little dish of sugar's un-fun cousin. "You go to a place that doesn't serve sugar."

"Sugar's bad for you," Theo says.

"Sugar is part of the circle of life."

He looks at me like, *does not compute*.

I settle for coffee with cream. The cream is actually really rich and delicious and probably farm fresh. It almost makes up for the lack of sugar. *Almost*.

"So, *then* you come here? After your workout?"

"No. This is special for you. But don't worry, it's not a relationship."

I sip my coffee really wanting sugar. I'm thinking about this little basement grocer we passed on our way in here. Two doors up the street. They would have sugar.

"I want you to know, you really can have your job back," he says. "Or if you don't want to work at Vossameer, I could help you get a job elsewhere. I have connections..."

"That's okay. I'm going to find some catering work while I get ready to move. I have a lot of catering friends. To be honest, I was going to quit after my bonus came through."

"You were using us for the bonus?"

"I earned it," I say. "My engagement numbers blew away your targets. I set you guys up with a great program. Of course it was an impressive bonus." I sit back with my coffee. "Far more than I expected."

"I like my employees satisfied."

"I like a boss who delivers," I say, finding his foot under the table. And suddenly I want to fuck again.

"The Instagram strategy. All those reports. Tell me." He looks serious. "It was yours, wasn't it? Everything that Sasha took credit for?"

"Not all of it. She did all those whitepapers. Like a demon."

He looks away, angry. I wouldn't want to be Sasha.

"Dude, people take credit for underlings' work at Vossameer all the time. It's a grim and competitive atmosphere. It's not good."

"The people who are attracted to Vossameer *are* competitive. They're the best of the best."

"I have a perspective from the bottom rung. I'm telling you. People are uptight and unhappy. They admire you in a kind of frightened way, and it keeps them from being relaxed and creative."

He seems surprised. "You think they're unhappy?"

Has nobody ever told him anything like that? "I know they are. You ban decorations, and even microwave popcorn. People love microwave popcorn!"

"Microwave popcorn is a ridiculous food. It has zero nutritional value and barely even any taste. It's like eating smell. And it distracts everyone else."

"Yeah, well people love it. Why not let them have it?"

"I'm not running a circus."

"Isn't a scientist supposed to be open to new evidence?" I ask. "You need to do something to help people feel more loose and easy. I don't know, praise them more. Let them have treats. Find ways to encourage them to be creative. Show they're appreciated, make them feel more secure so they don't have to work so late. You could make it so much better to work there."

He seems to be thinking about it.

"And while you're at it, get some color in there. Let people make it homey. Let them put pictures up." I stop. "I'm coloring outside the fuck buddy lines. I think it's the lack of sugar. It's amazing coffee, too, but so sad without sugar."

He's just watching me. I can't read his expression.

"But that microwave popcorn ban?" I continue, because apparently I can't help it. "No. If I were you, I'd supply them with awesome treats." I look down. "This coffee is a crime."

"We could go somewhere else."

"No, just..." I'm thinking about that corner store. It's like I can feel the sugar straining through the walls, trying to get at my coffee. "Excuse me for one second."

"Where are you going?"

"BRB." I go out onto the street and pop into the store. They only have sugar in two-pound bags. I buy it and bring it back and plop it down on the table.

"What the hell is that?" he growls.

"You know what it is." I rip open the corner, trying not to grin. I pour a long stream of it into my coffee as he watches sternly. I pour and pour, possibly a little more than usual. I stir. I taste. "Heaven."

He narrows his eyes.

"Want some?"

"Absolutely not."

"Is your body a temple?"

"I think I showed you the answer to that this morning," he rumbles.

I nearly snort out my coffee. I take a pen from my purse and I write my new phone number on the sugar. "You should bring this home with you. I think you need it."

"You're really moving to Fargo? Are you sure that's...what you want?"

"No, it's not what I want. Certain events caused my financial ruination, and it's hard to dig out of something like that in Manhattan. I'm only going for eighteen months. I'll help my parents with the pizzeria, and I'll do catering through one graduation season and two holiday seasons."

"So you have it all figured out."

"Yeah. I can work like a devil there, and I'll make bank with no overhead. I know exactly how much I can make. I'll restructure my debt and come back with seed money to open a bakery here. Like I had before, but better. It's not like anyone is going to rent a good space to me, what with my credit now."

"What if they do? What if the most amazing space falls into your lap?"

"That doesn't happen in New York. If it's cheap, there's something wrong with it." I stir my coffee, feeling sad. "It's just reality. I'll miss it here, though. I'll miss my friends."

"An ironic and dorky occasion cookie bakery," he says.

I smile. That's the description on my blog. Or maybe he saw my Instagram. "Somebody did their homework."

"I always do my homework," he says. "Did you ever think about looking for an investor?"

"No," I say. "I need it to be mine. It'll be all mine, and it'll be amazing."

He asks where I got the idea for my ironic cookies, and I tell him the whole long story, which involves a bet with a friend about the existence of Bathtub Party Day, and me rubbing it in through creative baking. Theo doesn't believe Bathtub Party Day is a real holiday, either, so I make him Google it. He finds it. Of course, he's disgusted. He's delightful when he's disgusted.

I tell him about Compliment Day and Donut Day and High Five Day. He thinks I'm making all of them up, and it's funny every time he discovers they're real, and we're laughing about it when a shadow appears over our table. "Excuse me. I'm sorry to interrupt."

It's a man with a pinkish complexion and a ball cap.

"I recognized you from the *Trib* article and I wanted to

thank you," he says to Theo. He tells us a story about his son falling off a ladder. Without Vossameer, his son would've died—apparently, the EMTs told him so.

Theo nods. He thanks the man politely, even tries to divert the conversation to the medical personnel's hard work, but the man is having none of it. He shows us three pictures of his kid playing in the park before he lets us get back to breakfast.

When the man is gone, Theo huffs out an exasperated breath. "Where were we?"

"Dude. Was that just an annoyance to you? Your product that *you* invented saved his boy. Doesn't that make you feel good?"

"It's a product."

"That saves lives."

"I think there were EMTs involved in saving his boy's life. Medical professionals who knew how to deploy it. I think that's what he needs to focus on."

"It doesn't make you feel good? Not at all?"

"I made millions selling blood coagulant. Does that make me feel good? Every time I look out my penthouse window at Central Park."

I watch his eyes, not buying it. And suddenly I'm thinking about his whole weird antihero thing. "I think you're full of shit right now."

"Oh, yeah?"

I shove at his leg with my foot. "I think you care."

Suddenly he has my foot. "You sure? Last I checked, I was the asshole of the century."

I shove at his thigh again. He starts working off my shoe.

"I'm going to need that shoe."

He has his dirty-sex look. "Not where I'm taking you."

"Fuck. *The fuck.* Off."

"You're a bad wake-up-call girl." He lowers his voice. "You've been nothing but trouble."

"If you think we're fucking in that bathroom, you are so wrong."

Theo lets go of my shoe when the waiter comes to pour more coffee while giving my giant bag of sugar the side-eye. Theo just gives me a sexy-eye. This guy. He melts me.

"Your family owns a pizzeria?" he asks when we're alone again. "That's where you'll work out of in Fargo?"

"It's not as glam as it sounds," I joke.

But there's this silence where that's not the issue. The issue is about ending whatever is between us that isn't supposed to be anything.

"You'll have to access an alternate food supply for your savagery," I say, trying to remind us what we are. Just two people who want no-strings sex. "To tear through and devour."

"Why not get loans or..."

"With my credit?"

"And you just rule out investors? Do you have any millionaire friends? Let me think..."

Himself, he means.

I give him a hard look. *Now entering full Mason flashback territory.*

"Sorry," he says. "No involvement in your business whatsoever."

I twirl my fork by one tine, like a music box ballerina, impressed at how well he can read my expressions.

Theo isn't oblivious at all. Or it's more like he's totally oblivious to everything on the planet except the things he's passionate about, and those things get the full force of his brilliance, the full spotlight of his passion.

And when that spotlight shines on you, it's beautiful. It's nearly blinding. Could it be dangerous?

"I want you to understand something. My ex, Mason, loved taking part in the business. He took over control little by little, and I let him. It's on me that I allowed it. I got lazy, I guess. Just wanted to believe a fairy tale. Anyway, he's the reason it crashed. He's down in the Caribbean or somewhere. With more money than I thought it was possible to squeeze out of me."

Theo's grim look is back. "The loan sharks were his doing."

"And I had no idea. I was so shocked when Lenny's guy showed up. Armed."

He grits his teeth, like he's angry on my behalf. "It wouldn't be that hard to hunt down your ex and try to get some of that back."

The dark pull of him feels so strong. Am I being a fool? "He probably hid it. Anyway, we don't know for sure that he's in the Caribbean."

"Yes, we do," he says.

"How?"

"Well...my PI tracked him as far as St. Thomas."

Alarm bells start going off. "Your PI? An investigator? You had me *investigated*?"

"I background everybody I deal with. And you were so elusive for so long..."

"So of course you had to dig into my background."

"It's not like that. Not in a sinister way."

He always does his homework. He always gets what he wants. Am I playing with fire? My Mason flashbacks are going full-tilt now.

I stand and grab my purse, feeling upset.

"It's just a routine thing. Nothing to be upset about."

"Routine to you, maybe, but think about it. You offered to invest in my company after I asked you not to get involved. And you had me investigated." I hug my purse, still wanting him so bad it hurts. "And here you are telling me I shouldn't be upset."

I wait. *Say something different,* I think. *Say something better.*

Finally, he says, "It's new for me not to be in the driver's seat. I'm not good at it." He looks back up, and I want to die in the beauty of his eyes.

My pulse races. "I *need* you to be good at it." I don't want to go, but it's time. I turn and leave.

TWENTY-NINE

Lizzie

I SPEND the morning networking until I find a caterer who needs a temporary baker. A friend of a friend. I go out to meet him at his place in Little Italy. His kitchen is cramped, but usable.

I get out of there feeling like I'm starting at the foot of the mountain, rolling the boulder upward, doing the kinds of jobs I did out of culinary school. I'm a better, faster baker, and a better businessperson than I was all those years ago, but in some ways, it's all actually worse, because I see the steps. I know what a long road it is.

Especially with an eighteen-month detour to Fargo.

I try not to think about all the things I'll miss—Mia, of course. Our quiet block with the quirky little grocer on the corner. The gang from La Dolce Vina where we all used to work. Pizza from Carpone's on 22nd. The street life. Biking the Central Park loop, the magic of the first snowfall in the city.

And somehow, Theo has crept onto that list.

Over the course of all those supposedly anonymous phone calls, we achieved a rare intimacy. If I had a Mount Rushmore for my life right now, he'd be one of the big faces.

But we can't be anything. We shouldn't even be fuck buddies.

Except I can't stop thinking about the way he swept into our little apartment. The way my whole body hummed when he finally touched me, one finger on my arm. The heat of us. How we tell each other brave, real things, or at least I do, but I think he does, too. His lab coats. His mysterious hatred of being a hero. The spanking I haven't gotten yet.

So the next morning when I'm lying in bed awake at the stupid hour of 4:29, I grab my phone and the little card with his handwriting, and I dial his number.

It's just a phone call, right?

"Wake up, motherfucker," I say when he answers.

"What was that?" he grumbles sternly.

"I'm sorry for the abrupt way I left breakfast," I say.

"Fuck buddies don't need apologies, haven't you heard?"

"I feel like this one does."

"I got into your business," he says. "You hate that."

"I do," I say. "Were you awake already?"

"Yeah," he says.

"Were you waiting for my call?"

"Yup."

"So what happens now? Do you have a home gym for your insanely punishing workout?"

"First I'm planning on taking a walk and watching the birds fall from the trees, stunned by my glory. And then the workout. What makes you think it's insanely punishing?"

"You're a bulletproof coffee-drinking workaholic with an unbelievably perfect body who sleeps four hours a night. Let's call it an educated guess."

He makes a little noise, something like a chuckle-groan, followed by rustling, like maybe he rolled over. I wish so hard I was there.

"Are you in your bedroom?" I ask.

"Yup."

"What does it look like?"

"You ruled out home visits yesterday. Are we sure about home descriptions?"

"Pleeeeease." I want to know. I want to picture him.

"There are three arched windows in front of me that face west. I can see the moon right now. Building tops. Lights. Long gray curtains on either side."

"Gray walls?"

"White walls," he says. "Dark wood floor. Most of my art is photography. Architectural photography. But some of it is shapes that the wind makes in sand."

"Really?"

"Sand. Is that surprising? The photographer is from Yemen. She photographs sand. It's beautiful."

"It's just funny, because sand seems so non-linear."

"Maybe it comforts me to trap it in a square frame, control freak that I am."

I snort.

"What are you doing this afternoon?"

"I don't know how I feel about that as a transition," I say.

"Tell me."

Heat steals over me. "Maybe I'm calling wake-up clients who are less assholey than you."

He growls, and shivers slide over me. He loves when I'm being impudent, and so do I. It's probably all sorts of wrong, but I don't care.

"I don't know. Errands and things."

"Keep the afternoon open," he says in the rumbly tone I've come to love. "Just keep it open."

"Why?"

"Because I need to teach you and your smart mouth a lesson."

I swallow past my dry mouth. And then he's gone. Before I can even OMG him.

Later that morning, at a far more decent hour, a courier delivers an envelope with the logo of the Rowell Hotel. Inside is a key card and one of Theo's business cards with a room number and 2:15 p.m. scribbled in his crisp penmanship, underlined twice.

The underlines are such a nice Theo touch. I bring the card to my nose and inhale, picking up the faintest traces of a sweet-sharp scent. Like melon and pepper.

I tell myself I shouldn't go. I don't like Theo telling me what to do...except maybe I might like it when it's in a room at a fabulous luxury hotel.

The Rowell is dripping with luxury, as it turns out, from the chandeliers up top to the lusciously thick rugs underfoot.

I ride a deluxe elevator up to the top floor and find the room empty. There's a note on the bed with just one word: *Strip*.

I sit down and check my phone instead. Because Operator Seven doesn't follow rules. Operator Seven has worn one of the sack dresses. Operator Seven is so impudent, it's not even funny.

Theo comes in without knocking. He takes one look at me and shakes his head, stripping off his overcoat with brutal efficiency. His stern manner makes me quiver deep inside.

I hold up the note. "If I recall, I quit Vossameer. You are no longer the boss of me, Drummond."

He rakes me up and down with his gaze. No humor, no lightness. Only hunger. I'm trembling so excitedly, it's a wonder I don't rocket right out the window.

I stand and rip up the note, let the pieces flutter to the posh carpet.

"Damn," he says.

I shiver as he stalks over, skin too tight on my body. He takes my hair in his fist and uses it to spin me around and push me face-first to the wall. He presses the bulk of his weight to me.

The wallpaper is smooth and cool on my cheek. His breath is ragged in my ear, all desperate desire and vulnerability.

Massive hands grip my ass, massaging it, grinding my pussy against the wall, kind of making me hump the wall.

Humping the wall is definitely not an activity I would've thought up on my own, sitting around bored on a Saturday night or whatever. I'd reach for the vibrator long before I'd go for humping the wall, but it's incredibly pleasurable with him lewdly pressing my flesh.

"I've been thinking about this ass all day long," he says. "I've been thinking about *this* all day long."

I want to say something sassy, but the language-formation part of my brain seems to be offline. Maybe the pleasure center of my brain annexed it, needing more space to put up dome-topped skyscrapers and rocket launch pads and other phallic things.

He slides his hands around to the fronts of my thighs, pulling up my dress, baring my legs. "What the hell do you think you're wearing?"

"You don't like it?"

He rumbles his displeasure. "Do you like being impudent?" he asks, pressing a finger into my wet folds. My breath hitches at the contact.

"Yes, I like it," I say, trembling with excitement. "Yes, I do."

Liking it more by the minute.

He grabs my hair and yanks my head back, looking into my eyes while he does me with his finger. Observing and assessing, sexy scientist that he is, adjusting his stroke for maximum, delicious, excruciating pleasure.

"What was that?" he asks, voice gravelly with desire.

"Yes," I breathe, melting in his hands. "I like being impudent."

"God. That smart mouth...that smart..." Instead of finishing his sentence, he kisses me while stroking me nearly to oblivion.

Nearly.

Just before I'm about to come, he releases my hair and lets off on my pussy.

I'm about to protest, but I don't—his feral gaze steals my words away.

He grabs the neck of my dress in a two-fisted hold. With just one harsh yank, he rips it asunder—simply tears it in two. I gasp at the suddenness of the motion. At the blast of cool hotel room air hitting my naked skin. Rough fists yank down my bra.

We're doing the savage thing now. It's savage go-time!

He pulls me flush to him. His breath saws in and out, gravelly with desire. He holds me so tightly that the hard circles of his suit coat buttons jut into my flesh. "You come here," he growls into my ear.

It's an unreasonable thing to say, being that I can hardly be closer to him...unreasonable and awesome.

Without warning, he begins pulling and tearing off the last bits of my clothes. Desire throbs in my veins, right down to my clit.

He pulls me from the wall and bends me roughly over a chair.

I clutch the arms, heart racing.

"Wider." He kicks my legs apart.

I can barely breathe. He's doing something back there. What? My whole body yearns for him to touch me again.

I press back, nudging him with my ass. "Where'd you go?" I

say. "You know the wake-up-call girl can't spend all day with just one client."

"What's that?" he growls.

"You heard me," I say.

Suddenly he slaps my ass. Actually spanks me! "The wake-up-call girl will spend as long as I need."

I'm trembling. I can't believe he spanked me! It's embarrassing and totally exciting, all at once. "You're a bad client," I say.

He slaps my ass again.

"Oh my god," I whisper. He smooths his hand over my skin. The back-and-forth between sting and softness makes my nerve endings tremble and swoon. "You are my worst client!"

He slaps my ass even harder.

"Okay, okay!" Every molecule on my skin is alive, afire. I press my face into the chair.

"You think you get to say when this stops?" he asks, skimming gentle fingers over my ass. It's a barely-there touch, but it sizzles, sending ripples of heat through me. My sex aches for him.

He reaches around to my pussy just then, stroking, caressing. I melt a little more with his every stroke.

"Do you?"

There's a question there, but I don't care. My thoughts have disintegrated into the pleasure of his touch. "More," I say. "More."

"More what?"

"More...just you."

Time suspends in the vulnerable truth of that. For a moment, it's just the two of us, alone in the spinning world.

He leans over me, sheltering me with his body. Warm lips press onto my shoulder blade. "I gotcha, baby."

I feel his thick crown nudging at my entrance, probing. His breath is rough in my ear. I need him so bad I feel crazed.

"Theo, yes."

He presses in slowly, filling me, owning me, thick and heavy inside me. He pushes in, all the way deep. He stills, and it's like the earth stills. He runs his hands up and down my hips, a small electric contact. "This," he says, beginning to pulse into me. "This."

"So good," I mumble. I reach between my legs and stroke myself while he pushes into me, seeming to swell inside me.

He groans. "Babe, you should've warned me you were going to do that—it's so hot, I almost lost it."

I rub my clit even more dramatically while he fucks me. He says nonsensical guy things where his tone matters way more than his words.

We lose it pretty fast, orgasming almost together, and then we fall into bed, shaky and excited. I want to tell him he's my favorite guy I ever had by miles. And I think he wants to say it, too, but we're fuck buddies only, and I'm on my way out of the city, so we just sprawl there.

Afterward, we take a shower and have sex again. Then we put on the hotel bathrobes and collapse on the bed. I snuggle into the pit of his arm.

"This is way hotter than what I imagined," he says, brushing the hair from my forehead with the pad of his thumb.

"Me, too." Hotness is safe territory. Fuck buddy territory. "Though I still haven't gotten my lab-coat fuck."

He knits his fingers into mine.

"Tell me more of yours," I say. "Of what you imagined us doing."

He's silent a bit, like maybe he doesn't want to tell. He pulls our joined hands to his mouth and presses his lips to my knuckle.

I feel like I could get used to this. Probably not the best thing.

"You drive me so crazy with those calls," he says, "tormenting me. I spend all this time at my desk looking at the data, but all I can see is your pussy spread before me, and it drives me crazy, and I can't concentrate on my lifesaving formula."

"If people complain, tell them, 'Buzz off, I was thinking about pussy.'"

He snorts and kisses another knuckle. "And I come and find you. You're laughing."

"So impertinent."

"You're in your pjs. I put you over my knee. I slide them down over your ass, and I spank the shit out of you. Then we fuck." He kisses my next knuckle.

"So you really don't spank all the girls?"

"Just you. Only you." He kisses yet another knuckle.

"You're running out of unkissed knuckles."

"I know," he says sadly. "I have to get back to work anyway."

There's this silence where I don't want him to go.

"I really have to hurry up and get that formula figured out," he says. "And I can't."

"Why is it so important to dehydrate?"

"It makes it portable. It could be issued to soldiers. Cops. Schools. Put in first-aid kits. It would be huge for gunshot victims. I should've had it nailed by now."

I sit up and set a hand on his belly, smoothing down the scant hairs. "Is there some kind of rush on it?"

"Besides people dying?" he says.

"Right, of course," I say.

He looks miserably at the far wall.

It sounds like an important invention, but I'm suspicious about how much pressure he's putting on himself about it, like it has to be him and he can't have a life until he nails it.

In a serious tone, he says, "Sometimes I think it's beyond my abilities."

My heart breaks for him a little bit, for how bereft he seems.

I'm about to tell him he can totally do it—he is the great Theo Drummond, right? But I realize that's probably what anybody would say to him. *Of course you can solve it, Theo! You can do anything!*

I think about what he said, how the stories about him as some hero make him feel really alone. I say, "Maybe you won't get it. Maybe you will, but maybe you won't. But things will still be okay."

"Things won't be okay if I don't get it."

"Why? I understand that it would be great if you solved it. But there are other chemists in the world. Maybe they could take a crack."

"I'm the one on the trail of it," he says. "And people need it. People are dying for the lack of it."

"Okay." I rest my chin on his shoulder and put my hand on his chest. "You have such a good heart. I never saw it before."

"A good heart doesn't get the formula solved," he says.

I'm stunned at how merciless he is with himself. "Well, you invented the other formula. So it's not like you're some slacker in the saving-lives department."

"Tell that to the people who die for a lack of the dehydrated version. It drives me crazy, because I know it's there. Just out of my reach."

I press my hand harder onto his beating heart, and he puts his hand over mine. We lie like that for a while. It's nice.

I say, "Who's the hero now, biotches?"

He snorts. "What did you just say?"

"You heard what I said," I say.

He rolls me over, pins me to the bed. "You are terrible."

"What, you're wounded? Maybe you should've tried not to get wounded."

He narrows his gray eyes, like I'm being amazing and terrible all at once. "I can't believe you just said that."

I shrug. Say nothing.

"You should've tried not to get wounded? Jesus." And then he flops back down and laughs.

And then I'm laughing.

"Uh," he says.

I prop my head up on my elbow. We just look at each other for a while. And we're not playing a game; we're just looking at each other. And it's as if the world stills. Everything stops. The wind in the trees. The cats riding the vacuum cleaners. Everything.

And then he kisses me. And I kiss him back.

It's a sweet kiss, not a *wanna-fuck?* kiss. Not a *naughty wake-up-call girl* kiss. Not a *jackalope-boss* kiss.

Just pure affection.

In other words, it's the most dangerous kind of kiss we could have.

I'm the one to stop it. I sit up and put a hand on his arm. To an outside observer, it might look like an affectionate touch. But I suppose it's like baby goat faces—something that looks nice but is pure vicious survival. A reminding touch. To remind ourselves of the fuck buddies-only pact.

When I look into his eyes, I know he knows it.

"Okay," he says. Because we don't need the words. Which makes it all the sadder, I suppose.

I grab my phone, just to mentally reset myself. I find a goat video I saved for him. I make him watch.

He smiles even though he tries not to, because he's a serious scientist who shouldn't love baby goat videos. But really, who can resist baby goat videos?

I go into my cloud to find him another really good one. We watch it together and he laughs.

He's always so happily astonished by them; that's what makes it fun to show him. It makes me feel like I'm showing him wonders from the future or something.

After that, I show him a bunch of photos from my phone. Mia and me in the Catskills. The pizzeria attached to the home where I grew up. My mom and dad and me celebrating Three Musketeers Day, a holiday we made up for ourselves. "We didn't have much money, but we were together in a fierce way," I say. "March twenty-first. We'd eat all our favorite foods and do our favorite activities. No matter what day of the week it fell on, Mom and Dad would take off work. Sometimes they'd get me out of school early."

"It's coming up," he says.

"I know. I'm going to miss it this year." I flick past. No sense in going down there when I'll be there at the end of the month.

I land on another sad image. "This space was for rent a few weeks back. I know they would never rent it to me with my credit, but I had to see it. Look at it. There's a restaurant going in now, but look at the tin ceiling."

He's not looking at the tin ceiling. He's looking at me. "Why would you go and see it if you know you can never have it?"

"You're gonna laugh," I say.

He traces the line of my jaw. "This is me." Something strange happens in my heart when he says that.

"I have a dream board," I say. "I know you're a scientist and everything—"

He kisses the words off my lips. "You put the image on your dream board."

"Yeah. I feel like it helps to have pictures of what I want. Though to be my ideal space, it would have to be on a corner. And really small and cozy like my old space. I would have one table outside, but none inside. I have a whole rationale about it."

He wants to hear my rationale, so I tell him.

Everything feels so real suddenly, and so far from fuck buddies. His face on my personal Mount Rushmore is getting huger by the second.

"I should go," I say.

He closes his hand around mine. My heart pounds. For a moment, I think he might not let me. But then he does.

THIRTY

Lizzie

I KEEP the wake-up calls going.

Every morning at 4:30 we talk on the phone while the rest of the world sleeps. Sometimes it's super sexy. Sometimes we talk like friends.

I keep Theo updated on my search for the perfect subletter to take my place living with Mia, and we discuss my worries about my current top contender. I tell him about my walks with Mia up along Ninth, sometimes Tenth, to her delivery job. I'm spending as much time as I can with her. I'll miss her like crazy.

I tell him things I'm afraid to tell Mia. Like my worries that Mia will find a new friend, or that she and I will grow apart. Eighteen months is a long time.

On one of the calls, Theo tells me that he has a long-distance friend from college he texts with all the time. He thinks their friendship has stayed strong because they keep up with each other's everyday minutia. He reads me a few texts he sent.

One is about running-shoe laces, and I give him shit about that, but it makes me feel better.

Theo tells me about his struggles with the formula, using super layperson's terms.

He's just so intensely driven, almost like he's racing time. It's noble, but I still don't like the grim, hard-ass pace of it.

One of the articles that's out there about him suggests he could've cashed out way bigger if he'd gone with big pharma, but he decided not to, because he didn't want to lose control over the pricing, and he couldn't get a guarantee that it wouldn't be inflated.

I ask him if that part's true, too. He lowers his voice, like he's making this big confession, and tells me that it was more that they wouldn't meet his demands that microwave popcorn would be banned on the premises where Vossameer is produced.

I laugh and tell him to screw off.

He goes on about something else, but I'm lying there, phone in hand, thinking that's a little bit heroic, too, to not want the price high. He'd admire it if it were anybody else, but Theo lives in a different world where the bar for goodness is harshly high.

Sometimes he pushes it, though. Like when he presses me on whether I really, really have to go. And I have to explain my reasons all over again. A free place to live and cater out of while I renegotiate the debt and save money. The fact that I can't start making money without a bakery space, and I can't get a bakery space without repairing my finances. Especially not while living in one of the most expensive cities in the world.

The decision is hard enough without him questioning it.

One time, he texts me a rental listing of a space that would be perfect for me. His message says, "Let's figure this out. We can make this work."

I grit my teeth. Is this not what I asked him not to do? Like a masochist, I click through it, looking at each and every picture, wanting just to cry. I call him up. "Don't do that. Don't send me these."

"It's the perfect space."

"The perfect space they'd never rent to me. And I couldn't afford it even if they did say yes."

"You could afford it if I invested. Cosigned."

"You mean if I let you be my sugar daddy and rent it for me? And then you'd be able to take it away on a whim?"

"I wouldn't do that."

"Theo—"

"It's ridiculous to move away when you don't have to."

"It's not ridiculous to me," I say. "Do you not understand why I need to do this on my own? However you dress it up, this plan would give you power over my existence. I know it seems unreasonable to you, but I want you to respect it's a thing with me. Okay?"

He sighs.

"Don't show me any more real estate."

He's silent. Then, "I won't show you any more real estate."

I meet him out at hotels during the day a lot. He always sends a car unless it's within walking distance of where I am. What with these fancy hotels, I feel a little bit like a cross between a princess and a call girl, which I can report is a highly sexy combo.

Our sexy games never get old; they just get more exciting. We do endless variations on stern boss and impudent employee. Sometimes it's angry client and wake-up-call girl. Other times it's suit-on-the-street driven crazy by my hotness and sassy tone. Or "what the hell are you doing in my hotel room?"

I sometimes wear my prairie dresses, like offerings to the savage dress-ripping god. Sometimes I wear lingerie. We have hot sex. Outrageous sex. Wild sex.

The one thing we never have is sweet sex as ourselves. Like

that's just too bold—for me, at least. Because I'm not ready for a relationship like that, and I'm leaving, anyway.

Theo would go for it. He sometimes does, but I always pull us back to the sassy game.

Maybe I'm a coward. It's just that sweet sex is a boundary I can't cross with him. It's too much risk, too much heartache.

So we keep meeting in strange hotels, sexy thieves, stealing what isn't ours.

I think about him alone in bed at night. I think about him when I'm waiting for the subway, or interviewing possible subletters.

I think about him when I'm waiting for something to come to a boil at the catering gig. Sometimes I'll slide a finger over my arm, my cheek, and I'm back with him. Or I'll remember a conversation. I'll smile at something he said.

I thought he was so oblivious, so antisocial.

I was so wrong.

When it's nice out, Theo and I walk around together outside the hotels where we meet before going back to our lives. Now and then, he asks me to come to his place, but I always say no, because that's a line in the sand for me. The hotels keep everything out of reality.

But reality does creep in.

Like the afternoon we're stuck in the back of Theo's town car on the Third Avenue Bridge. We're going back from a hotel, and his whole demeanor changes. I think it's the traffic that's getting him down, but then he lowers the privacy partition.

"I'm sorry," Derek says. "There was construction over on..."

Theo's voice is calm. Too calm. "Ask next time."

"I really am sorry."

"It's fine. Next time..."

"Absolutely," Derek says.

Theo raises the shield.

"What's wrong?" I ask.

He gazes away, bitterly, almost. "That would be out of the fuck buddies purview."

"Theo," I say.

He shakes his head. Says nothing.

That's when I know. This is *the* bridge.

It's not just something I know, it's as if I can feel his heart, still raw about it, twisted in on itself. I reach over and take his hand. I squeeze it, sensing his pain so acutely.

What's happening to me? I vowed to myself not to get close to a man, especially not one as personally powerful and consuming as Theo. But here I am. So close.

After a long while, he squeezes mine back.

Traffic moves at a crawl.

"The spot they went through is back there," he finally says. "All this metal, and he managed to find the one loose part, the one damaged part, to blast through."

I stay holding his hand. Theo doesn't like a lot of chatter when he's feeling emotional. We're starting to move. He looks over at me. "Screw it. Okay. Okay, then."

"What?" I ask.

He lowers the partition. "Take us down to the water once you're off."

"Will do," Derek says.

"Down to the water?" I ask when he doesn't explain.

"We've come this far," he says simply.

And I wonder: does he mean *this far* in terms of distance to the bridge? Or *this far* in terms of being honest with each other?

A few minutes later, we're parked near a giant docking and loading area for barges. It seems deserted. Maybe because it's still cold, maybe because there's not a lot of freight traffic today.

He grabs two beers out of his back-of-the-car cooler. "Come on." He gets out and walks. I follow, pulling my jacket tight. The afternoon sun doesn't do much to cut the chill from the wind that blows off the Harlem River.

Everything around us is huge and hulking. There are piles of cement things here and there, and a large sign for the river traffic that we only see the metal back of. I catch up to him and follow him along the railed edge of the concrete slab and down some steps toward the dirty green water.

He puts out his coat on the lowest step. I sit.

He hands me a beer, then he turns and lifts his in a toast, as if toasting to the bridge.

I toast my own beer, and then hold it in both hands on my knees, waiting solemnly for whatever he wants to say.

He's showing me a piece of himself, and that means a lot. Because in spite of everything, I want to be connected with him, whether it's the hottest sex or the deepest, darkest pain. I never felt like that with a man before.

"I didn't take you here to feel sorry for me." He swigs his beer. Stays standing.

"I know," I say.

He nods. He knows I know.

"See the third section? And how the bridge is darker right down from it? That's the repaired part. You can still tell."

"Where they went off. The accident." It's not really a question.

"It wasn't so much an accident, really. Accidents are unexpected. This was inevitable."

I wait. Listen.

"You could see it coming from miles away," he says. "My dad, the world's most high-functioning drunk. He kept a good job. Managed to handle his responsibilities, but couldn't resist driving. He just loved to drive us around. I don't know what the hell was in his head. It especially terrified Willow. She'd cry when he'd make her ride. He saw it as a criticism, and he'd just do it all the more."

I stare out at the bridge with its crisscrosses and thick, gray geometry. Cars streaming over, right past the spot where his parents went off. None with any idea of the lives that ended just feet away.

"That's why Willow worked so hard for those scholarships," he continues. "I mean, she was in her bedroom programming from morning to night when other girls were doing whatever girls that age are supposed to do. It was her ticket out. The shit he'd say. Those terrifying rides. Willow and I always hated rides at the fair. Roller coasters. That type of thrill was never fun for us. We had the real-life version."

"Sounds like," I say softly.

Seagulls screech nearby. One swoops into the air with a hunk of something in its mouth. The others chase.

"When I was fifteen, I started standing up to him and taking away the keys. I'd refuse to ride. Refuse to let Mom ride. Sometimes hide the keys and just take what came. But he was still a lot bigger than me. I could sometimes stop the rides, but not always."

He's silent for a while. I want to go up next to him and put my hand on his arm, but I know not to. That's not what he needs.

"At one point, Dad went out of town on a business trip, and it was just Mom and me. We were out of his orbit long enough that we felt what it was like to be free of his power. I had my mom talked into leaving. It was going to be just us. Build our own life. I had enough savings for a place in Queens. A sad little studio in a piece-of-shit building, but it would've been ours. I really thought I had her on board, but then he came home, and nothing changed. Except the fights over the keys got worse. Finally I left. I managed to get a job." He turns around to face me, leaning back on the railing, picking at the edge of the label on the bottle. "I was so damn angry. At him, but also at her."

He says nothing for a while, just looks at the river.

"I glowered at her as I left, angry that she was too weak to come along. That was the last time I saw her. Because she was too weak to take the keys away from him herself. And I knew that."

"Theo—"

"That was my role. Getting the keys. It was how I kept the three of us alive."

"Like it was your fault? She was an adult. She could've taken the keys."

Cars whiz past up there in the distance. "In theory, yes. In reality, she couldn't have taken them any more than she could've pole-vaulted over the house."

"So you think it's *your* fault?"

The look he gives me breaks my heart. It's a *yes*, tattooed deep in his heart. "It was inevitable."

"That is such shit!" I say. "It was her job to take away the keys. To be watching out for you."

"In a perfect world," he says.

"In *this* world."

He's silent.

"What does Willow say? Surely she agrees."

"She doesn't know. I mean, she knows they went off. She knows I left, but she's never thought it through in terms of cause and effect."

"Maybe because there isn't any cause and effect that involves you."

He keeps peeling his label, and I know with every bit of

certainty inside me that I'm the first person he's confessed his guilt to.

His supposed guilt.

I get up and stand next to him. "You should tell your sister."

"I'm not going to tell my sister. Especially now. She has problems of her own."

"You can't carry it like this. You need to talk about it."

He looks over at me, then. "Isn't that what fuck buddies are for?"

"No, actually."

It's here I wonder—is that why he's so crazy to get the formula? Is there some invisible balance sheet he's trying to even out?

He gets off some of the label and shoves it into his pocket. A river full of litter and he won't add to it. "They always tell that story like I'm a hero. You can see now why I'm not a fan."

"God, Theo."

I slide a hand onto his arm. I really want to hold him, but he'll resist. This is the most affection he'll tolerate right now—a small touch.

"I'm going to come back to your place with you," I say. "And make you some nice hot cocoa."

"I don't want a pity visit."

"It's not a pity visit. I just want to." And I don't want him to go back to work tonight. That's what he'll do. It seems wrong. "You think you can stop me?"

His eyes lower to mine. "Yeah."

"You think you're the boss of me?"

His lips twist. This is one of our sexcapade lines. "I don't have stuff for cocoa," he says finally.

"I do. In my bag. From the caterers."

He touches the lip of his bottle to the underside of my chin, tips my head up. "You just want more of my savage and uncivi-lized loving."

And just like that, we're back on familiar ground. And we both pretend that sex is what my visit will be about, or at least, I do.

Because it's easier than acknowledging the significance of us.

THIRTY-ONE

Lizzie

THEO LIVES in an ultramodern building with giant windows and large balconies. "Which is yours?" I ask.

He points to the top. Penthouse. Of course.

The doorman lets us into a lobby that could double as a mod lighting showroom. A woman in a uniform—some sort of concierge, I suppose—comes out from behind the desk with a silky black garment bag for Theo. He groans when he sees it, then he takes it and thanks her, and we make for the elevator.

The black bag has some sort of European-style crest on it, and when I look closer, it's the name of a dry cleaner.

"Do just you despise dry-cleaning?" I tease as we head up.

"It's a tux for a ridiculous banquet. I despise ridiculous banquets."

"Too *kumbayah* for you?"

"Pretty much."

The elevator opens into a small, sleek foyer. He hangs the

dry-cleaning bag on a hook, and we head through an archway into a huge, airy space.

I spin around, taking it all in. It's as cool, severe, and utterly gorgeous as Theo, a somber mix of natural wood tones with browns and blacks and whites, and some crystalline lighting. And the black-and-white photography. The sand he told me about. The only actual color in the room is the bright blue sky out the window.

I go look down over Central Park. You can see a faint haze of green on the sea of brown trees. Spring is coming. "I've never seen it from so high and near like this. The paths look even curvier."

He comes up beside me. "They made them like that so there wouldn't be horse and carriage races," he says.

"Doesn't slow the bikes."

"No," he says, sliding my hair over my shoulder.

We head to his kitchen, which is lots of steel and crisp white tile. I find the kettle. "You can't blow off the banquet?" I ask.

"No. It's one of the hoops I have to jump through for the Locke Foundation partnership." He takes the kettle from me and fills it with water from a special drinking spigot.

"I thought you and Henry Locke were friendly."

"We are, but it's not just him. He has a whole board. They want to ensure that I'm good in public. Not an asshole and all that. Apple pie and smiles for everyone."

"Oh, you are so apple pie and smiles for everyone."

He sets it on the burner and turns on the gas. "I can be when I have to be," he says, eyeing me. "When I want something."

"Because you always get what you want."

He smiles.

We drink our cocoa, and later we order Chinese and eat it while we watch an Avengers movie on his couch. It's the most couple-ish thing we've ever done. When it's over, I stretch out and lay my head in his lap. "What should we do now?"

He looks down at me, and for once I can't read his expression. My belly tightens as his hand slides onto my cheek. He leans down and kisses me, all spicy and sweet; then he kisses the crook of my neck.

There's no forbidden game to it at all. I've never felt so naked with him. We feel like a couple, exactly what we can't be, for oh-so-many reasons.

"Why do you even need the Locke partnership so bad?" I ask, forcing us off the romantic slippery slope. "You have wads of money and your own company."

He stills. "They have relationships and trust built up with charitable organizations across the world," he says. "It's a lot less hassle to jump through their PR hoops than to set up my own network. Giving is actually more complicated than people think."

"Well, the Locke people should be grateful. That's what I think."

"They're into image. A strong image attracts the best people and makes them more effective. I can appreciate that."

"You just don't want to bother," I say.

"No." The tip of his finger traces my jawline. "They'd be especially grateful if I'd worked out the new formula."

"More gratitude, motherfuckers," I say.

He chuckles softly. I feel it from his lap. "Yeah, mother-fuckers."

He traces my jawline back the other way, and a strange thrill stirs through me, wonderful and dangerous.

This is nice, I think, and I suddenly want to say it. But I don't. I can't.

He touches my right cheekbone. "This is my favorite freckle of yours. My second favorite is the one on your right thigh." He touches my right thigh. "Here." His touch is a magic wand, awakening my thigh and nearby pussy.

"I never think about that one."

"I always do. And there's another one here at two o'clock from your belly button." He sets a finger over the spot. My belly undulates under his touch, but it's his gaze that gets me. "I like every place on you, Lizzie."

My belly lurches. He's not doing any kind of look, not playing any sort of game. It's just him, open and frank.

"I don't want you to leave," he says.

"Theo—"

"Please stay."

"It's impossible."

"Unless we decide to make it possible."

"Don't. We talked about this. You said you wouldn't get involved."

"Maybe it's time for you to change your mind," he says.

"I can't change my mind on an emotion."

He gazes miserably out the window.

"Please respect that I need this to happen on my own steam. I need you to stop trying to change my mind on it."

He sighs.

I sit up and touch the inner edge of his right eyebrow. "This is one of my favorite places on you."

He doesn't want to play anymore. He just stares out the window, secret thoughts flowing behind stormy gray eyes.

"Your other one whorls perfectly, but this one refuses to whorl. It marches to its own drummer. It's something you don't see until you're really up close. A secret eyebrow rebellion."

He finally meets my gaze. "Do I need to quash it?"

"Maybe," I say.

He contracts his brows.

"Still there. You can glower and furrow all you want." I kiss it. "You're not the boss of this eyebrow."

He still looks sad.

"You think you're the boss of everything," I add, sliding a finger over his lips, another favorite place. I let my finger linger there, pushing in a little.

He watches me, rebelling along with his eyebrow, refusing to play.

I smile and slide my finger back and forth over his bad-boy lower lip. The energy between us is shifting.

The subtext to our interaction is that if he wants to fuck, he has to do the stern boss thing.

Suddenly he growls and nips my finger. I squeal and pull it out, but he has my wrist. And then he slides his hand around my waist. Because in the end, Theo's a man with a cock.

He flips me over and presses me down to the couch, holding me still. "Everything always has to go perfectly your way. Is that it?"

"Yes," I say. Because that kind of *is* it. "What are you going to do about it?"

He begins undoing my buttons. "I think you know."

What he does about it is to carry me to his bedroom, and go down on me, and then he plunges into me, thick and hard, breath warm and ragged at my neck.

I TELL myself I shouldn't sleep over. Lying in his bed, legs and arms twined perfectly with his, I do a positive visualization of myself getting up and gathering my clothes. I picture myself putting my outfit on. I would then grab my phone and kiss him goodbye. And then I'd head down and get a Lyft. Even as I'm drifting off to sleep, I'm picturing it.

I wake up with an inexplicable glow of well-being blazing through me. I open my eyes and meet his.

And I know he was watching me sleep—in a sweet way, not a creepy way.

I love this. I love his eyes on me. My belly does a nervous little twist.

"Good morning," he whispers, kissing my cheek.

"Good morning," I whisper back. "Wow."

"What?"

"Here it is, morning," I say. "How did that even happen?"

He props his hand on his head, creating folds in his stubbly cheek. He smiles sleepily. "An effect of my amazing, savage lovemaking—"

I smash my fingertips onto his lips, heart squeezing. Is this all too good? Am I getting too close to the fire?

"What are you thinking, baby?"

I'm thinking a man has never made me feel like he does. I'm thinking I want nothing more than to spend the day making him as happy as he makes me.

I slide my fingertip over the bad-boy bump on his lower lip. I'm thinking I would give him anything. It makes me scared as hell.

"I'm trying to decide which microwave-popcorn-of-the-month subscription to order for you," I say. "I've narrowed it down to empty cheesy aroma or whiff-of-buttery-nothingness delight. What do you think?"

He kisses my finger. That's what he thinks.

I grab his shirt and go to the window, as if I really, really need to see the view.

THIRTY-TWO

Theo

SHE WRAPS herself up in my shirt and wanders over to the window. The sunrise lights the mussed edges of her pale brown hair, a goddess tipped in flame.

She stands there a long time, gazing out over the park, and I have this sense that she belongs here, that she's always been here in some impossible way. As if her being here stretches beyond time.

I want to tell her that, but I don't. One strong shift in the breeze and she'll disappear like a wisp of fog.

I want to thank her for going to the bridge with me, too. For being who she was there. For listening and saying what she did. Not that she changed anything. I don't feel absolved, much as she wants me to, but there was this sense—just for a moment—of her sharing the load. Carrying it with me, if only for a little while.

This nameless, faceless woman who was so easy to talk to on the phone is ten times the miracle in person.

What we have is something special, and I feel like she's killing it with her plans to leave. She's killing it before it has a chance to grow. I wish she'd see that.

I wish she'd come back to bed, too. I want to kiss her cheekbone freckle. She smiles in a lopsided way every time I do that—a happy, what-the-heck smile. The eye-rolling version of a smile. The smile of a woman who doesn't get how hot she is.

Lizzie Lizzie Lizzie, I think.

I reach out. "Get over here," I growl, giving her the edge she likes, just stern enough so that she can tell herself we're back to playing wake-up-call girl.

That's what that jackass Mason did to her—he made her skittish for an honest relationship. Ruined her financially to the point she has to move.

To freaking *Fargo*.

I'd like to find him and wring his worthless neck.

I can't let her leave. I just can't. But for now, I need her back in bed.

I lower my voice to a deep register. "Now."

She comes. I wrap her up in my arms. I kiss her on the freckle and hold her against me, the clench of a lover, even as my words are cold. "You're going to stay right here as long as I require your services."

She snorts.

I require her services on top of me, as it turns out, and then on her knees in the shower.

Eventually we find our way out to the kitchen. I start some coffee and pull her huge bag of sugar out of the cupboard.

"You kept it!"

I crowd her against the kitchen island, growl in her ear. "It has your phone number." I kiss the shell of her ear. "How the hell else would I call you?" I kiss her neck.

Of course I kept it. It's so her. So wonderfully, perfectly her.

"Do you have eggs?" she asks. "Veggies?"

"Yeah." I pull back. "I have eggs and veggies. But I don't have the stuff for breakfast."

"You just listed the stuff I'd need to make breakfast."

"Not so sure about that."

She slides a finger over my chest, tracing the edge of my left pec through my T-shirt. It's hard not to grab her and carry her back to bed. She turns me primal in a way no other woman has. Sometimes I barely know myself.

But I fight the caveman urge. I like how she's touching me. I've shunned affection for so many years. Now this woman has me like a beggar.

More, I think.

"Thank you," she says.

"For what?"

"Telling me about the bridge."

My heart soars at this.

She trails her finger down my abs. "And I accept the challenge. I'm going to make an amazing breakfast for you. Right here."

A few minutes later, we have coffee going, and she's riffling through my kitchen, disgusted, while I sit on the counter, enjoying the way the long-tail cut of my Oxford brushes against her perfect thighs. She's all about breakfast, like I knew she would be.

"You have no butter, no oil, no pan." She spins around to look at me, mystified.

"I told you."

"What are you doing with the eggs? Poaching them somehow?"

"I thought you were the kitchen expert here."

"Do you microwave water and poach them like that?"

"You can do that?" I ask.

She narrows her eyes. "You're not hiding kitchen stuff?"

"What? No. This is all I have. Coffee maker and a blender."

"Have you been throwing the eggs off the balcony at people? Is that what you use them for?"

"I blend them," I say. "It all goes in the blender. Veggies. Raw eggs."

"What? Yuck."

"Food is fuel. Not recreation."

"Are you one of those people who wouldn't eat at all if you didn't have to?" She holds up a hand. "Don't answer that. God, at least you're consistent. What if you want meat? Don't tell me you put that in the blender."

"It's called restaurants," I say.

She presses her hands to the counter, thinking.

"You're hot when you're stymied." I jump down and slide my hands around her waist.

In the end, my shitty kitchen is no match for her. She poaches eggs in a coffee cup full of boiling water while we wait for a delivery of a loaf of warm rosemary bread from a bakery she has a catering relationship with.

The concierge texts, then comes up with it. And I'll admit, it smells like heaven. She cuts the bread and toasts the pieces over the gas burner and puts the poached eggs on top.

"Ordering isn't fair," I say, biting into the insane deliciousness of the simple meal.

"I know," she says. "But please. What you're doing? It's like those pills that astronauts used to eat for food."

"Astronauts are efficient."

"Why don't you just feed yourself to the worms and get it all over with?" she asks. "That would be even more efficient."

"Because I have things to do. I have to nail this deal with Locke," I say. "I need to develop the dehydrated version."

When I look up, she's gazing at me sadly. As though what I just said was incredibly tragic.

"We need to get you a few pans," she says. "Jesus."

WOMEN ARE FREQUENTLY DISGUSTED with my one-track, workaholic mind. It's not something I cultivate, but sometimes it works out.

Case in point: the disgust that compels Lizzie to take me to the kitchen store down the block, a store that may as well have sold bagpipes as far as I was ever concerned.

But these are her people. "He doesn't have any basics whatsoever," she says to the woman who helps us. "He doesn't even have a good egg pan."

The woman looks concerned. "A man needs a good egg pan."

Apparently, a man needs several good egg pans, a selection of pots, a pepper mill, and the utensils made of the same material as the space shuttle.

She buys an entire kitchen's worth of stuff—more than we can carry. I have to call Derek to come with the car.

Back up in my kitchen, we start unwrapping things, and she finds a specific place for each and every implement. She holds up a flat metal sheet with an evil grin. "For cookies."

I go to her. "In what universe?" I kiss her head. "In what universe am I making cookies?"

"Maybe you want to impress some date."

Everything inside me stills. I know it was a joke, but it's not funny. That's not a universe I'm interested in inhabiting. Not unless the date is her.

I kiss her head again.

"Or whatever." She turns away and picks a place for the cookie sheet. I unwrap more things, and she finds more places.

She's in the middle of explaining what large utensils go in which drawers when Willow bursts in through the archway, holding the black garment bag in the air. "Are you even planning on trying it on to see if the alterations worked? Dude, you're going to be on a Jumbotron holding a Locke Award statue and making a speech. You can't be all—" She freezes when she sees Lizzie there. "Oh, I'm sorry."

Willow has keys, of course. My doorman knows her. I've always been fine with her coming in. She smiles, trying to cover her surprise at finding a woman in my kitchen.

"Hi." Lizzie's smile is friendly, but she's standing straighter, a little standoffish, and in a flash, I see that she's feeling territorial. I find that I like that.

Willow lays the garment bag over a chair and comes around the island. "Hi! I'm Willow, Theo's sister," she says.

They shake. Is Lizzie relieved? I like to think she's relieved. Willow's overjoyed that a woman's here.

Lizzie looks over at me. "So the ridiculous banquet is for you? For you to get the Locke Award? The Locke Award is a big deal!"

"I know, right?" Willow says to her.

"A ridiculous award?" Lizzie says, marveling.

"Is that what he called it?" Willow shakes her head, disgusted.

"You're giving a speech," Lizzie says. I see it when things click in her head. "And speeches will be given about you."

"That's right," I say. Speeches will be given about me. Tales will be told about me.

Lizzie nods somberly. It means everything that she gets it. That she's with me, at least in this.

"It's a very huge honor," Willow says.

Lizzie keeps her gaze on me. We're our own world.

"I'm off," Willow says. "I came to drop a few things—"

"No, look at the time," Lizzie says. "I have to go to work." She grabs her purse, her jacket.

"Please don't go on my account," Willow says.

"I really have to be at work. There are quiches to make. It was great to meet you, though." She turns to me. "Thanks for...*breakfast*," she says in the tone of air quotes.

"I'll walk you out," I say, taking her arm, giving her no choice. I walk her through the foyer to my elevator and hit the button for her.

She turns to me. "It's a huge honor. Even though I know you'd rather get poked in the eye with a stick. Or have people sitting there flipping you off."

"I would so prefer it."

"You're terrible."

I touch her collar. My affection feels bigger than my heart. Bigger than me. "Come with me," I say. "Be my date. Be the one there that flips me off."

"I can't, Theo."

"Because of our fuck buddies thing?"

"Um...yes?"

"Screw it. You're leaving in two weeks." I pull her to me, slow and hard, whisper into her ear. "Rules were made to be broken."

She snorts, as if I'm being ridiculous.

"Come. It'll be a delicious dinner if nothing else. Henry Locke knows how to put out a damn fine spread." I kiss her ear. "There will probably be lavish desserts. And then you can sit in the audience and flip me off." I kiss her neck and draw back, look her in the eye. "Be the one person who's with me, really, really with me."

She shakes her head. "Theo."

"I'll get that *Funny Face* dress back for you."

"Don't. You can't."

I shrug. "You're not the boss of me."

She gives me a sad smile. "It can't happen."

"Why not?"

The elevator has arrived, though. I growl and pull her to me. I give her another kiss, just a quick one, and then I turn and walk.

I don't even look back when the doors squeech shut.

Back in my place, Willow is surveying the sea of kitchen store packing materials. "What happened here?"

"Apparently a man needs an egg pan," I say. "And an egg pan needs an entourage."

She's searching my face. "I'm so sorry I ran her off."

"She would've gone anyway."

"I like her," Willow says. "She actually gives you crap."

"Isn't that your job?"

"You had her in your *home*. You let her take you shopping. Did you ask her to the Locke banquet?"

"Are you trying to get out of being my date?" I ask.

"Did you ask her?"

"Yeah," I say. "She doesn't want to go."

"But you had her at your home. She seems so..."

"Perfect?"

Willow leans over the counter, sets her chin on her hands. "Yeah."

"She's coming off a bad experience. She's moving away in a couple of weeks. She just wants to be fuck buddies." I move to the window and look down. If she crosses the street, I'll see her down there.

I hear Willow come up behind me after a bit. "But you so want more."

I so want more.

I HEAD into work for a blissful Saturday of no people around. Well, it used to be blissful to have no people around.

I pass by the whiteboard and go to the window, look down at all the Saturday people doing their Saturday things. Buying pastries and flowers or whatever.

Flowers, the most useless crop.

Does Lizzie like flowers? What kind would she buy? I twirl my marker, thinking I need to ask her. It would be some outrageous kind. Bright and ruffly and huge. Peonies or something.

And then I realize I'm thinking about flowers instead of formulas, and I go back to the board.

I'd hoped to have dehydrated Vossameer nailed in time for the Locke banquet. I really had hoped to use the occasion to announce it; the foundation would get the publicity bump, and our partnership would be off to a positive start. We could work together to expedite the testing.

It won't happen now.

The fact that I won't have the thing solved by the banquet is bad, yet it feels like far less of a disaster than it might have a month ago.

My race for the formula used to be the only thing on the landscape of my life. Now it exists alongside kitchen things and ironic cookies and hotel trysts and long afternoon walks when I should be working. It lives in a world where conflicted emotions can be contained in one simple, fierce word over the phone.

Where beauty is an asymmetrical freckle. Where baby goats play. Where I can wake up and Lizzie is the first thing I see. And I lie there loving everything about her so hard that it wakes her up.

I return to the whiteboard before I think too hard about her leaving, about the very real possibility that I might not be able to prevent it, hard as I might try.

And really, those baby goat videos. The ridiculous way they hop while they're running. Or more like they pop into the air, mid-run, and it's so cute, you can't look away.

The baby goats seem to inspire each other to jump more—one starts doing it, and then the others follow. Each one acts on its own, like individual kernels of popcorn, pop-pop-popping. I think about that for a while, how it's random, but there's a certain strange logic to the sequence.

I'm staring at the board, and that's when I see it—a round-about way to link the remaining water molecules together to keep a stable compound while still removing enough of them to get the dehydration I need.

It is possible? Is this it?

Heart pounding, I go to my other board and start capturing it, capturing everything, writing as fast as I can.

The ideas pour out. I scribble, feeling like I'm in a trance.

This is it.

The answer is right here. It was there all along. It's magnificent.

THIRTY-THREE

Lizzie

"DID you make microwave popcorn for him yet?" Mia asks as we head under some scaffolding. "You so need to do that before you leave."

The space to walk is too narrow for going side by side, so we walk single file for half a block, which is just as well, because I don't want her to see the sadness in my eyes. "We're not at that point in our fuck buddy relationship," I say over my shoulder, as breezily as I can.

It's a Wednesday, and I leave a week from Saturday. The things I don't do now with Mia and Theo, I might never do them. I have a subletter lined up who travels a lot for work. The woman seems good.

"Yeah, fuck buddies. Whatever you say," she says when we come back together. "You know you're gonna go to that banquet."

The dress arrived this week, as promised. I gave Theo shit about his persistence two days in a row, but he knows how much

I love it. He wants me to keep it no matter what. As if I'll have a reason to wear it in Fargo.

"I vowed I wouldn't get wrapped up with a guy like him," I say.

Mia says nothing, like she always does when she disagrees with me on something.

"It's better for him, too," I add. "He's been making great progress with his formula over the past week. He needs that mental bandwidth for his work."

She just grunts.

"What?"

"It just seems...wrong. You two are good together."

"We are, but it's how it has to be."

"Says who?" Mia says.

"Says the complete crushing of my life that was Mason."

"Is Theo that much like Mason?"

"They're both suit-wearing guys who are very into getting their way," I say. "And I'm still recuperating."

"Not strong enough to withstand his influence?" Mia asks.

"Exactly," I say.

We stop at a DON'T WALK sign and wait with a crush of people. She says nothing. Full disagreement mode.

I move nearer to her. "True, he doesn't try to influence me like Mason always would. Mason thought he knew everything."

"And Theo, I'm sorry, that dress?" Mia says. "On his own, he bought you a gown you love, in your size. It's like, an Olympic gold medalist level of boyfriend achievement." She holds up her hand before I can correct her that he's not my boyfriend. "I'm just saying."

"Theo is a scientist. He observes things with laser-like intensity. That's his job." Even as I say it, I realize the bullshit of it. It's not about his job, it's about his passion.

"It's sort of funny," I continue, "I was telling him the story about how I fell into the theme cookie niche, and I kept trying to shorten the story, because Mason would get bored with stories like that, but Theo was all, 'Wait, back up. I want every detail.'"

"Dude, please," Mia says. "He's fascinated with you."

Goes both ways, I think. "And he never tells me what to do. He respects my instincts. In a weird way, I feel...admired."

"So weird!" Mia jokes.

I want to go under another scaffolding and cry. I'll lose so much when I leave. So much.

I pull out my phone at the next light and poke through random things, clearing and organizing. The most recent text from Theo kicks off with a purple devil emoji. I forbid myself to read it.

A few rows down, there's a text Theo sent from his sister Willow's phone number when he was out of juice one time, and I think, I should put Willow in as a contact now that I have her number, just in case!

And then I think, what's the point? I'm leaving.

That makes me want to cry even more.

Meanwhile, Mia is furious at her phone. "Uh!" she says. "Are you fucking kidding me?"

I perk up. "What?" I really need something to distract me.

The light turns, and we're walking. "Stupid work stuff. " She shoves her phone into her pocket and narrows her eyes at something across the street. "Oooh." She grabs my arm.

"What?"

She points. "For your dream board."

That's when I see it. A tiny corner place for rent. "Oh, no!" I say. "I love this block. This is the perfect block!"

"Let's go look!"

"I don't know if I can bear it."

"You need it for your dream board. You have to."

I let her drag me across to the tree-shaded side of the

street, up past a sushi place and a jeweler. We look in the window together. Tiny counter. Huge windows. Tile floor and walls.

She gasps. "The ceiling."

I look up. Pressed tin. My heart sinks. "It's so..."

"Amazing," she says.

"Perfect," I add. "If only it was eighteen months from now."

"Why not call and find out the rent?"

"It has to be so much money."

"For comparative purposes." She moves around to look in the other side. "Oh, Lizzie!"

I go over to join her. It's even better from the side. It's just the size for baking stuff and a counter. It's got fans. "Kill me now." I take out my phone and get a few shots.

She takes my phone and makes me stand by the door. She gets a few shots of me, then one of us together.

An older woman comes up the street with a bag from the hardware store. She smiles. "Can I help you?"

"Sorry, are you...is this your place? Are you the one leasing it out?" Mia asks.

"Yeah. We just put up the sign."

Mia kicks me.

"Just out of curiosity, what's the rent?" I ask.

She names a reasonable price for the neighborhood. A lot, in other words. "Want to see it?" She's unlocking the door.

"I'm more interested in it on an aspirational basis," I say, at exactly the same time as Mia says, "We'd love to!" She grabs my arm, whispering, "Vision board!"

We go in. It's more perfect on the inside. The kitchen is better than my old one.

"What sort of operation are you thinking about?" the woman asks. "I'd say this space is ideal for retail or small food prep and carry-out."

"She's looking for a Cookie Madness space," Mia says to the woman.

The woman's gaze swivels to my face. "Cookie Madness? With the fun frosted cookies?"

I smile wanly. "Yeah."

"That was her," Mia says proudly.

"We loved Cookie Madness," the woman says. "We couldn't understand why you closed."

"Her ex was a con man," Mia blurts. "He took her for everything!" She starts telling the sordid story; I practically have to seal her mouth with my hand to shut her up.

"I'd rather not have that get out," I say. "I'm not in a position to put down a security deposit or anything, really, right now, but I'll be back on my feet." I let Mia go and scribble my cellphone number on a slip of paper and hand it to the woman. "If this place comes up again the summer after next, or if you have anything else like it, I'd be in a position to rent it."

The woman studies my card. "We'd love a Cookie Madness in here. It's the exact sort of thing we envisioned." She looks up. "Would you be open to something entrepreneurial?"

"What do you mean?"

"A percentage of net instead of rent?" the woman says. "We really were fans. We always loved the concept."

My blood races. A percentage of net means I wouldn't have to pay anything until the bakery made money. Mia squeezes my arm.

"We don't want something corporate in here," the woman explains. "I'd have to discuss it with my husband, but would you be open to it?"

"What sort of percentage?" I ask, trying desperately not to freak out and hug her.

"Maybe we could both come up with a number and see where we are, maybe arrive at something we both think is fair.

It's the kind of business we've always envisioned for this space. Of course we'd do due diligence."

"I would be extremely interested, and I'd be happy to supply the police report, anything. Though I am getting ready to relocate somewhere cheaper for a while..."

We set up a lunch meeting for the next day.

I walk out of there with Mia like everything is totally normal.

We're silent as nuns for almost half a block. Then, when we're a safe distance away, I death-grip her arm and squee.

THIRTY-FOUR

Lizzie

TWENTY-FOUR HOURS LATER, I'm walking in the front door of Vossameer. I wasn't planning on talking to Theo until the next morning, but I want to tell him the good news about the space. Perfect location, perfect landlords. Our meeting was like a lovefest. I brought them cookies, of course.

I have to have a lawyer look at the papers, but the deal seems fair. I won't need any money up front, and I'll end up paying them the equivalent of what I'd pay in rent, possibly more, once profits start rolling in. I couldn't have hoped for better.

And it was my reputation that landed it. Plus luck.

So I'm heading in there, imagining his face. And growing nervous as hell. Because staying changes things. Our end-of-March expiration date was a kind of safety net.

Theo wants to get serious, but I'm just not ready. Or am I?

Worry and uncertainty and utter excitement rage inside me all the way down the block to the Vossameer building.

I push through the front door and get hit.

With color. Art.

In the Vossameer lobby?

A trio of large, colorful abstract-art banners hang down one side, very vertical, and a horizontal hangs over the elevator. And there's new lighting—bright pendulums. A small collaboration space with comfy chairs.

"Ms. Cooper." I look over, and there's Marley in his gray security uniform, same as always. "We've missed you."

"Hey, nice to see you." I go up and lean in conspiratorially. "What's with the art?"

"A fancy decorator lady came through here."

"Does Mr. Drummond know?" I joke.

Marley shrugs.

I nearly collapse when I get into the elevator and see that the gray panels have been replaced with colorful ones. And when the door opens on the accounting floor to let in another passenger, I smell microwave popcorn.

Microwave-freaking-popcorn!

I smile at the woman. She seems to recognize me. She probably thinks I still work here. It's only been a few weeks.

The elevator stops on the marketing level, and I spot Betsy coming out the marketing/HR door. She brightens up the moment she sees me, and it would be too weird to keep going up, so I slip out, taking my chances that Sasha isn't there.

Betsy gives me a long hug. We do a quick catch-up and I tell her about the microwave popcorn I smelled in accounting.

"You have no idea. You have to see something." She grabs my arm and pulls me in the door, around her desk, and past the rows of cubicles.

"Uhh," I whisper as heads swivel.

"Ignore," she says. We arrive in the back room where I was fired. Except it's all different. There are comfy chairs, an espresso maker, a new microwave, and a giant basket of treats. "These are deadly," she says, holding up a pack of chocolate-covered pretzels. She picks up another. "Cheese microwave popcorn. Food of the gods." Another. "These caramel things? Best-kept secret in the baskets. Every department has a basket like this."

"How is this allowed?"

"Mr. Drummond promoted Fernice from HR to employee well-being oversight, and suddenly these appeared."

I pick up a pack of cookies, feeling weirdly excited and hopeful. It's a basket of treats that feels like more than a basket of treats. It feels like a sign or something. A big sign that says *yes*. Or maybe *this way out of fuck buddy-only territory*.

"IT ran through theirs," she confides. "And another appeared."

"Wow."

"I know we're trying to get that deal with Locke Foundation, but it was thoughtful. It's not as if they'd ever know about something internal like this."

"Yeah," I say. "How would they know?"

"When Mr. Drummond does something, he doesn't go halfway," Betsy says. She asks about the job hunt as we head back up to the front.

"I'm working for a caterer, but I just signed a lease deal for an amazing space for a new Cookie Madness on Ninth."

"Lizzie! You got a space?"

I grin. I kind of can't not. "It's so perfect—right where Hell's Kitchen meets Midtown. A lot of foot traffic. I wouldn't have been able to afford it, but the landlord knows my reputation and she wanted me in there. It's this older couple—I think they have a lot of money and they just really want what they want. A tiny little place on a corner. So gorgeous."

"That's where the big food festival is," she says.

"You're opening a Cookie Madness on Ninth?"

I spin around and come face-to-face with Sasha. I stiffen instinctively, but what can she do to me? If anything, she should feel stupid around me, though judging from her haughty stare, she doesn't.

"That's right," I say.

"Where on Ninth?" she asks.

I hesitate to reveal the intersection, but what's she going to do? Come in and trash the place with a baseball bat? "Ninth and 43rd. It's going to be awesome. So amazing."

"Huh," she says. It's a significant *huh*. A foreboding *huh*.

"What?"

She just smiles. "Nothing."

I give her a smile of my own. I'm done letting her intimidate me.

I get out of there and continue on up to Theo's office. Everything is still Gulag Drummond up there. The gloomy anteroom. Theo's drab workspace.

Theo doesn't get nice things even when everybody else does. He's working at his whiteboard, totally absorbed.

Wearing his lab coat. The lab coat.

"Art? Microwave popcorn? What have you done with Mr. Drummond?"

He turns. Our eyes meet. White-hot energy bolts through me as he comes to me, slow and steady. Stalks to me.

I back up to the door. Most of me backs up, anyway. The butterflies in my belly are freaking out to get to him.

He pushes the door closed behind me, caging me against it.

"How can it be?" I say. "I'm afraid you're going to have to fire yourself for promoting a climate of fun."

"I'm a scientist," he growls, kissing me. "I test things out. Even wild theories from wake-up-call girls."

"Seriously." I push him away. "You promoted Fernice to

oversee employee morale? That's brilliant. I was just down there. I think it's already working."

"It wasn't really my idea," he says. "I hired an executive coach, and we brainstormed finding somebody with people skills to complement my chemistry skills. Valerie, that's my coach, is all about the carrot over the stick. Or the gift basket, as it were. The microwave popcorn was my addition." He kisses me. "If productivity goes up, they'll get more colors and more treats."

"And if it goes down?"

He draws a finger across his throat.

I slide past him and walk to the middle of his office. I feel like I'm on the edge of a cliff. A good cliff, maybe, but a cliff all the same. I go to his board. Is he still making progress? "I have news, too," I say.

"Uh-oh," he says. "You sound serious."

I turn. "I might've found a space." Suddenly I can't stop smiling. "And it's amazing."

He tilts his head. "A space?"

"For the bakery." I fish out my phone and show him the pictures. "I know. It wasn't going to happen. But look. Check it out."

He flips through. "Wow. Even your ceiling."

"Is it amazing or what?" I tell him the story of the landlord couple, or at least I think they were the landlords. The entrepreneurial deal. "I didn't think I could get one on my own with no cash and my credit totally shattered. But I did. I got it on my reputation. I did it myself."

A dark cloud seems to pass across his gaze, but then he brightens back up. "You're staying."

"I have to figure out how to break it to the subletter. My parents will be sad, but if I really hustle...I mean, with a space like this, I know how to make money."

"You're staying."

"Yes!" I'm just laughing now. "I'm staying!"

He picks me up and twirls me around, and I scream, and for a second, we're like a normal couple. Simple and happy. A normal couple where something good doesn't mean something scary.

He sets me down on his worktable and slides a knuckle along my jaw. His touch feels potent. Electric. Far too honest. Everything's new now, because I'm not leaving. And before I can pull away, he kisses me. I take hold of the lapels of his lab coat and hold tight.

"Thank goodness." He tips his forehead to mine. "I wanted you to stay, Lizzie. More than anything."

I narrow my eyes and glance at his whiteboard. "More than anything?" I ask, meaning, even the solution to the formula?

"More than anything."

My pulse skitters. More than anything in the world, he means.

He pulls away and pins me with his eyes, the gritty gray of storm clouds. "Let's not play games anymore." He takes my hand and holds it palm up.

"No more games?"

"I don't mean no more games *ever*, but it's not a game right now. Not for me." He plants a kiss on the tender middle of my palm. Shivers bloom across my skin, bloom so hard I can't speak. "You want to try it?"

I gaze into his eyes, this guy who is everything. "Okay, but I don't know where we're going. It feels like free-falling."

"I don't know, either, but I know we're together, so it's okay, right?"

"I don't know." I swallow past the dryness in my mouth. "I feel like we're on one of those maps they used to draw before they figured out that the world is round. Those maps where they thought you fell off the edge."

He slides his hands over my arms.

"And they would write 'here be dragons' around the edges," I continue. "Because they didn't know what was out there, only that it was something scary."

He bends so that his gaze is level with mine. "We'll go there together. We'll fight the dragons together."

Together. I take a deep breath. "Okay, then."

"And you know what a badass I am in this lab coat," he says into the kiss.

"Oh, you get to joke around, but I don't?"

"We can do anything we want, Seven."

And I know right then that he couldn't—wouldn't—trash my life the way Mason did. No, this man could utterly obliterate me. Yet here I am, in the palm of his hand. Can I do it?

But then I look into his eyes, and I know that I can. That we can. "Then let's do this thing. See where it leads."

He heaves out a breath. "Yes." He kisses me again—deeply. It's an all-consuming kiss, and I think, *this is what it is to be really kissed.* I melt into him, molding to him. He kisses my neck, begins to unbutton my blouse.

I'm half kissing him, half mauling his shoulders and arms with my greedy hands, enjoying him, daring to go there with him. I lock my legs around him, pulling him fully to me, fitting the steel of his cock between my legs.

With trembling hands, he yanks the hem of my shirt up from my skirt. He pulls it up over my head and throws it.

"The door."

He goes to the door and locks it, then turns back, strolling toward me, watching me with a kind of wonder that I enjoy. "You are so beautiful," he says. Like he's stunned that a beautiful woman is sitting in her bra on his worktable.

I hold out my arms.

He comes to me and we kiss. He pushes my skirt up with jerky motions as I shimmy-help him. "I need you so bad." His voice is ragged. He feels out of control.

"Need you, too," I unbuckle his belt with clumsy fingers. It's the truth. One real thing.

And soon enough he's got me mostly naked, but he's still wearing the lab coat, and he's just on that point of entering me, and I'm looking into his beautiful eyes, reveling in his sweet and peppery scent.

And it's like nothing else.

"Theo," I whisper. I twist the lapels of his lab coat. My heart feels so big, I want to scream.

"I'm here." He pushes in, slowly, filling me deliciously, moving inside me.

In every way that's important, it's us having sex for the first time. Us inside each other. It feels like he's fucking me all the way up to my eyes, or maybe my soul.

"Look at us. Fitting perfectly," he whispers.

"Perfectly," I agree, too blissed out for creative words. I kiss his perfect chin. His bad-boy lips.

Having sex without the game feels like a journey, an odyssey. We're mindless, but also really together.

I press the back of my hand to his warm belly, enjoying the feeling of him inside me, and then I do myself. He swears under his breath, because it gets us both off.

A little later I have my clothes back on, and I'm lounging in his desk chair.

Everything feels different. I grab a carrot stick from his little Tupperware, and then I kiss him one last time. "I have to go deal with this subletter."

"Wait. Saturday? Will you come to the banquet?"

The dress. The Cinderella experience. "I'm in."

He grins. "Good."

I grab his hand. "I'm going to warn you, don't be mad at me if I get scared or weird, okay?"

"Roger that," he says.

"I'm serious. Mason tried to control my life, and he took everything away from me."

He furrows his brow, like he can't even bear to think of it, then kisses my right cheekbone the way he sometimes does, and everything's good again.

I smile. "So if I'm ever weird..."

"Noted." He kisses my left cheekbone.

"It feels like a leap, okay? This whole thing. Scary."

"We got this," he says.

A sparkly feeling comes over me. "Dinner tonight?"

"Now who's being presumptuous?"

I grin and slap his shoulder. "Where are you in your—" I nod at his whiteboard.

"I'll hit a stopping point around six. Meet you at seven? You pick."

"Wait, this wasn't a stopping point? Were you running equations this whole time we were..." Fucking isn't the right word, but making love feels too *something*...

"The whole time we were off the map?"

I put my hand to his heart and kiss his stubbly cheek. My chemist who carries the world on his shoulders. Who thinks he doesn't deserve nice things because he didn't get the car keys so many years ago. "I'm into it," I say.

"Me, too. I'm into your animal videos and your pointless, awesome cookies and your snarky comments at four in the morning. I want a hundred and ten percent."

"You're not much of a scientist if you think you're going to get a hundred and ten percent," I joke.

"You make me believe in impossible things," he says.

THE SUN REFLECTS off the polished floor of the Vossameer lobby. The new artwork seems almost to glow. And I feel like I'm flying.

Everything was so gray and somber for all these weeks, but now there's color and hope and trust and *us*—two people who are maybe shitty at relationships, me because of what happened with Mason, and him because, well...I'm grinning stupidly thinking how standoffish he is with people in general, but it's different with me. He shows me a side of himself he doesn't show other people.

He makes me want to be a fierce dragon fighter. I want to go back up and tell him that, but I resist the urge. There's time now.

I see Marley at the guard stand talking with somebody. Sasha. Marley says something, and she turns and smiles in a way that I don't like.

I smile back. Nothing can bring me down.

Even so, I want to be instantly outside and away from her.

That's not what happens. Sasha pushes off and comes for me, clicking along, following a path designed to intersect with mine.

I tell myself that *she's* the one who should be avoiding *me*. I tell myself nothing she can say can upset me.

And then she opens her mouth. "Such a fierce business-woman. With your amazing new space you got with your fabulous reputation."

"If you're trying to do a whole *zinger* thing on me, you shouldn't use facts I feel awesome about."

"No?" She tilts her head with an exaggerated frown. "But that's what's so funny. That you think you got it on your reputation. Did you check who actually leased that space?"

"What are you talking about? I leased it."

"You *sub*leased it. From Theo. Setting you up so you can play bakery. Isn't that nice!"

My belly drops through the floor, but I don't let her see it—I won't. I cross my arms over my chest.

"You can check with Petey Sanger in accounting if you don't believe me." She crosses her arms, mirroring my pose. "That better? For my zinger?"

I force a smile. "When impersonating me doesn't work, there's always petty jealousy, isn't there? It doesn't become you."

She puts on a fake pout. "No? Okay. But letting you know what an idiot you are? That for sure becomes me."

I turn and head back to the elevators, mind reeling. I'm thinking about that dark look that flashed across Theo's face when I told him how happy I was to have gotten it on my own steam. I'm thinking about all those times he asked about my bakery dreams, the pictures for my dream board that he seemed so interested in.

"Uh-oh!" I hear her laugh behind me.

Her laughter is a whisper compared to the thundering despair inside me.

THIRTY-FIVE

Theo

THERE'S a formula for utter misery. You have to start off happy. Preferably with your heart soaring higher than you can remember. Extra points if the world feels new, if for once in your worthless life, you feel like you're not the piece of shit you always believed you were.

Maybe you're looking out the window, because you want to catch one last glimpse of her.

And maybe it's a little bit of pride, because you did it—the woman you're falling for is right there with you, falling back.

More extra points if you still feel her all over your skin, but especially in your chest where she touched you, where she pressed her hand to feel your heart beating out of control.

But she doesn't appear on the sidewalk below. She's coming in the door.

I turn, happy to see her, even after a few minutes of separation. I assume she forgot something...until I see the devastation in her gaze.

"What happened?" I go to her.

She puts up a hand. The hand that was on my heart, connecting us just moments ago, is marking a wall between us.

She knows.

"How could you?"

I move my lips, but no words come out.

"I can't believe you!"

"You were leaving, Lizzie. You needed help and you wouldn't take it—"

"That's because I wanted to do it on my own! Me. Without a man lording over me. A man with the power to take it all away. You knew that. I asked you to respect that."

"I'm so sorry."

"Having control of my own destiny was so important to me."

My pulse bangs in my ears. "But you would have control. It would be all yours."

"No, it would be fake control that you grant me. You didn't even ask me. You just did it! Oh my god."

"I didn't want to lose you—"

"And that woman? She and her husband acting like they love Cookie Madness...were they actors?"

"They were brokers."

"*Brokers* who were acting out a script that you gave them."

"But the contract was real," I say. "The terms protect you. The success would be all you. I don't want money. I don't care about controlling you. I want us. I want to undo some of the wrong that was done to you, so that you can have the success you deserve."

"Do you not see the problem here? Do you not see how monumental the deceit is? I asked you to respect a thing that's important to me and you tricked me."

"I didn't want to lose us. I didn't want to look back and

think, if only I hadn't..." The words die on my lips. The hurt in her eyes is breaking me.

I want to go to her, touch her, hold her, but I caused the hurt.

She looks away. "What is the one thing I asked of you?"

I hesitate, desperate for some way to take away the pain.

"What is the one simple thing?"

"To respect your wishes. To not try to control you."

"And what did you do?"

"I fell for you."

"You tried to control me."

"I know," I say. "I messed up."

"No, missing a date because you're absorbed in your work would be messing up."

"Please," I say helplessly. "Give us another chance."

"I can't," she says.

"You can't just leave."

"It was always going to happen." She looks around. "Thank you for..."

"No."

I go to her, but she puts up her hand. "Don't follow me, either. I'm asking you for that one thing."

"I don't want to live without an *us*."

She regards me with that gaze that used to hold so much trust. It's all gone now.

"I'm sorry," I say.

I know. She mouths it. Maybe she whispers it. My pulse is whooshing too hard for me to tell. *I know*.

And with that, the most precious thing in my life walks out the door.

Everything in me yearns to follow her. I ball my fists, force myself to stay. Disrespecting her wishes, that's how I got into this mess.

The one thing I asked you.

I stand there for the longest time, twisting with torment. I always find a solution to everything. A hole I can break through to find the answers, but this thing is frozen solid. There's no hole anywhere, unless you count the one in my heart.

After what feels like forever, I go back to my board. So many promising pathways and new discoveries. All irrelevant.

I wander to the window, but I know I won't see her. She'll wait to cross the street until she's out of my view. She'll think of that out of kindness, so that I don't see her walking away from this building one last time.

I press my hand to the glass, feel the rumble of Manhattan. The crash of this relationship.

I wander around after work. Streets that won't have her on them. I head home, earlier than usual, at a loss for what to do with my free time.

I sit out on the veranda where we ate pizza once.

I tell myself I'll be able to concentrate on finishing the dehydration formula now, but the mad frenzy of it is gone.

Ironic that I'd make my breakthrough as soon as my frenzy to make it disappeared.

Or maybe not—maybe I made my breakthrough *because* the frenzy disappeared. Because Lizzie helped give me perspective that widened my world. Because she bothered to look beyond my moods and my accomplishments. With her I'm real. Was real.

Why couldn't I have let her go to Fargo?

I could've visited her there. Flown her back here. Supported her in ways she'd appreciate. Respected and supported her. Instead I did the opposite.

She has every right to be angry.

I text her later that night.

I'm sorry.

Thursday night I take a long run in the park, as if I can pound the misery out of myself, but it seems to compound.

I text her again. I tell her I'm sorry. I add a heart emoji.

Later that night, I pull my new egg pan out of my cupboard, just to touch something she picked out for me.

I turn it over and over, musing about the nature of space and time. How close yet distant that moment was. How happy I felt. It seems baffling that I can touch something she touched last, put my fingers exactly where hers rested, but the whole world is different.

I order some groceries and teach myself to make an omelet off YouTube. As if that might bring her closer in some vague way.

It only outlines her absence.

Now I'm just a man who can make himself an omelet.

Out on the streets, the crowds seem thicker and angrier. The décor and treats throughout Vossameer are pathetic.

I call Sasha into my office to fire her. She seems to be expecting it, but what she doesn't expect is the news that Lizzie went to bat for her when I was going to fire her the first time. I tell her what Lizzie said about her being a hard worker, a dedicated employee, deserving of another chance.

"You blew that chance," I say. "She showed you honesty and decency, and you blew it."

Which makes two of us.

"I wasn't thinking," she says.

"No," I say. "And now it's too late." I call security to escort her out.

I go over to Lizzie's building on Friday night, but nobody's home. Supposedly. She might be ignoring me. After all I've done, I'm not going to bust in, too.

"What did you do?" Willow asks when I call to tell her that

Lizzie is gone, that she for sure needs to be my date for the banquet.

I tell her how I engineered things to make Lizzie stay. How I scoured the different walking routes she and Mia take for a space she'd like. How I found one and bought out the current tenant to make it available. How I figured out the timing of her walks so my broker could be there.

"Wow. It's impressive. Not in a good way."

"I know," I say.

"She was going to move temporarily. It didn't have to mean the end of a relationship."

"You think I don't know that?" I say.

"She was different."

"Yeah," I say.

"She'll be back in eighteen months."

I nod. It's not entirely helpful. "On the upside, I've taught myself to make omelets. You want one?"

THIRTY-SIX

Lizzie

I WALK home from my catering gig enjoying the rich tapestry of noises and smells that make the city feel so alive. I'll miss that. I'll even miss the people who stand at the top of the subway steps.

I probably won't miss the conundrum window.

Mia and I put on fun outfits and hit happy hour at our favorite place for one last time, a fusion taco place that has crazy margaritas.

She doesn't have any auditions this weekend and my catering job is really slowing.

After margarita number two, Mia talks me into going to the old restaurant where we used to work, which seems like a great idea at the time. But then everybody finds out I'm leaving in a week, the drinks are suddenly lining up in front of us.

And we're laughing and feeling wild, except for the time when we cry so hard about how we'll miss each other that we get mascara spiders under our eyes, and then we laugh-cry.

The restaurant closes, but we stay around, having wild fun with our old coworkers. Mia dances on top of a table, but I'm not in the mood.

It's around 4:30 in the morning that I'm outside the bathrooms calling Theo. Or at least trying to call him. The numbers on my phone are so stupidly close together.

"No, no!" Mia rips the phone from my hand.

"What?"

"Friends don't let friends drunk-dial."

"I'm not drunk-dialing; I'm doing a wake-up call."

"You can't call him."

"I'm rethinking this leaving thing."

"Not while you're trashed," she warns.

"What if I was too hard on him?"

"That's a question you have to ask yourself sober."

I flop back against the wall. "I like him so much."

"I know."

"It's such a cute space, too. But how can I trust his heart? I need to trust his heart. That's the most important thing."

"The decision will still be there in the morning, won't it?" She hands me my purse, pretty much shoves it into my stomach.

Before I know it, we're in the back of a Lyft.

I look at my phone. "I wish he was on Facebook. I just want to know how he's doing. Or would that be torture?"

"Torture," she says. "Do I need to take your phone away for the night?"

"Maybe." I sigh and lean back.

"I want you to stay, Lizzie, but only if it's the right thing for you to do. Not as a tequila decision."

"Are tequila decisions so bad?"

"Are you honestly asking me that? You remember that guy you almost screwed last summer? The juggler in Clinton Park?"

I cringe.

"Do you remember the night of hate and gyros? When we got into that fight?"

"Yes," I say sullenly.

She hugs me close. "No tequila decisions," she whispers.

I don't know how I make it up the stairs to our place. I wander into my half-packed-up bedroom and collapse. I sleep long and hard, sleeping the sleep of the drunk until well into midmorning.

"THANK YOU." I'm leaning on the doorframe to the kitchen/living room. "For stopping me."

Mia's on the couch looking half dead. "You're welcome."

I collapse next to her. "It would've been cruel to call him and patch things up. Because today I'd have to break up with him all over again."

She says nothing.

"I have issues with guys controlling me and he wants to manage everything around him. It can never work."

I can tell by her expression she was half hoping I'd still change my mind and make a relationship-repairing call. That I'd take the space and stay in the city.

It's so tempting. Too tempting.

That's when I decide it. "I need to rip the bandage off," I say.

"Meaning what?"

"Leave today. I'm pretty much all packed. You have work and rehearsals all this week—you won't even be here."

"To stop you from giving him another chance?"

"Exactly," I say. "And last I checked, I could get that van early."

"I'll be here a little bit..." But I see in her face that she gets it.

I'd just be waiting here alone to leave. Trying not to call him. "Honey."

"And you can help me load this way."

She snorts. "Oh, I see. I get it now."

Of course the day would be beautiful. Sixty and sunny with that fresh, crisp March air. We find a parking spot for my rented U-Haul right in front of our building. A whole passel of our friends from last night show up to help me.

The hauling goes fast—almost too fast. We have a farewell meal of pizza and beer in the empty space that was once my bedroom.

I eat the pizza sans beer—I've got a long night of driving ahead of me. I want to at least get to Pennsylvania before midnight.

We say our tearful goodbyes. Mia promises again and again to make a summer trek to Fargo.

I head out.

Midtown is jam-packed with Saturday evening traffic. Everybody heading out to dinner before Broadway shows. It makes me sad.

Not that I ever go to Broadway shows, but I could've gone to them, and now I can't.

I tell myself it's only temporary, that I'll be back. I'll again be one of those people who could go to Broadway shows but doesn't. I'll once again be hanging out with friends and going to restaurants in the same five-square-block area I love.

My pep talk to myself goes on.

In Fargo, I'll work alongside my parents, and we'll be the Three Musketeers again. I'll be able to see stars in the night sky. I'll drive my own car, and there will be giant parking places everywhere I go. There will be grass all around. Green grass. It will be awesome.

And I'll get on my own two feet and nobody will be able to control or manipulate me.

There's construction everywhere, including on Harlem River Drive—my detours have detours and eventually I'm in a sea of honking cars on Willis Avenue Bridge, being carried along in the massive crawl of traffic.

And there, just up the river, I see the Third Avenue Bridge. *The* bridge.

The crawl slows, and eventually it's gridlock. And I'm stuck there with the memory of Theo's intense guilt echoing in my heart. The tragedy of his family. The sense of responsibility that seems to drive him.

He thinks if he'd stuck around and taken the keys away from his father, that his mother would be alive.

It's probably not true, but he thinks it is.

Just like he thinks it's up to him and him alone to invent something to save wounded people from dying of blood loss in remote regions. The whole world on his shoulders.

The ultimate control freak. How can I be with somebody like that?

But as I go over it now, locked in a parade of honking horns, an alternate perspective takes shape in my mind.

He handed me something of vast importance that day under the bridge—a vulnerable secret truth from deep in his heart. Something he'd never told anybody ever before.

He told me a secret, but it's more than a secret—he gave me the ability to see him in a way other people can't. To see what drives him.

Theo is a controlling guy who thinks he's responsible for everything. I thought that doomed our relationship.

Now I see what his control issues really are—they're dragons. Dragons that we can fight together. Because we're good together like that.

You make me believe impossible things.

I feel as if some kind of fog has lifted. I want to turn around. I want to find him and apologize. But what if it's too late? He apologized so many times on text and voicemail, even tried to see me.

I ignored him. I gave up the fight too soon. I ran from the edge.

What have I done?

I call Theo, but I get his voicemail. I take a look at the time—after six. He's at his banquet. The eating part has already started. He wanted me there. So badly.

I call Mia.

She picks up on the first ring. "Lizzie? Is everything okay?"

"Yeah," I say. "I mean, I'm just stuck in traffic. But I'm wondering, should I have listened to the tequila?"

"What?"

"Was I hasty? With leaving?"

"Well..."

"I'm thinking I was."

She sucks in a breath. "Are you sure?"

I tell her my thoughts, ask her whether I'm being stupid.

"He's not Mason," she says.

"Why didn't you say anything?"

"I did! I said exactly that! Before we found your storefront. Remember?"

She did, yeah. "Well, I'm coming back."

"Oh my god."

"But I need you to do something."

THIRTY-SEVEN

Lizzie

PEOPLE ALWAYS COMPLAIN about time flying by too quickly. They gripe that they wish they could slow it down.

Those people should try renting a U-Haul, double-parking it outside the massive Sturdyven Concert Hall in Midtown on a rainy Saturday night, and having people honk at them nonstop. Do that, and the minutes feel like hours.

I make the universal *I'm sorry* gesture to the drivers who pass by, hoping a cop doesn't come.

Sleek cars pull up in front of me, one after another, and discharge glamorous people in eveningwear.

I hope I'm not too late. I want to be in the audience for him, to be the one person really with him.

A cop comes by and makes me move. I drive around the block and park again.

Finally there's a knock at the passenger window. It's Mia with the dress. She slides into the cab, and I undress and put the thing on, which is a combination contortionist and bra-exhibitionist show. She helps me fix my hair, then takes over the wheel.

"You good?"

"So good," she says.

I jump out and run down the sidewalk with my purse, smoothing down my hair. I hit the red-carpet covered steps and pop up them, toward a pair of doormen who aren't holding the doors open anymore. "Ticket," one of them says.

"I'm a friend of Theo Drummond's." I point to the sign on the easel that proclaims him to be the winner of this year's Locke Award. "I need to get in and see him. It's very important."

"You'll have to talk to him another time."

I peer helplessly in at the vast expanse of red carpet under glittering chandeliers, at the set of doors on the far side. Probably leading to the auditorium. Theo will be accepting his award in there. Feeling alone onstage. Like nobody knows him. Like nobody gets him. Like nobody's with him.

I'm here.

I'm with you.

I turn away and text Willow. I still have her number from when Theo texted me from her phone that one time.

It's Lizzie. Outside. I messed up. Can you get me in?

After what seems like forever, she texts back.

:(

A frown. What does it mean?

I go back to harassing the doormen. "You have to let me in," I say. "He needs me there. It would mean everything."

"Then he should've given you a ticket."

"He asked me, but I thought I couldn't at the time," I say. "I was moving away, but I changed my mind over Willis Bridge. I turned my entire U-Haul of stuff around—"

"That was you out there with the U-Haul?" The one

doorman shakes his head. The U-Haul detail doesn't help my case.

"Please," I say.

"We're going to have to ask you to move on," the one grumbles, already sick of my story. "Now."

I start down the steps, wondering if I could sneak in some other way. Or at least wait for him on the sidewalk?

"Hey!"

I turn, and there's Willow, holding open the door.

"What's going on?" she asks.

I run back up the steps. "Your brother," I say breathlessly. "I have to see him. I need to apologize and tell him...just so many things!"

Willow turns to the guards. "She gets to come in. She's Theo's important friend."

"Not without an invitation," the guard says.

The other guard is on his phone, probably with the cops. Nervously, I smooth down my red dress.

"Come on, I'm Theo Drummond's sister." Willow points to the sign. "I'm his sister."

"I don't care if you're the Pope," the other guard says.

There's another figure in there, a woman in a green dress crossing the lobby. At first I think she's carrying a fuzzy white purse, but then I realize it's a little white dog—possibly the cutest dog I've ever seen.

She pushes out the door. "Willow? What's going on out here?"

"Vicky," Willow says. "This is Lizzie. We need to get her in. She's with Theo."

"You can't have pets in there," the first guard says.

"He's not a pet," Vicky says. "He's Smuckers. A very important member of the Locke family." She turns to me. "God, I love your dress. You're with Theo?"

I don't know what to say to that. I left him. But now I want to be with him. "It's a long story, but I need to be in the audience. He needs to know I'm there."

"Cosign," Willow says, with a hand on my back. "It would mean everything to him."

"Come on, we'll get you in." Vicky thanks the guards and leads the way. Willow and I follow. The little dog peers back at us, riding happily, wee little tongue poking out his mouth.

"Thank you," I say to her.

"Thank Smuckers for having to pee." Vicky leads us down a side hall and pushes open a door. "Shhh! Go on," she whispers.

Willow and I sneak in and the door closes behind us. The vast ballroom is a dark sea of tables covered with white tablecloths. Bright dresses glow softly in the candlelight. There's somebody on the stage talking about construction. Green buildings or something.

Willow takes my arm. "At the next break, I'm gonna lead you to our table up front. You can take his seat."

"Are you sure?"

"More than sure!" She squints at the stage. "He's up soon, I think."

"How's he been?" I whisper.

"Miserable. He's just been holed up in his lab. I don't think he wrote any kind of speech. Certainly not the dog-and-pony show that the older members of the Locke board want to see."

"I feel so bad."

"Don't. Trust me, I know how he can be. He'll be so happy to see you." Willow squeezes my hand. "I know he messed up."

"So did I. But I feel sure we can work it out."

People start clapping.

"Now," Willow says, dragging me around the edges of the ballroom to a table in the front. There are two empty seats together.

An announcer comes on and starts talking about Theo, about inspiration being found in tragedy. It's bright up onstage.

I whisper to Willow, "Can they even see us from up there?"

She shrugs and shakes her head.

He finally calls Theo's name.

There's applause as Theo walks out in a tuxedo. Theo in a tux is even hotter than Theo in a lab coat. He accepts the shiny award, and shakes the man's hand.

The room hushes.

He thanks the Locke Foundation, talks about how honored he is.

I wave at him, but his eyes glide right over me—over all the audience. He can't see with the lights burning onto him—just as I feared.

He goes on to speak about how much he wanted to partner with Locke. He then starts in on his struggles with dehydrated Vossameer.

"Wow," Willow says. "I didn't know he was going to talk about all that."

"Inspiration comes in many forms," Theo is saying. "I've been trying to nail this formula with all my might. Power it out. And then one day..." He steps aside. There's something in his hand. He raises it to the screen and a goat video flashes up. Little goats playing. Everybody laughs.

"Oh my god, he's gone insane," Willow whispers.

I'm just grinning. Theo is showing baby goat videos at a giant banquet. He's talking about randomness, about chemical structures. How he was looking at things in a too-rigid way. How the goats at play showed him something. A way to solve the problem.

My smile stretches ear to ear, like it might break my face.

The people are eating it up. Well, who doesn't love baby goats?

He announces that they're gearing up for clinical trials that will be expedited once they have FDA approval. He hopes they can get the new formula out into the field as quickly as possible. People clap. They all know what it means.

"I was going at it all wrong," he says, and that's when he sees me. Or squints at me, like he thinks it's maybe me. They turned the lights down for him to show the goat videos. Willow and I both wave like crazy.

Then I do it, there in the dark. I raise my middle finger.

I know you. I'm with you.

His lips twitch. He's looking right at me.

He sees me.

Theo, I mouth.

"Wake-up calls come in many forms," he says, looking directly at me now. "Sometimes baby goats show you you're being too linear. And sometimes it's a literal wake-up call that wakes you up to a world that's wider than you ever imagined. Let's never stop discovering ways to make it better and more beautiful. Thank you." He raises the award to thunderous applause.

"Shit," Willow says. "He killed it."

I smile stupidly as he fits the mic back into the holder, as he comes off the stage and shakes a lot of hands. His gaze never leaves mine.

Because in the end, we're the only people in the room.

I finally get to him, or maybe he gets to me. "You came." He cups my cheeks, looking at me like he can't believe it.

"Theo—" There are too many words. So I kiss him. He groans and pulls me closer, kisses me back.

"I was wrong," I say, pulling away. "Wrong to just leave."

"No, I was wrong. I know I was wrong."

"But I was wrong to not believe in our power to get past it.

We can figure this out. I feel like we can figure anything out. I love that we can figure anything out."

His eyes shine. "You can't even imagine what it was like to see you out there. I wanted to yell."

"Probably good you didn't." I grab hold of his lapels. They feel cool and silky. "I'm home. I don't want to leave this." *Ever*, I think.

"You're staying? In the city?"

"Yes."

He wraps his arms around me, wraps me into a hug. There are no words.

And then we have to separate, because it's picture time. Henry Locke, who runs the Locke empire, wants a picture with Theo. Then they bring the little dog into the picture. Then it's Theo and some other people.

I have to figure out what to do about the subletter. Figure out about a job. Theo may have rented the awesome space, but those are all details. I catch Theo's eye as the press takes a few pictures of him with his award. The main thing is that I'm staying.

Willow hands me a glass of champagne. "He made an omelet for me this morning," she says.

"He did?"

"It was terrible."

After a lot of mingling, the party breaks up, but the night's not over—Henry and Vicky invite Willow and Theo and me out for drinks and desserts. Henry wants to toast the partnership.

We end up in a cozy, candlelit bar in one of the famous Locke boutique hotels. The five of us commandeer a big, comfy booth and drink to the partnership with champagne that I don't dare ask the price of.

We talk about the goat videos, and Willow explains a data initiative her company is doing. Vicky's excited that I'm the

Cookie Madness person. It turns out she makes jewelry, and we have fun bonding over crafty stuff while we pet the little dog, who might just be the cutest dog in the universe.

Henry Locke can't say enough about how much he loved Theo's speech. They've known each other for a while, but I get the feeling the partnership is a new level in their relationship. He compliments him on the firm's engaging online presence, too.

"That's mostly Lizzie," Theo says.

"So that's where you two fell for each other?" Vicky asks. "When you worked at Vossameer?"

Theo and I exchange glances.

"It's a long story," I say.

Willow snorts.

Playfully, Vicky narrows her eyes. "Okay, you don't have to tell. *Now...*"

I have a feeling she's going to extract every detail some-day. And I wouldn't mind it. I like her. Mia would like her, too.

I go home with Theo after the party breaks up. We kiss in the limo and then later in the elevator. Theo slides his hands over my hips. "I just want to rip this off you."

"Don't you dare! It's my favorite dress ever!"

He chuckles.

In the end, he doesn't rip it off. He carries me to his bedroom and he undoes the zipper for me, kissing my back every few inches.

We make love in his big bed with the moon shining in the arch-top windows. Afterward I tell him about going over the bridge, and thinking about what he said, and we dream together of how we want things to be with us.

"We're talking about our relationship," I say. "It seems so weird. But in a good way."

"A very good way." He touches his finger to the tip of my nose. "And you know what I'm going to do tomorrow morning?"

"What?" I ask.

"I'm going to make us omelets!"

"Hmm!" I say, trying to sound excited.

The next morning, we collaborate on the omelets, thankfully. He's surprised at the things he was doing wrong.

I put in a call to my parents. It's a hard call—they're crushed I'm not coming but they're thrilled I might have a space. Theo told me it's still empty. It's something else we'll work out. I promise to come visit soon for a nice long time. A late Three Musketeers celebration. I'll bring special cookies.

Later that morning, we head to my old place. With the help of Derek and Mia and a few other guys Theo rounded up, we make quick work of unloading my carefully packed truck and putting all my stuff back in my room. The subletter hasn't moved in yet, luckily, and Theo has a place to offer her—apparently, Vossameer owns a few apartments to put up overseas visitors, and one of them will be open for a couple of months.

After everybody leaves, Theo and I drink lemonade on our couch.

Mia comes out in her outrageous delivery girl uniform. She has to deliver sandwiches dressed as a cat.

She looks ashen.

"What's wrong?" I ask. She hates wearing the uniform around people she knows, but this is different. She looks actually upset.

"They changed my delivery area," she says. "It's...not good."

"You think it'll be a bad tip area?"

"No, it's a nicer area, but it includes Maximillion Plaza," she says.

"No!" I gasp.

"What's wrong with Maximillion Plaza?" Theo asks.

I look over at Mia, unsure how much to divulge.

"I have history with somebody there," she says. "My high school nemesis works there. And if he ever saw me delivering sandwiches in a cat suit?" She shakes her head, like it's too horrible to comprehend.

"Or if he ordered one?" I add.

"Oh, my god," she says. "And he would. If he learned that having me deliver a sandwich in a cat suit is a possibility in his life, he'd be all over it."

"Can you switch territories?" I ask.

"I'm going to try. Because I would rather die. Literally die."

"Would it be that bad?" Theo asks.

"Yes," we say in unison.

Mia thanks Theo again for offering the subletter a temporary free apartment.

"Everything's perfect," I say.

"Except the conundrum window," Mia says. "Beware, it's almost summer."

We explain the horrible dilemma of the window to Theo—too hot when it's closed, too stinky when it's open.

He goes over, but he doesn't seem to be looking out the window. He's looking at the part of the wall next to the window, studying one of Mia's cross-stitches, hanging right next to it. "What is this?" He takes it off the hook.

Mia turns to me, jaw hanging open. It's here I realize—that's the *Sex with me is a dirty, savage affair. Utterly uncivilized* cross-stitch.

He turns, holding the thing up. "Care to explain?"

"Um, no?" I squeak.

He smiles his sexy, stern smile.

"Gotta go," Mia says, getting out of there.

I lock up behind her, and Theo presses me to the door. "You are a totally impudent wake-up-call girl who needs to be taught a lesson," he rumbles.

"Am I?" I start unbuttoning his shirt. "Am I, really?"

In fact, I am. All afternoon I am.

EPILOGUE

Theo
New Year's Day; eight months later
Fargo, North Dakota

I stand at the front of the tiny prairie church, adjusting my cuff links. There's a fiddler, a friend of the Cooper family, playing wedding songs in the corner.

I adjust my sleeve, trying to get it even with the other sleeve.

Willow pokes me in the back. "They're fine! You're perfect!"

I turn to face her.

Per-fect, she mouths.

She's standing up with me as my best woman, in a blue gown that matches Mia's, who's over on the bride's side. Lizzie's side.

Lots of our Manhattan friends came out for this. Henry Locke provided the Locke jet and pilot as a kind of wedding gift, so that everybody could ride here together. He and I have become quite friendly, and the four of us hang out all the time.

Over the summer, my PI figured out exactly where in St. Thomas Lizzie's ex was living, and we tipped off the cops. The guy was extradited to the United States to stand trial, and while Lizzie didn't get all her money back, she got some. Enough to take over the space I found for her and stand on her own with the bakery.

Lizzie's mother, Fredericka, sits in the front. I catch her eye and she smiles. We've gotten to know each other pretty well over the past few weeks of my being here, celebrating Christmas and doing wedding prep.

The way the Coopers have brought me into the family—this feeling of being part of her generous family—is something I never dreamed of for myself. Something I never expected when I fell in love with Lizzie.

I can't remember the last time I had a real Christmas. To me, Christmas was always a pain in the ass, with extra obligations and most of my favorite restaurants being annoyingly closed. Something to get through.

But an actual Christmas? The Coopers do every dorky thing there is—the mistletoe, the singing, the whole nine yards. There have been dinners and presents. There have been long, snowy walks and even skating on the river, with hot apple cider breaks. And caroling.

And I've loved it all.

The Coopers were sad Lizzie didn't move back home, but they were thrilled she found a place for Cookie Madness.

And really, they're fine. Lizzie's parents are a hugely romantic pair with a rich, fun life full of friends. And they never stop learning and growing. This spring they'll be taking a month-long trip to a French chateau to learn some kind of foodie technique. Food is definitely a family passion.

Sometimes I secretly study Lizzie's parents for clues of how to have a good marriage—out at dinner, sitting around the fire, when we drop by the pizzeria. Lizzie laughed when I told her that, but I never saw a successful marriage up close, and that's what I want for us.

There are dark pink flowers all around the church—peonies. That's Lizzie's favorite flower, as it turns out. She told me once that they make her happy—the color, the shape, the size, the scent. So I'm thinking flowers might not be so useless after all.

The music changes and I straighten. Everybody twists around, waiting for Lizzie to appear with her father, Joe, who will be walking her down the aisle.

My pulse races. I have the urge to adjust my cufflinks again.

But then the doors open and there's Lizzie, madly gorgeous in a white dress and elegant hairdo, smiling brightly, clutching a riot of peonies. My nervousness goes, and everything's right. Because she's with me. Whatever happens, we're in it together.

I love you, she mouths.

I whisper it back. *I love you.*

Because we're two dragon fighters, traipsing through life together. Falling off the map together.

$\sim$ *The End* $\sim$

AFTERWORD

Thank you for reading Theo and Lizzie's story! I hope you love them as much as I do.

———

But there's more—Mia is still wearing that sandwich delivery cat suit, and can you guess who found out?

Can you guess who is making her deliver a sandwich to him —tomorrow?

Max Hilton, her high school nemesis turned billionaire, one of the wealthiest and most notorious playboys in all of NYC —that's who.

Mia's thinking about quitting her lunch delivery job—that's how much she can't stand the idea of being mocked by Max.

But then her friend tosses her a copy of the pick-up guide he wrote.

One of those how-to-pick-up-girls-by-being-a-jerk guides.

She's decided to use his guide against him. She's going to bring him to his knees!

Grab *Breaking the Billionaire's Rules!*

"...so hilarious that my jaw was hurting. It made my heart so full and happy. I couldn't stop smiling and swooning. A must read of 2019."
~PPs Bookshelf

ACKNOWLEDGMENTS

I seriously don't know what I'd do without my beautiful, badass, book-loving friends out there. So many of you lent your love to this book!

Thank you, Joanna Chambers, for your tough, OMG-smart, wizard-level feedback over two full iterations of this book. And Molly O'Keefe, I'm wildly grateful for your amazing insights, for thinking of things that made this book so much better. Massive thanks also to Katie Reus—you came through with character ideas and tweaks that made the text sing. Thank you, Christine Maria Rose, for reading this over and using your chemistry expertise to help me get this book right, and to make Theo into a credible chemist. And thank you to Courtenay Bennett for your many book-saving catches, and for keeping me out of the tool and rod club! And to Trisha Wolfe for kickass tweaks! And to Rylie Finn from Book-Bosomed Book Blog for eagle-eye catches!

And to you, Nina Grinstead—you have become such a fierce friend and ally, you blow me away with your warmth and fun and badass strategic mind. Thank you to the whole Social Butterfly gang—Brooke, Sarah, Chanpreet, Shannon, and everyone else.

And Melissa Gaston, I don't know how I got so lucky as to be hooked up with you—thank you for your creativity and warmth and smarts! Thank you also to editor Deb Nemeth for wonderful developmental edits, and to Sadye Scott-Hainchek, Judy Zweifel, and Lea Schafer for fabulously expert copyediting and proofing polish. Any mistakes in here are my own because apparently I can't stop fussing with every little thing!! And major hugs to Michele of Catalano Creative for this amazing cover.

I'm grateful to too many bloggers to name—I deeply appreciate the care you take with your reviews and recommendations—my heart does a little flutter when I see you've read and reviewed my books, and your passion inspires me to always reach higher.

I want to thank my husband, Mark for always being there and for patiently reminding me of all the other times I freaked out and thought the book I was in the middle of writing was a doomed mess, but later felt happy about it. Not that it kept me from a mid-book freakout this time around. Maybe next time, baby!

Huge, warm, tackle-hug thanks to my amazing friends in the Fabulous Gang—you are the smartest, funniest, sweetest group there ever was. You guys mean the world to me! Special thanks to gang members Darlene Good, Erica Stennett, Catherine Ojalvo, and Cindy McGriff for coming through with perfect heroine, friend, and sister names. And my Awesome ARC gang – I hope you know how grateful I am that you are on this journey with me. You all so rock!!

ALSO BY ANNIKA MARTIN

Find a complete list of books and audiobooks at
www.annikamartinbooks.com

ABOUT THE AUTHOR

Annika Martin is a New York Times bestselling author who sometimes writes as RITA®-award-winning Carolyn Crane. She lives in Minneapolis with her husband; in her spare time she enjoys taking pictures of her cats, consuming boatloads of chocolate suckers, and tending her wild, bee-friendly garden.

newsletter:
http://annikamartinbooks.com/newletter

Facebook:
www.facebook.com/AnnikaMartinBooks

Instagram:
instagram.com/annikamartinauthor

website:
www.annikamartinbooks.com

email:
annika@annikamartinbooks.com

Thank you for reading!

xox Annika

Printed in the USA
CPSIA information can be obtained
at www.ICGtesting.com
LVHW010801260823
756374LV00037B/1100